*Pride is the mask of
one's own faults.*

–*Jewish Proverb*

MYSTERIES *of* LANCASTER COUNTY

PRIDE AND PETTINESS

MYSTERIES *of* LANCASTER COUNTY

Elizabeth Ludwig

Guideposts

Danbury, Connecticut

Mysteries of Lancaster County is a trademark of Guideposts.

Published by Guideposts Books & Inspirational Media
100 Reserve Road, Suite E200
Danbury, CT 06810
Guideposts.org

This is a work of fiction. The village of Bird-in-Hand, and Lancaster County, Pennsylvania, actually exist, and some places and characters are based on actual places and people whose identities have been used with permission or fictionalized to protect their privacy. All other names, characters, businesses, and events are the creation of the author's imagination, and any resemblance to actual persons or events is coincidental.

Every attempt has been made to credit the sources of copyrighted material used in this book. If any such acknowledgment has been inadvertently omitted or miscredited, receipt of such information would be appreciated.

Scripture references are from the following sources: *The Holy Bible, King James Version (KJV). The Holy Bible, New International Version (NIV).* Copyright ©1973, 1978, 1984, 2011 by Biblica, Inc. Used by permission of Zondervan. All rights reserved worldwide. www.zondervan.com

Cover and interior design by Müllerhaus
Cover illustration by Bob Kayganich, represented by Deborah Wolfe, LTD.
Typeset by Aptara, Inc.

Printed and bound in the United States of America
10 9 8 7 6 5 4 3 2

CHAPTER ONE

Mary Classen Baxter's stomach rumbled as the door to the Bird-in-Hand Family Restaurant & Smorgasbord swung open, and the delicious smell of warm, yeasty rolls wafted out. Despite the harsh February wind whipping across the parking lot, she came to a standstill and took a long whiff.

"Mmm. Do you smell that?" She glanced over her shoulder at her sisters, Elizabeth and Martha.

"I'd smell it better inside." Martha huffed and rubbed her gloved hands over her arms. "Come on, Mary. It's freezing out here."

Mary sighed and pulled the door open wider for her sisters to step through. Martha was sensible and organized, but sometimes it'd be nice if she put all that aside and stopped to enjoy the little things in life…like the smell of buttery steamed carrots and roasting chicken.

Her mouth watered as a waitress in a crisp green shirt and black vest strode by carrying two plates piled high with food.

Elizabeth's eyes grew round, and she rubbed her tummy. "Goodness, I didn't realize I was so hungry." She motioned toward the hostess desk. "I'll go get us a table."

"Okay." Martha pulled off her gloves and shoved them into the pocket of her coat. Dodging another hustling waitress, she unwound the muffler from around her neck. It quickly went the same way as the gloves. "Wow, this place is busy."

Mary looked around as she shrugged out of her coat. "It does seem busier than normal, but it's Thursday night. Maybe people are just getting an early start on the weekend since the weather is supposed to turn bad later."

Martha's nose wrinkled. "Hmm. Maybe."

Elizabeth returned, her red woolen scarf draped over one arm. "They'll page us when our table is ready." She eased closer to Mary as a group of teenagers angled past. "Where did all these people come from?"

Instead of stopping at the hostess booth, the teenagers made a beeline for the back dining room. Noise like the buzz of a full stadium filtered out as they entered.

"What's going on back there?" Martha asked, craning her neck to see.

Mary snapped her fingers. "The job fair."

Elizabeth glanced at her watch. "Is that tonight? I thought that didn't start until next week."

Martha shook her head and scooted out of the way of another group of teens. "No, Mary's right. I forgot all about it. No wonder this place is so packed." She glanced at the line forming behind the hostess table. "Looks like we got here just in time. They're going to be really busy once the job fair lets out. Did they say how long the wait would be?"

"Twenty to thirty minutes." Elizabeth gazed longingly at a plate of steaming roast beef drifting by atop a tray on a waitress's shoulder. "Not sure I can wait that long."

Mary slanted a glance toward the back room. "Well then, why don't we check out the job fair? We have plenty of time, and it'll keep our minds off the food."

"Why not?" Martha took hold of Elizabeth's arm and led her away from the smell of the savory beef. "Let's go."

Elizabeth sighed, her feet shuffling along the floor as she trudged behind Martha.

Mary was hungry too, but she quickly forgot the rumbling in her stomach when they ducked into the back dining room. Tables had been pushed along the walls, and lines long and short extended from each one. Most of those in line were kids, Mary noted, probably students looking for part-time work after school or during the summer, but there were plenty of adults present as well.

She leaned in toward Elizabeth. "I didn't realize there were so many jobs available."

Elizabeth grabbed a sheet of paper off the table nearest the door. "Here's the list." She squinted a little as she read over it. "Cooks, cashiers, stage usher, maintenance worker…it's a pretty wide variety."

"I'll say. Stage usher?" Martha shrugged then pointed over toward a table with a sign that said COUNTRY ACRES CAMPGROUND. "I'm going to check that one out."

"Just don't apply for anything," Elizabeth teased, bumping her arm playfully. "As busy as we've been lately, we can't afford to lose you."

Martha smiled and melted into the crowd.

Mary motioned toward the far end of the room where the tables were smaller and the lines a little shorter. "Looks like a few of the newer businesses showed up this year." She elbowed Elizabeth and shot her a teasing grin. "How come we've never thought about signing up for a booth? We could use a little more help around the store."

"Business *has* been pretty good," Elizabeth said with a laugh. "Do you want to look around?"

Mary nodded. "Sure. Let's go."

They wandered slowly down the rows of tables, neither one speaking. The lively chatter would likely have drowned them out anyway. When they neared the end, Mary stopped to pick up a brochure touting a list of benefits and competitive pay rates.

"Mary?"

Hearing her name called by a voice she didn't recognize, she lifted her head. A couple of tables down, a woman with shoulder-length dark hair and a wide smile beckoned.

"Over here."

Elizabeth pressed into her shoulder. "Who's that?"

"I have no idea." Mary frowned and then did a double take as the woman's cheery smile stirred a distant memory. "Wait, is that—?"

The woman rounded the table and stuck out her arms. "Mary, it's me. Paige Schiller." She put her hand to her chest. "I used to be Paige—"

"Hathaway." Mary set the flyer down and moved in for her hug. "Goodness, Paige, I haven't seen you in, well, since we graduated, right? Are you back in town?"

She stepped away as Paige nodded.

"Unfortunately, yes." She chuckled and held up her left hand. "I mean, I'm glad to be back in Bird-in-Hand. I just hate that it's because of my divorce."

"Oh, I'm so sorry."

Her smile faded. "Thank you, but it was sort of inevitable, really."

Though her tone remained light, the lines around her lips and eyes spoke of a wealth of heartache—something Mary remembered from her own divorce. Other than that, the years had been kind to Paige. She still had the slender, athletic figure Mary remembered from high school, and a sort of fresh, youthful energy about her Mary could easily envy. She turned and introduced her childhood friend to Elizabeth. Paige stuck out her hand and gave Elizabeth's a shake. "Pleased to meet you."

Elizabeth smiled at her. "It's good to meet you too," she said.

Paige motioned around the room. "Crazy, huh? The number of people that turned out for this is way better than I expected."

Mary followed her gaze. "I'll say." She pointed to Paige's table. "So, what are you here for?"

"I just opened a beauty salon and could really use some help." Her gaze flicked from Mary to Elizabeth. "Any chance either of you do nails?"

Elizabeth shot Mary a sly smile. "Say, that's something you haven't done before."

Mary laughed and followed Paige back to her table. She'd held a variety of jobs over the years, from coffee barista to teaching art lessons, but she'd never worked in a salon. "Sorry,

Paige, my sisters and I aren't looking for a job. We're just here for dinner."

"Aw, that's too bad." Paige smiled and handed her a sheet with the details of the position and the pay. "In case you change your mind."

Mary laughed and tucked the paper into her purse. "So? What have you been up to? Any kids? Or grandkids?"

Paige shook her head. "No grandkids yet. Kailey, my daughter, just turned fifteen." She glanced at Elizabeth. "I was thirty-six when she was born. Jack and I didn't think we could have kids. She sort of surprised us both when she was born."

"That's one of life's *good* surprises," Mary said.

Paige smoothed the edges of the tablecloth next to her display and nodded. "Absolutely. Wouldn't trade her for the world. Of course, Jack wasn't too happy when I decided to move away from Pittsburgh to come back to Bird-in-Hand, but…" She dropped her gaze and shuffled the papers on her table into a neat stack. "Anyway, I did what I thought was best for Kailey and me. She wasn't very happy at her old school. It was too big, and Kailey's so shy, she felt lost. I thought moving to a small town would be good for her."

Strain marked Paige's features, and Mary knew how tough the decision to uproot her family must have been for her. She reached out and squeezed her hand. "You'll have to come by our shop. We reopened Secondhand Blessings, the thrift store and gift shop my parents used to run in the barn on their old farm. Do you remember where it is?"

"I do. Oh, I used to love that old Victorian farmhouse. I remember your mother always hung that beautiful red, white, and blue bunting on the porch railing every Fourth of July. And those gorgeous stairs that led up to the porch." She feigned a dreamy roll of her eyes. "Does it still look the same?"

Mary smiled proudly. "Pretty much. We've made a few renovations inside, but for the most part, we wanted to keep it looking the way it did when we were growing up."

"Well, I'm glad to hear it's still in the family." Paige's eyes sparkled with excitement, and she returned the squeeze on Mary's fingers. "I can't tell you how good it is to see a familiar face. It makes me feel so much better about everything."

Warmed by Paige's words, Mary smiled. "I'm so glad."

"Mary." Elizabeth held up the pager, which was flashing bright red. "Our table is ready."

"Oh, we've got to go." Mary dropped Paige's hand and jerked her thumb toward the main dining room. "Do you want to join us? I'm sure we could add one more person."

"I'd love to, but I can't." She frowned and tapped the stack of papers. "I'll be here for another hour at least. But I'll definitely stop by your store."

"Great. It's open Monday through Saturday, though we close a little earlier on Tuesdays." Mary circled around the table and gave her friend one last hug. "Bye, Paige. I can't wait to meet your daughter."

"Bye, Mary." She waved to Elizabeth. "Nice to meet you."

"You too." Elizabeth smiled and then waited for Mary before heading toward the dining room. "She seems nice. Why don't I remember her?"

"She was into a lot of sports in high school. Plus, she was pretty shy." Mary waved to Martha, who extricated herself from the cluster of people gathered around the campground booth and joined them.

"Is our table ready?"

Elizabeth held up the pager and then wove toward the hostess stand. In minutes, they were seated and digging with gusto into the variety of home-style items the smorgasbord offered. And, almost as quickly, the noise of the job fair melted into a cloud of fluffy mashed potatoes.

Mary yawned and stepped away from the cash register in Secondhand Blessings. It was only two thirty, but the busy morning, combined with a late night tossing and turning, had put a kink in her back and left her wishing for a nap. A lock of her hair fell into her eyes, and she immediately thought of Paige as she pushed it away. How good it would be to have a friend from high school back in town!

The doors whooshed open, and as though she'd been conjured by Mary's musing, Paige ducked into the store. Next to her was a girl with hazel eyes and long hair the same dark shade as her mother's.

Mary smiled and circled the counter to greet them. "Hey, you found us." She stopped in front of the girl and held out her hand. "You must be Kailey. It's such a pleasure to meet you."

The girl neither responded nor looked Mary in the eyes. Instead, she slipped one hand around her waist and laid the other limply in Mary's palm.

Paige draped her arm around Kailey's shoulders. "Kailey, this is Mary Baxter, an old friend of mine from high school."

A blush colored Kailey's cheeks, making her look even more like the friend that Mary remembered from high school. She pulled her hand away then ducked her head and shuffled her feet, her discomfort obvious.

Mary offered a kind smile. "Welcome to Bird-in-Hand, Kailey. How do you like it so far?"

"It's okay." She glanced at her mother. "Can I look around?"

"Sure, baby." Paige dropped her arm and nodded encouragingly. Kailey disappeared down one of the aisles.

"She's beautiful," Mary said. "She looks just like you at that age."

"Thank you." Paige shook her head sadly. "She's really having a tough time with the divorce though. She used to be a lot more outgoing before Jack and I split up."

"Hopefully that will come back in time," Mary said gently. A customer approached the cash register, and she frowned apologetically. "Sorry, I need to help this person."

Paige fluttered her hand. "No, no, you go right ahead. I'm going to go find Kailey and then have a look around."

Mary was soon wrapped up in helping customers. A short while later, Paige reappeared at the cash register, an antique pair of barber's shears in her hand. Kailey hovered at her elbow, a slim and silent shadow.

"Ooh, those are nice." Mary ran her finger along the finely scrolled blades. "I forgot we had them."

Paige set the shears on the counter. "Something for the salon. I thought they would look neat mounted in a shadow box on the wall in my office."

"Absolutely." She looked past Paige at Kailey. "How about you, Kailey? Find anything you like?"

Kailey jammed her hands into her pockets, and her gaze jerked toward the door. "We don't have a lot of room in our apartment."

Mary glanced at Paige. Kailey's sharp words sure sounded like an indictment. Paige ignored it and handed Mary a twenty-dollar bill. Mary started to push the money back to her, but something in the steady way Paige met her eyes told her she didn't want that. She rang up the sale and handed Paige her change.

"So, Paige, I've been looking for a good hairdresser." Mary reached under the counter for a bag to package up the shears. "Tell me about your salon. Have you been open long?"

Paige pulled her purse strap over her shoulder. From a pocket on the side, she pulled out a business card and handed it to Mary. "It's been a couple of weeks. We moved here after the holidays, but it took me a while to find a place and get set up. Plus, it took us a few days to get settled in our new apartment."

"Of course."

"I'd be happy to do your hair," Paige continued. "I mean, if you're serious about looking for a new hairdresser."

Mary tucked the card into her apron pocket and then pushed the bag with the shears across the counter. "Oh, I'm serious. Do I need to make an appointment?"

"Nope," Paige said, her expression brightening. "Just come on by. I'm taking walk-ins until I can build up my client list. And if you like your hairdo, maybe you can tell your friends?"

She widened her eyes hopefully then pretended to bite her nails.

Mary laughed. "Of course I will."

Mary waved as Paige and Kailey made their way to the door. "Thanks for coming!"

More customers lined up at the cash register, so Mary concentrated on the task at hand. Eventually, though, she was ready for a break and was only too glad to hand the job over to Elizabeth.

"Maybe we'll need to take on that additional help sooner than I thought," Elizabeth joked, tipping her head toward the customers coming in through the door.

Mary sucked in a breath. Wade Jameson paused just inside the entrance, his customary baseball cap in his hand and sunglasses tucked into the collar of his shirt.

Elizabeth tilted her head. "Hey, isn't that—?"

"The high school baseball coach," Mary said.

"And Bird-in-Hand's most eligible bachelor," Elizabeth said, echoing Mary's thoughts. She slanted a sly smile at her sister. "Wonder what he's doing here."

Catching sight of them, Wade lifted his hand and stepped toward them, a wide smile on his lips. "Hey, Mary. I was hoping you'd be here today."

At his words, Elizabeth snorted playfully and disappeared down one of the aisles.

Mary dropped her hand to her shirt, smoothing the wrinkles from the deep blue fabric, and circled the counter to meet him. "Good afternoon, Wade. Something I can help you find?"

A dimple appeared on his right cheek. "Last time I bumped into you, I mentioned I might stop by, remember?" His smile widened, and he leaned in closer. "Were you leaving?"

Mary took a steadying breath. "Actually, I was just about to take a short break."

"Then my timing is perfect." A twinkle lit his hazel eyes, and he motioned toward a patch of sun glinting through one of the shop windows. "Mind if we talk a minute?"

Not at all sounded too proper. *No* was too abrupt. Mary pressed her lips tight and led the way to the back of the store.

Wade was tall and lean. No wonder women swooned when he passed. Okay, so maybe that was an exaggeration, but he still made Mary's heart beat fast. She crossed her arms over her chest and turned to him.

"What can I do for you, Wade?"

The smile slipped a bit, and a glimmer of uncertainty shone in his eyes. Mary groaned. She was coming across all wrong. She dropped her arms and smiled. "I'm surprised you were able to get out of class."

He grinned and slid one hand into his pocket. "This is my conference period. I thought I would try to catch you before I head to practice."

"Baseball practice already?" She glanced out the window at the light dusting of snow on the ground.

"Spring training is just around the corner. I'm working on lining up some scrimmages."

"I see." She waited.

He shrugged. "So, Mary, I was wondering, if you're not busy tomorrow, would you like to catch a movie or something?"

"Saturday?" Her pulse ratcheted. Were her palms sweating? She clasped her hands. They were definitely sweating. "Uh, yeah, that sounds fun."

"Yeah?" He lifted one sandy-brown brow and thwacked the baseball cap against his leg. "Cool. How about five thirty? That would give us time to head over to Lancaster for something to eat before the show."

She hesitated. "Could we make it a little later, say around six? The store closes at five, so that will give me plenty of time to get ready. N-not that I need an hour to get ready." She stumbled to a stop, heat flooding her cheeks.

Wade laughed. "Okay. So I'll see you then?"

She nodded. "Looking forward to it."

"Good." He pulled a business card out of his pocket and handed it to her. "Here's my number in case anything comes up. See you tomorrow, Mary." He paused, a funny sort of half smile on his face as he looked at her. Finally, he clapped the cap back on his head and turned, freeing her to breathe normally.

Martha poked her head around a bookcase, her gaze darting from Wade's retreating back to Mary. "Was that Wade Jameson, the baseball coach?"

"It was." Mary scrambled to pull Paige's card from her pocket. Across the front, the words PAIGE'S PLACE scrolled in flowing brown script. "Hey, Martha?" she asked distractedly.

Her sister stepped out from behind the bookcase, eyebrows raised questioningly.

"Would it be all right if I take off a couple of hours tomorrow?" Mary smiled and lifted her gaze from the card in her hand to the man outside the window climbing into a shiny new Dodge Challenger. "I'm going to need to get my hair done."

CHAPTER TWO

Bright yellow tape fluttered across the entrance to the parking lot outside of Paige's Place early Saturday morning. It was no surprise. Even though Paige took walk-ins, Mary had called for an appointment just to be sure she could get in and out of the salon quickly, and Paige had warned her the lot was under construction.

Mary flipped on her turn signal and angled the car around the back of the salon toward the alley. Only one other vehicle occupied the narrow space. She slipped in behind it then climbed from her car and hurried toward the rear entrance.

A sharp wind pinched Mary's fingers as she reached for the knob, reminding her how hard Bird-in-Hand's winter weather was on her skin. Wishing she'd thought to grab her gloves, she jerked the door open and ducked into a dark hall.

Blinking as her eyes adjusted to the dim light, she called out, "Hello? Anyone home?"

"In here." Paige poked her head through the opening at the end of the hall and waved. On her hand was a blue latex glove. "Come on in. I'm just finishing up with a customer."

Mary fumbled with the buttons on her coat as she wove past a metal shelf lined with beauty supplies, a rack of metal hooks draped with aprons, and a laundry basket stacked high with clean towels.

"Sorry about the mess." Paige ducked into view and pointed with the tip of her scissors toward the hall. "I keep meaning to sort all of that out but there never seems to be enough time." She smiled and shrugged, then laid her hand on the shoulder of the woman sitting in her stylist chair. "Mary, do you know Chelsea White?"

"No, I don't think so."

The young woman peeked up at her through the strands of damp hair clinging to her face. "Hi."

Since Chelsea was draped in a cape, Mary didn't offer to shake her hand. Instead, she just tipped her head to her and smiled. "Hi, Chelsea. Nice to meet you. I'm Mary Baxter."

Paige picked up a comb and swiped a straight, even part through Chelsea's brown locks. "Mary is an old friend of mine from high school."

"Not that old," Mary joked. She settled into the stylist chair opposite the one occupied by Chelsea. "How do you know Paige?"

"Actually, we met a couple of days ago at the job fair." She smiled up at Paige, who winked at Mary and waggled her brows.

"Chelsea is a nail tech. I offered to do her hair in exchange for my nails."

"It's a trial run for both of us," Chelsea finished.

Mary leaned back in the chair and crossed her ankles. "That's a pretty good deal."

"I think so." Chelsea glanced into the mirror. "I look better already."

Paige finished up the last few snips on Chelsea's bangs and then reached for a hair dryer. Soon, a cherry-scented cloud wafted from Chelsea's head. "I'm almost done here, Mary."

Mary waved her hand. "No rush. I really appreciate you rearranging your schedule to fit me in."

Paige shrugged and talked a little louder to be heard over the dryer. "No problem. The lady who was supposed to come in was happy to take a later slot."

"Well, it is Saturday. Most people like to sleep in on their day off."

"Are you speaking from experience?"

Mary laughed. "I wish. I'm usually at the store first thing." She looked over at Chelsea. "My sisters and I run the resale and gift shop called Secondhand Blessings on the other side of town."

"Oh yeah. I've heard of that place."

"You should check it out." Paige clicked off the dryer then ran her fingers through Chelsea's hair to give it one last fluff before spritzing it with hairspray. "It's a really neat place. They even have some baked goods."

Chelsea raised her eyebrows. "Really?"

Mary nodded. "I know that's probably not what you would expect from a resale shop, but one of my sisters loves to bake. And if you're into handmade Amish goods, we stock a little of that too."

Her face heated a bit while she mulled the next words. It always felt a little prideful when she told others about her art-work, but she was learning to overcome that. "I've also taken up painting again. Every now and then I put a few of my things up for sale."

Paige gaped as she rested her hand on the chair. "I didn't know you painted. You mean that lovely landscape I saw by the store window was yours?"

Mary nodded, glad that she'd noticed.

"That's awesome, Mary. You're very talented."

Chelsea slid off the chair and reached up to unsnap the cape from around her neck. "I'll have to check it out." She caught her lip with her teeth and glanced at Paige. "In the meantime, should I wait for you to call me?"

Paige extended her hand to admire her new manicure. "I'm happy if you are. When can you start?"

Chelsea's face lit with a smile. "That's awesome. Would a week from Monday be okay? I need to give the grocery store where I work time to find a replacement."

"Next week would be perfect." Paige motioned around the salon. "Maybe by then I'll be finished pulling all of this together. If it's okay with you, I thought I would put a table over there, next to the window, for you."

"Absolutely. Great light there."

"Good. Now, what about nail polish, files, clippers, all of that? Is there anything I need to purchase?"

Chelsea shook her head. "I have all my own supplies." She picked up her phone and keys. "I've been working out of my house part-time. I have my license," she added quickly. "I just couldn't afford to rent my own building, so this"—she motioned around the salon—"is perfect."

The two shook hands and then Chelsea headed for the door, a small skip in her step.

"Hey, that worked out, didn't it?" Mary said as she slid into the chair Chelsea had vacated.

"I'll say." Paige shook out the used cape and dropped it into a laundry basket next to her station. She opened a drawer, pulled out a new cape, and draped it around Mary's shoulders. "Chelsea is going to rent the space from me, which will be a big help in cutting some of my overhead."

"I'm glad, Paige." Mary smiled at her friend in the mirror. "Have I mentioned how thrilled I am to have you back in town?"

To her surprise, tears welled in Paige's eyes. She blinked them back and offered a wobbly smile. "Thanks, Mary. That means a lot to me, especially since not everyone in Bird-in-Hand feels the same way."

Mary swiveled the chair around with her toe. "What are you talking about? Who's not happy?"

Paige crossed her arms over her chest. "Well, Vanessa Bancroft for one. My ex-husband, for another."

Mary tilted her head curiously. "Who's Vanessa Bancroft?"

"You remember," she urged. "Her name used to be Wyland. She was really pretty, long hair, always wore it in a ponytail."

Mary snapped her fingers. "Now I remember. What about her?"

Paige laid her hand on the back of the chair and gently spun it around so Mary faced the mirror. "Vanessa and I have a long history, going all the way back to high school."

"What sort of history?"

"Not a good one, I'm afraid." Paige grabbed a comb and began running it through Mary's hair, gently weeding out the tangles. "She thinks I stole her boyfriend."

Mary frowned at her in the mirror. "You're kidding."

Paige's brows rose.

"Oh, come on. People don't really hold on to grudges for thirty years over something so petty, do they?"

Paige laughed and put the comb down, then smoothed the cape around Mary's shoulders. "To be honest, there was a lot more to it than that, but apparently, she's still not over it. I ran into her at the job fair, and she barely said two words to me." She tore off a strip of cotton gauze and stuffed it into the gaps at Mary's neck.

"Maybe she didn't recognize you."

"Do I look that different?" Paige patted her hips with a laugh. "I mean, I know I've gained weight since high school, but—"

"Ha." Mary groaned and eyed Paige's slender figure. "Whatever exercise routine you're using, it's working."

Paige laughed and ran her fingers through Mary's hair. "So, speaking of different, what are we doing to your hair today?"

"I was thinking a cut and a color. Maybe something to brighten me up a little bit?"

Paige nodded and removed a color sample book from a tall wooden cupboard. While Mary flipped through it, Paige laid out a water bottle, her scissors, a comb, and a box of thin foil wraps on a clean, white towel.

Satisfied with a color, Mary pointed it out and then handed the book back to Paige. "So, what about your ex-husband? Why was he unhappy about the move?"

Paige sighed and went to the cupboard to mix the color Mary had chosen. "He lives in a small town just outside of Pittsburgh, which is a little over four hours away. Basically, he feels I'm trying to keep Kailey away from him. I tried explaining it wasn't about that, but Jack..." Her shoulders sagged, and she closed the cupboard door with a sigh. "Well, let's just say it was a pretty messy divorce, and there are plenty of hard feelings on both sides."

"So he's not likely to believe anything you tell him."

"Unfortunately, no."

"That's too bad."

Paige shrugged and pulled a tall tray on a stand over to the chair. "Anyway, I do what I can to make sure Kailey spends time with her dad, but it's never enough. Jack can be pretty ruthless when it comes to getting what he wants."

She dropped her gaze on the last few words and turned her face away, as though there was more to the story she was too embarrassed to share.

Compassion swelled in Mary's heart. How well she understood those feelings! She'd lived with them for months after Brian left. Elizabeth and Martha would say she'd been comforted so she could offer comfort. In this case, she agreed with them 100 percent. She reached up and patted her friend's hand.

"I've been there, Paige. Things were pretty tough after Brian and I divorced. I found that coming back to Bird-in-Hand was a good choice, and I know it will be for you too. In the meantime, if you ever need someone to talk to, you know where to find me."

When she looked up, dampness clung to Paige's lashes. She fumbled in a drawer for a tissue. "I appreciate that. I really do."

Prompted by the hurt in her eyes, Mary twisted around to look her in the face. "I hope you don't mind my asking, but have you and Kailey thought about getting involved with one of the local churches here in town? It's a really good way to make new friends, put down roots, that sort of thing."

"I've thought about it, but that's as far as it's gone," Paige admitted, wiping the tissue across her eyes and under her nose. "To be honest, Kailey has been a little reluctant, and I haven't pushed her."

"Well, our church has a really awesome youth group. If you're interested, I'll text you the information and worship times. No pressure. Just something for you to think about."

"I…" Paige hesitated, but then nodded eagerly. "You know, I think I'd like that."

"Great." Mary smiled and settled back in the chair. "I'll get it to you."

"Thanks." She paused and squeezed Mary's shoulder. "I mean it. Thank you so much for being such a sweet friend."

"Always." Mary swallowed down the emotion rising in her throat and smiled. "Now, as far as a trim, I was thinking maybe a couple of inches off. What do you think?"

"Couple of inches it is," Paige said, brandishing the scissors.

She set to work, and before long, Mary sat in the far corner of the salon, her hair covered in color and strips of tinfoil.

"You know what this reminds me of?" she asked, reaching for a magazine while Paige checked that the strips of tinfoil were secure.

"The scene from that movie with the guy and the two kids sitting in front of the TV with tinfoil cones on their heads to protect against aliens?" Mary gaped, and Paige laughed. "I know. I hear it all the time."

A bell chimed, and she motioned toward the back door. "Let me check who that is. My next appointment isn't due to come for at least another thirty minutes."

Mary held up her hand. "Before you go, would it be okay if I wrapped up in a towel? I don't want to risk getting any color on my clothes."

"Of course." Paige crossed to a cabinet, pulled out a brown towel, and carried it back to her. "Here you go. Let me know if you need anything else. I'll come check on you in about thirty minutes."

"Okeydoke."

Thirty minutes of sweet, quiet bliss. Mary put her feet up on a stool, then spread the magazine over her lap. The salon was L-shaped, so she could hear Paige and another woman's voice carrying on a conversation around the corner, but she couldn't see them—a fact that suited her just fine since she hoped to relax in private.

She scooched lower to prop her elbows on the arms of the chair and thumbed lazily through the pages of the magazine. In one article, a famous actor gushed about being six months sober. Another bemoaned the aches and pains of the latter stages of pregnancy. Mary flipped past that story in a hurry. She loved her children, Michael and Jennifer, but she was happy with her current phase of life and had no desire to go back to her child-rearing days. Finally, she settled on an article about the newest addition to England's royal family. Before long, the lull of muffled voices tugged on her eyelids.

"Hey there, sleepyhead."

The magazine slipped off her lap to the floor as Mary jerked her eyes open. A few feet away, Paige watched her, a smile on her lips. "You doing okay?"

"I'm fine." Mary pushed up in the chair and rubbed her fingers over her eyes. "Wow. I must have been tired. I actually dozed off."

"It happens a lot." Paige's gaze rose to Mary's hair, and she frowned.

"What?" Mary lifted her hand to her head.

"Something doesn't look quite right." She crossed to pluck one of the strips of foil from Mary's hair then tsked. "Would you mind coming over to the sink? I want to check to see how your color is developing."

"Sure." Mary draped the towel over her arm then followed Paige to a nearby chair situated in front of a deep sink. Unlike the dryers, the sinks were in the long portion of the salon. Mary's gaze locked with the other customer's in the mirror. The woman was middle-aged, with a sleek look to her clothes and makeup that marked her as one of the high-society types that Mary rarely rubbed elbows with. Her hair was perfectly coiffed, despite the fact Paige hadn't cut her hair yet, and her nails French tipped and polished. Mary gave her a nod before turning her attention to Paige.

"It's been a while since I've had a color. Do you think maybe I should have washed my hair before I came?"

"It shouldn't make any difference." Paige patted the chair. Once Mary was seated, Paige angled the back downward so Mary's neck rested comfortably in a rounded notch that allowed her hair to hang into the sink. "Let's take a look."

Paige pulled off another piece of tinfoil, and then another. Something about the look in her eyes made Mary's stomach muscles tense.

"What is it? Is something wrong?"

Instead of answering, Paige began removing all the pieces of tinfoil and dropping them into the sink. She worked quickly, her lip caught between her teeth.

"Paige?"

"I don't… Something…" She blinked rapidly and grabbed the handheld sprayer to douse Mary's head in warm water. The longer she rinsed, the more nervous Mary felt. Finally, she reached up and grasped Paige's wrist.

"You're going to have to tell me what's going on."

"I can't." Paige grabbed a towel and pressed it into Mary's hands, then set the chair upright and reached for a mirror. "Mary, I…I have no idea what went wrong. Honestly. It's a new-to-me brand, so when it was different, I…I don't know what to say." She hugged the mirror to her chest and shook her head.

Mary pressed the towel to her head, soaking up most of the water. Finally, she reached for the mirror. "Give it to me, Paige. Let me see."

Tears welled in Paige's eyes as she reluctantly handed over the mirror. Mary sucked in a breath then flipped the mirror around to see her reflection. A gasp escaped her lips at the sight that met her eyes.

Instead of the glossy blond with honey-colored highlights she'd expected, her hair was a brilliant shade of neon blue.

CHAPTER THREE

Mary stared at her reflection. Even after several seconds, her mind refused to process what her eyes told her. She fingered one lock of brilliant blue hair then let it plop onto her shoulder.

Don't panic. It's just hair. It'll be fine.

So why did she feel sick to her stomach? Next to her, Paige shuffled her feet, her hands flitting in agitation around Mary's head.

"I have no idea what could have happened. Truly. But I'll be happy to fix it, no charge, of course. Oh, Mary, I'm so sorry."

Tears flooded her eyes, and Mary had to blink back a sudden burning in her own. She sucked in a slow breath. "We were talking. Do you think maybe you were distracted and grabbed the wrong bottle of color?"

Paige's shoulders rose to her ears. "I don't see how I could have. They are all on different shelves, sorted by color. Granted, I've been really busy trying to get everything stocked and ready for opening, so one could have been in the wrong place but—"

Across the room, Paige's other customer leaned forward in her chair and cleared her throat loudly. "Excuse me?" She waited until they looked at her and then frowned. "Is everything all right over there?"

"I'll be right with you, Mrs. Randall." Paige turned her back to the woman, hiding Mary from view. "Just stay put," she whispered to Mary. "I'll let her know I'm not quite finished with you and ask if she can reschedule."

Mary grabbed her arm and lowered her voice. "Won't that be bad for business?"

"Yes, but…" She motioned helplessly to Mary's hair. "This wasn't what you asked for, and you have a date tonight." She shook her head firmly. "It's my fault you have blue hair. I'll take care of it."

Mary slid her gaze around Paige to Mrs. Randall. The woman made no attempt to hide her curiosity. In fact, she eyed Mary's blue hair with suspicion and reached toward the floor for her purse.

Mary tipped her head in the woman's direction. "You can't afford to lose any customers. I'll just call Wade and tell him something came up."

Smiling brightly despite the pit in her stomach, she pulled the cape off her shoulders and turned. "Thanks so much for the great color, Paige. It's absolutely fabulous. Just what I wanted."

"But…but…," Paige stammered. She leaned close and lowered her voice. "You don't have to do this."

"No, no, don't worry about giving me a blow dry," Mary chirped, waving her hand. "I'll take care of it at home. And thanks so much for squeezing me in at the last minute. You're a gem."

She pulled Paige into a quick hug. "I'll call you later to schedule an appointment," she whispered, then slipped her arms into her coat. Smiling, she wiggled her fingers at Mrs. Randall as she strolled toward the back door. "See you later, Paige."

Paige's eyes shone with gratitude. "Bye, Mary."

In the alley, Mary let her shoulders sag. The cold air on her damp head was a bitter counterpoint to the hot tears gathering in her eyes. She lifted her chin and hurried toward her car.

"For goodness' sake, it's not like this was your only chance for a date with Wade Jameson. Besides, there was a point in your life when you wouldn't have minded blue hair," she muttered to herself as she dug through her purse for her keys.

Of course, that was a long time ago. She was a different person now, and she'd worked hard to prove she was better at making sound decisions. Blue hair certainly didn't fit into the scheme. And what would her sisters think? Or Wade?

She stuttered to a stop as her foot connected with a small plastic bottle, sending it bouncing along the pavement. As it passed the garbage cans, a small cat shot out from behind the cans in a blur of black and white and then froze, hair on end and green eyes wild. Mary knelt and held out her hand. "Here, pretty kitty," she said. "I didn't mean to scare you."

The cat—kitten, really—backed away, turned, and took off down the alley.

Mary stood and went to pick up the bottle she'd kicked. It was brown and unmarked, the white cap's seal unbroken.

She rolled the bottle in her palm. Only a sticky patch of glue remained where the label should have been, but she recognized it as one of the hair color bottles from the rack in the salon. Why would an unopened bottle of hair color without a label be in the alley?

Suspicion formed in her brain. Could it be that the unfortunate state of her hair wasn't an accident? She shook the thought away. That couldn't be. She'd made the appointment at the last minute. No one could have possibly known she would be Paige's next customer, or even that her next customer would request a cut *and* a color.

Noise rattled from the end of the alley. Mary looked up in time to glimpse a man dressed in dark garb rounding the corner. Had he been watching her? Paige's claim that not everyone was happy she'd returned to Bird-in-Hand rang inside Mary's head. Would someone really be so cruel as to try to sabotage her business before she'd really even started?

Shivering, Mary carried the hair color bottle to her car and climbed inside. Then she pulled her phone from her purse and dialed Paige's number. When she answered, Mary spoke quickly.

"Paige, it's Mary. Don't say anything. When you can, I need you to grab the garbage can that has the bottle of color you used on my hair and bring it outside. Pretend you're just tidying up. Okay?"

"Uh…sure, that will work."

"Good. See you in a minute."

She disconnected then tapped the steering wheel impatiently until the back door swung open, and Paige stepped out carrying a clear plastic garbage bag that was only half full. Mary jumped from her car and hurried to meet her.

Paige's brows winged upward. "Mary, what on earth—I thought you went home."

Mary took the bag and jerked it open. The empty bottle of hair color lay near the top. The brand wasn't familiar, but the bottle was identical to the one she'd found on the pavement.

She snatched it out then handed the bag back. "Paige, how long did you tell me the salon has been open?"

"Just a couple of weeks."

"And have you had many customers?"

"It's been steady, I guess. I mean, the first couple of days were slow, but I've had several walk-ins a day since then." Her gaze flitted nervously toward the door and back to Mary. "Why?"

Biting her lip, Mary concentrated on lifting the edge of the label with her fingernail. It peeled back easily. Paige watched in silence, her head tilted to one side.

"What are you doing? Why did you want me to—"

"Aha!"

At Mary's exclamation, Paige stammered to a halt. Mary lifted the bottle triumphantly, then pulled it back. Her hunch had been right, but that wasn't a good thing.

"What is it, Mary? What did you find?" Paige asked slowly.

Mary licked her lips while she groped for words. "Paige… uh…I'm not sure how to tell you this."

"What?" Her gaze sharpened before dropping to the bottle clutched in Mary's fingers. "What's wrong?"

"It's the label." Mary cleared her throat then lifted her hand to touch her damp hair. "Someone put a blond color label on the blue color bottle. Someone is out to get you."

CHAPTER FOUR

Elizabeth hummed a happy tune while she chopped the potatoes for the beef stew she was making for supper. At her feet, Pal, their border collie, and Tink, their mischievous dachshund, watched with ears pricked and eyes peeled in anticipation of any stray pieces that rolled to the floor. The cat, Butterscotch, showed less interest. He merely observed from the windowsill, his tail twitching occasionally as he stared with disdain at the dogs.

John would be joining them later, a thought that brought a smile to Elizabeth's lips as she scraped the potatoes off the cutting board and into the steaming pot. John Marks was a fine, upstanding man, and a distinguished member of the East Lampeter Township Police Department, but what she respected most was the generosity he exhibited toward the people he considered friends. Cooking for him was a pleasure, especially since, as a widower, he was so appreciative of a home-cooked meal.

The kitchen door scraped open, and Elizabeth looked up from the pot bubbling on the stove.

"All done closing up the store?" she asked as Martha stepped inside.

"Yep." Pausing by the windowsill, Martha gave Butterscotch's ears a tickle. Shrugging out of her coat, she smiled and took a deep whiff. "Mmm, smells delicious. What are you cooking?"

"Beef stew. I hope you're hungry." Elizabeth placed a lid over the stew and then wiped her hands on a clean dishtowel. "Supper will be ready in about an hour."

"I'm starving. I'll go wash up and come back to help you finish." Martha sighed and draped her coat over a hook next to the door wearily.

Elizabeth frowned. "You look tired. Still not sleeping well?"

Martha shook her head. "It's the strangest thing. I've never had trouble before, but the last few nights, I wake up at almost the exact same time, and then it takes me forever to go back to sleep."

Elizabeth crossed the room to pat her on the shoulder. "Do you want to try lying down before we eat?"

"But supper—"

Elizabeth shook her head. "Don't worry about coming down to help. I can get it. Anyway, Mary should be home any moment."

As if to punctuate her statement, a car door slammed, and both Martha and Elizabeth directed their attention to the door.

"There she is now," Elizabeth said, shooing Martha toward the stairs. "Go on up. I'll call you when it's ready."

"Maybe I will…" Martha trailed off and stared out the door.

"What?" Elizabeth followed the direction of her gaze. Instantly, it was apparent what had shorn the words from her lips. She laid her fingers over her mouth in shock. "Oh, Mary."

The door swung open. Mary didn't look at either of them as she stepped inside.

"You dyed your hair blue?" Never one to mince words, Martha folded her arms over her chest. "What on earth made you do that?"

"I didn't do it on purpose," Mary said with a sniff. She took off her coat and hung it on the hook next to Martha's. "There was a mishap at the salon."

"Well, can you get it fixed?"

"Martha." Elizabeth touched her arm and gave a small shake of her head.

Martha shot an apologetic glance at Mary. "I only mean that your hair is so pretty as it is. Why would you want to mess with the color?"

Catching sight of Mary's reddened eyes, Elizabeth left Martha to cross to her. "What happened, honey? I thought you were just going to get a cut and a touch-up to the color?"

"That *was* the plan," Mary said, reaching for a napkin. She fluttered it in the air before pressing it to her nose. "Paige says it was an accident, but I'm not so sure."

Martha's brow furrowed in concern as she joined them at the door. "You think Paige dyed your hair blue on purpose?"

"Why would she do that?" Elizabeth asked in almost the same moment.

"No, you misunderstand. I don't think it was Paige. I think it was someone else."

The look of confusion on Martha's face mirrored the one Elizabeth felt. She gestured toward the table. "Why don't we sit down, so you can explain," she suggested, leading the way. She pulled out a chair and then nodded to Mary. "Okay, start at the beginning. What happened?"

Mary drew a deep breath and recounted the events of the day.

"I really don't understand why Paige wasn't more concerned about the man I spotted outside her salon," Mary finished.

Elizabeth scratched her head. "Was it someone she knew? Are there other businesses nearby? Why would he be there?"

"To be honest, I didn't get a very good look at him. And Paige kept saying my finding the bottle and seeing someone leave could just be coincidence."

"Even after you showed her the covered label?" Martha asked.

"And what about her ex-husband? He wasn't happy about her moving back to Bird-in-Hand. Isn't she worried it was him outside her salon?" Elizabeth added.

Mary shrugged and rested her arms on the table. "I asked her all of that. She called it an 'unhappy accident' and said the double label could have happened anywhere, even at the factory."

Elizabeth narrowed her eyes. "But you aren't convinced, are you?"

"Not really. I mean, it could have been an accident like Paige said, but…" She bit her lip uncertainly. "Anyway, Paige offered to fix my hair for free, but I didn't want to make a big deal of it. She had another customer in the shop, and with her business being new, I didn't think she could afford to lose any customers. I'm supposed to call her to reschedule."

Elizabeth patted Mary's hand in sympathy. "And speaking of rescheduling, what are you going to do about your date tonight?"

"Wait a minute." Martha frowned and held up her hand. "What's this about a date?"

Mary scrunched the napkin and rose to throw it in the trash. "Wade Jameson came into the shop yesterday."

Martha crossed her legs, then her arms. "Isn't he the baseball coach at the high school?"

Mary nodded. "He asked me out on a date, which is why I went to the salon to see Paige. I figured I'd freshen up my looks a little before we went out." She snorted wryly and pinched a lock of hair between her thumb and forefinger. "Talk about backfire. No way I want to go anywhere looking like this." She pushed away from the counter. "I'd better go call him. After that, I'll be down to help you with supper, Elizabeth."

Elizabeth glanced at the pot simmering on the stove. She still had biscuits to make to go with the stew, but there was plenty of time for that. "No rush," she said.

Mary disappeared through the door, and Elizabeth sat drumming her fingers on the tabletop while she thought over everything Mary had told them. Finally, she frowned and turned to Martha.

"I have to say, I agree with Mary about this whole thing being a little more concerning than just an 'unhappy accident.' What do you think?"

Martha lifted her palms helplessly. "I agree, it's strange. But if Paige isn't worried, there's not a whole lot we can do."

"Maybe not." She got up from the table and crossed to the cupboard and took out a large bowl for the biscuit dough.

Martha leaned forward to rest her arms on the table. "I don't like that look on your face. There's something else worrying you, isn't there?"

Elizabeth pursed her lips as she pulled a bag of flour from the pantry. "It's probably nothing."

"I doubt that. You've a good sense about these things. Spit it out."

She plunked the flour on the counter and turned to Martha, a heavy feeling settling in her chest. "I just don't think Paige should be so cavalier about this, especially since we don't know who the person is that Mary saw outside her salon. I've read a lot of stories of abusive spouses wreaking havoc on their ex's lives. What if this is another case of a man causing problems for his ex-wife because of a grudge?"

Concern glowed in Martha's gaze, but she said nothing for a moment. Elizabeth could almost see the wheels inside her head turning, until finally she sat up straight and gave a small nod, as though she'd reached a decision.

"First of all, I'm not sure we should assume Paige's ex-husband is abusive. It makes sense that he would be unhappy she moved away. Given the situation with their daughter, I would likely feel the same way, wouldn't you?"

Elizabeth considered the idea of being separated from a child, then nodded in reluctant agreement. "You're right. I'm jumping to conclusions."

"But I do agree that Paige may be taking what happened a little too lightly." Martha paused for a moment to rest her chin in her hand. "I guess it wouldn't hurt to keep an eye out around town in case her ex-husband shows up. Do we know his name or have any idea what he looks like?"

"His name is Jack, but that's all I know. Mary might have an idea what he looks like. I'll ask her when she comes down for supper." Noting the weary lines around Martha's eyes, Elizabeth patted her hand. "You still have time to catch a quick nap if you want."

Martha lifted one shoulder and got up to check the stew. "At this point, it would probably just make it harder for me to fall asleep later."

The front doorbell rang, and Martha tipped her head toward it. "Didn't you say John was coming to supper? That's probably him. Why don't you go let him in and let me finish getting the food ready?"

The offer was tempting. Elizabeth ran her hands over her apron and glanced at the flour still sitting next to the empty bowl.

"Oh, go on," Martha insisted, smiling as she reached for a spoon to stir the stew. "There's not much left to this, other than making the biscuits and getting the tea ready. I'll make drop biscuits. They're faster, and Mary likes them better anyway."

Her sister's thoughtfulness warmed Elizabeth's heart. She wrapped her in a quick hug then slipped out of her apron. Outside, a light snow had begun to fall. It was above freezing so it wouldn't stick, but it was still beautiful. And cold. She hurried down the hall to let John in. His smile as she opened the door stole her breath.

She touched her hair nervously and then waved him inside. "Hi, John. Come on in."

"Hey, Elizabeth." White flakes dotted his dark hair and coat as John stepped past her into the hall, a plain white box balanced carefully in both hands. "Hope you don't mind. I stopped by the Village Bakery on my way over and picked up an apple pie for dessert."

"Mind?" Elizabeth took the box from him and dipped her head to inhale the warm scent of vanilla and cinnamon. "Thank you so much. This smells delicious. Today was so busy, I only had time to work on the stew."

"Beef stew?" John's smile grew as he patted his stomach. "Sounds great, especially with it being so cold outside. You keep feeding me like this, and I won't fit into my uniforms."

Elizabeth stifled a pert smile. John was tall, but even without his height factored in, his broad shoulders and trim waist made it obvious he kept in shape. "It'll take more than a bowl of stew and slice of apple pie," she retorted, surprising herself with her frankness, then lifted the box as she felt her cheeks warm. "Let's go put this in the kitchen. I'll stick it in the oven to keep it warm. I think I even have a tub of ice cream in the freezer that will go perfectly with it."

His answering smile wiped away any trace of awkwardness she might have felt. Her steps light, she turned for the kitchen. She and Mary needn't worry about Paige. With officers like John Marks and others keeping watch over their quaint little town, she would be perfectly safe.

What could possibly go wrong?

CHAPTER FIVE

Mary pulled her stockinged feet up onto her bed and stared at the plain white business card in her hand. The front was stamped with the high school logo. On the back was Wade's name and contact information, along with the link to the school's athletic page on the district website.

From the floor, Tink shuffled her front paws and let out a low whine. The moment Mary looked at her, she exposed her teeth in a strange sort of doggie smile. Chuckling, Mary bent and lifted her onto the bed. Appeased, the dog circled once, twice, then curled up with a sigh—one Mary felt tempted to echo.

Cupping Tink's snout, Mary looked deeply into her soulful brown eyes. "What do you think? No sense putting it off, right? I have to call him."

Tink tilted her little head to the left and stared at her, unblinking. Mary reached for her cell phone. With one hand, she dialed the number. With the other, she grasped Tink's front paw and gently ran her fingers over the rough pads. Tink rolled onto her back in response, her four little legs jutting into the air like sausages.

"Hello?"

Mary caught her breath. The line hadn't even rung on her end. "Wade Jameson, please."

"Speaking."

She swallowed and pressed the phone tighter to her ear. "Hi, Wade, it's Mary. Mary Baxter."

Wade's voice instantly warmed. "Hey, Mary. Hold on a sec."

Dead air filled the space until he returned.

"There. I closed my door so we can talk in private."

"Oh. Okay." Unsure how she felt about the pronouncement, she licked her lips and dropped Tink's paw to rub her palm over her knees. "Listen, Wade, I'm sorry, but I'm afraid I'm not going to be able to make our date tonight."

He answered without hesitation. "I'm sorry to hear that. Is everything all right?"

"Everything's fine. I just…" What could she say that wouldn't be a lie, but wouldn't reflect poorly on Paige? She cleared her throat nervously. "It's been a long day, and to be honest, I'm just not up to going out. Could we possibly move it to another night? Maybe Monday, or possibly Tuesday?"

"Well, Monday I'm busy."

Her heart sank.

"But I'm free on Tuesday. How does dinner at Jennie's sound?"

"Sounds great!" She cringed at the too-eager tone of her voice. *Whoa. Rein in the enthusiasm.*

"I love their chicken potpies," she added, after sucking in a breath to keep her voice steady.

"Okay. Pick you up around six?"

"Six. Good."

"Great. I'll see you then. Bye, Mary."

"Goodbye, Wade." She pressed the END CALL button then dropped the phone on the bed and pulled Tink onto her lap.

"So, not a total loss. I would have hated to miss out on the chance to go out with Wade. He seems like a really nice guy." She tickled the dog's ears and then deposited her back on the floor.

At least, *she* thought Wade seemed nice. Martha apparently didn't agree. Or had Mary only imagined the look that crossed her sister's face when she learned they had a date? The question lingered as she headed back downstairs.

Voices carried from the kitchen, one of them male, and Mary paused at the bottom of the stairs. It sounded like John. Elizabeth had mentioned he'd be joining them for supper.

She glanced down at Tink, who waited patiently at her feet. "I'll be right back."

She bounded back up the stairs. Not to be left behind, Tink followed at her heels. Ducking into her bedroom, Mary grabbed a scarf and wrapped it tightly around her head.

"It's either this, or a hat," she said, flipping the end of the scarf over her shoulder. She braced her hands on her hips and glanced down at Tink. "What do you think?"

The dog gave an eager yip and jumped up to rest her front paws against Mary's leg. She laughed and bent to pick her up for a cuddle. "You couldn't care less what color my hair is, could you, girl?"

In response, Tink squirmed to lick Mary's chin.

"Okay, okay. We're ready now."

Cradling Tink in her arms, Mary traveled the stairs a second time then turned for the kitchen. Martha was just ladling the last of the stew into a tureen. At the counter, Elizabeth was busy filling four tall glasses with ice cubes and tea. John sat at the table, elbows propped as he related details of his last call out—

an encounter with a goat that ended with mud and slush covering his uniform from head to foot and the culprit trotting hap-
pily home. If he noticed the scarf on Mary's head, he didn't
mention it. She greeted him with a smile then set Tink on the
floor and went to help Martha.

"What can I do?"

Martha nodded toward a basket of biscuits, which Mary
carried to the table along with a stick of butter and a jar of
Martha's homemade strawberry preserves. After asking a blessing, they dug in, the pleasant meal enhanced by the funny
stories John told and the snippets the sisters added of things
that had happened at the store. When it was over, they lingered over coffee and pie until the doorbell interrupted their
conversation.

"I'll get it," Mary said. She pushed her chair back and then
motioned toward John and Elizabeth, and also Martha. "Don't
worry about the kitchen. I'll take care of the dishes since you
two got supper."

"What about me?" John asked, a smile on his lips. "I didn't
cook."

"You brought dessert. That counts in my book."

They laughed, and Mary slipped out to answer the door. Her
heart rate sped at the sight of Wade standing on their porch, a
brown paper bag clutched in one hand and his ever-present
baseball cap in the other.

She sucked in a breath and pulled open the door. "Wade,
what a surprise."

"Hey, Mary. Hope you don't mind." He held up the bag.
"When you said you weren't feeling well, I thought I'd stop by

with some chicken soup. It's not homemade, but I hear it's good." His lips stretched in a grin. "I got it from the Family Restaurant in town."

Panic set in in Mary's chest. Had she told him she wasn't feeling well? She didn't think so. She swallowed a sudden knot in her throat and shifted her weight to one foot. "Thank you. That was…so sweet."

She stepped back and swept out her hand toward the hall. "Would you like to come in?"

He reached for the zipper on his coat, then hesitated. "Are you sure you wouldn't mind? I mean, I don't want to keep you if you're not up to company."

"No, no," she said quickly. "I'd actually love—"

Was love too strong a word?

"—like a chance to visit. Please."

Wade's grin widened as he tipped his head back to look around the house. "So this is the old Classen place." He brought his gaze around to rest on her. "I've heard a lot about your family. You're practically famous."

"Infamous, maybe." She smiled and held out her hands for the bag containing the soup. "I'll take that."

He gave it to her then shrugged out of his coat. Draping it over his arm, he drew in a deep breath. "Uh-oh. Something smells fantastic. I take it you've already eaten."

"Afraid so." She smiled an apology and held up the bag. "But it's the thought that counts, and this will make a wonderful lunch for me tomorrow." She angled her head toward the kitchen. "We were just enjoying some coffee and apple pie. Would you like some?"

"Is that what smells so good?" He laughed and rubbed his belly. "I'm always up for pie. Lead the way."

Conversation stopped as Mary led Wade into the kitchen. She made the introductions, then put the soup in the refrigerator and went to fetch a cup of coffee and a plate for Wade's pie. Wade shook hands with John before taking the seat next to him at the table.

"You two know each other?" Elizabeth asked, looking from one to the other.

Wade clapped John on the shoulder. "This guy? We sure do. John helps out with the athletic boosters every chance he gets. We couldn't run the concession stand without him."

"Eh, it's nothing." John reached for his coffee cup. "So, how's the baseball team shaping up this year? Any chance we'll make the playoffs?"

Wade chuckled and leaned forward to rest his elbows on the table. "Well, it's a little too early to tell. I've got a good number of seniors coming back. That should give us a strong foundation to build on." He shrugged, then looked up as Mary set his coffee down. "Thanks."

"You're welcome. Would you like some ice cream with your pie?"

Across the table, Martha stood and began clearing dishes. Wade didn't appear to notice her silence, but Mary did. She eyed her sister curiously. Something in her manner was off. What had her so prickly?

"Ice cream sounds great," Wade said.

Mary nodded. "I'll get it."

Martha set the dishes in the sink then turned to face them. "Such a pleasure to meet you, Coach Jameson. Now, if you all will excuse me, it's been a long day, and I'm feeling a little tired. I'm going to turn in early."

"I hope you're not coming down with the same thing Mary has." Wade glanced over at Mary and flashed a winsome smile. "I only brought enough chicken soup for one."

"Mary, are you not feeling well?" Elizabeth asked, her brows lifting in surprise.

"I didn't realize that," John said, rising. "I shouldn't keep you."

"No, I…"

Mary fingered the edge of her scarf then looked over at Wade. "I'm afraid I may have misled you. I didn't mean to imply that I was sick. I wasn't able to keep our date tonight because something…unforeseen…came up."

He chuckled and waved his hand. "No problem. In fact, I'm glad it's not because you aren't feeling well."

John smiled too, then looked at Elizabeth. "I should be going, anyway. I have an early shift tomorrow."

He said his goodbyes and walked with Elizabeth into the hall. Martha also left, and Mary dished out a slice of pie, topped it with ice cream, then gave it to Wade and settled next to him at the table.

"I really do have to apologize again, Wade. It was so sweet of you to think of bringing me soup. I'm sorry that you wasted a trip."

"Wasted?" He leaned toward her, eyes twinkling. "To be honest, I may have read into your words just because I wanted an excuse to see you."

"Oh." She reached up to touch her hair, remembered that it was covered by a scarf, and fingered the handle of her coffee cup instead.

"It could have backfired, though."

Her gaze flew to him. "Backfired, how?"

He took a swallow of his coffee then shrugged. "You could have called because you had a change of heart. Since you rescheduled, I took a chance it wasn't just that you didn't want to see me."

"Oh, no. It wasn't that at all. I really did—"

His grin widened, and she knew he was teasing. Relaxing against her chair, she smiled. "Funny."

He put his cup down and picked up his fork for a bite of pie. "So, tell me about your hair."

She touched the scarf. "Uh…what about it?"

"Not the right shade of blue?" He tilted his head playfully.

"How did you—? Oh." The word blew from Mary's lips. She stood and stared at her reflection in the mirror fixed to the back of the china cabinet. Sure enough, a blue lock had escaped the scarf and rested in plain sight on her shoulder.

"So much for hiding my secret." She dragged the scarf off her head and dropped it over the back of her chair. "I'm so sorry, Wade. I had a little accident at the hairdresser earlier today. That's why I had to postpone our date."

He laughed and took her hand to pull her back to her chair. "You mean you didn't do this on purpose?"

She groaned and clapped one hand over her eyes.

"It's probably a good thing. You'll need a little less teal if you want to match the school colors."

"Trust me, that wasn't my intent," she said with a laugh.

Now that the truth was out, Mary felt better about her little mishap. While Wade finished his pie, Mary sipped her coffee, and they talked. Finally, he set his cup aside and glanced at his watch.

"Whoa, where has the time gone? I hate to call it a night, but I should probably be going. I have to get to the gym early in the morning. Some of the guys like to get in a workout before heading to church."

She felt a small flutter of disappointment but nodded and stood with him. "It'll be a long day for you."

He tucked his fingertips into the pockets of his jeans. "Eh, I'm used to it."

She motioned toward the fridge. "Thanks again for the soup."

"No problem. I hope you like it."

"I'm sure it'll be great."

He was so much wider and taller close up, and he smelled good—like fresh air and sunshine. And he was in no hurry to move away, she noted. He dropped his hands to his sides as he looked down at her, his gaze locked to her mouth.

She retreated a step and lifted her chin. "So, Tuesday?"

He blinked and took a deep breath. "Tuesday, right. I'll pick you up around quarter to six."

"Okay. I'll be ready."

"Okay." He smiled and pointed toward the hall. "This way?"

"Yeah. I'll just…" She moved past him and pulled open the door.

"Good night, Wade."

"Good night."

She watched through the glass as he climbed into his car and backed down the drive. When at last his taillights winked out of sight, she gave a contented sigh and ambled back toward the kitchen. This certainly was not how she had anticipated the evening would go, but she wasn't complaining.

Who knew a day of color confusion could end with such a perfect night?

CHAPTER SIX

Mary placed the last plate in the dishwasher, shook some powdered soap into the detergent cup, and set the machine to wash. While she wiped down the countertops, she rehashed the details of her conversation with Paige. Was her friend right? Were the labels on the bottles an innocent mistake? And if not, was this merely a case of a prank gone wrong? It was just color, after all. Nobody had gotten hurt.

The image of the man she'd seen outside the salon flashed into her head as she carried the dishcloth to the sink to rinse it out. He could have been anyone, really—one of the contractors working on the parking lot, a salesman, even the trash guy—and his presence could have been no more than a coincidence.

She wrung warm water from the dishcloth and walked over to the table. Was it plausible that the man she'd spotted was Paige's ex-husband? It was nearly four hours from Pittsburgh to Bird-in-Hand. Would he really travel all that way just to switch the label on a bottle of color? The act itself seemed pretty lame, especially if his goal was to drive Paige out of business. So if it wasn't him, then who was it?

She frowned. Maybe Paige *was* right. Maybe the two events were completely unrelated, and she needed to stop obsessing over it.

A soft footfall sounded from the hall behind her, and Mary glanced over her shoulder to see Martha shuffling toward the fridge. Butterscotch darted in behind her and sat just inside the door, licking his paw.

Mary wiped the last of the crumbs from the table and deposited the dishcloth in the sink. "I thought you were turning in early."

Martha stretched her arms over her head wearily. "That was the plan, right up until my head hit the pillow. Now I can't sleep, so I thought I would fix myself something to drink."

Noticing the shadows under Martha's eyes, Mary crossed to rest her hand on her back. "Can I get you some warm milk?"

"Warm milk." A fond smile curled her lips. "That was always Mama's favorite remedy whenever we had a bad dream. Remember?"

"I do." Mary shooed her to the table and took the milk out of the fridge. "Say, Martha, have you and Wade met before?"

"Met him?" Martha averted her gaze and adjusted her fluffy pink robe. "No, we've never met. Why?"

Mary crossed to the stove and took out a saucepan. "I sort of got the feeling that you weren't all that crazy about him."

Martha looked decidedly uncomfortable as she ran her finger along the seam in the table. "No, that's not it. He seemed nice enough."

Mary unscrewed the cap and let the milk gurgle into the pan. That done, she turned the burner to warm, then replaced the milk in the fridge and went to sit next to her sister. She'd learned long ago that Martha wouldn't be pushed to speak before she was ready, so she waited with her fingers laced atop the table while Martha fished for words.

"I've had a lot on my mind recently."

"Mm-hmm." Mary fidgeted with a string on her sleeve. "Is that why you haven't been able to sleep?"

"Partly, yes."

"Do you want to talk about it?"

Their eyes locked, Martha's dark and troubled. She reached out to cover Mary's hand. "You struggled for a long time after you and Brian divorced. I've been really glad to see your confidence blooming."

Mary gave a confused smile, unsure as to where the conversation was going. "But..."

"But I'm a little worried that you might—"

The ringing of the doorbell cut off what she'd been about to say. Mary glanced at the microwave above the stove. The clock read eight thirty.

"I wonder who that could be." She pushed up to check.

"I'll go see," Martha, said waving Mary back to her seat. She moved away quickly, leaving Mary to wonder if she'd changed her mind about their conversation and was looking for a way out of it. She frowned as she went to check on the milk. What was Martha concerned about, and why did she suddenly not want to talk about it?

She removed a cup from the cupboard and filled it with milk just as Martha returned with Bill Richmond on her heels.

"You have another visitor," Martha said. This time, there was no mistaking the worry in her eyes. She grabbed the cup from the counter and gave a nod to Bill. "Nice to see you again." To Mary, she said, "Thank you for the milk," before slipping out the door.

Unable to decipher her sister's odd behavior, Mary shook her head and shot a smile at Bill. "This is a surprise. What brings you by?"

Bill had been a friend of the Classen family for years, but Mary had always felt a particular fondness for him, especially after he helped fix up the barn so they could reopen the shop. "Can I take your coat?"

"Uh...no, that's all right. I won't be staying long." His gaze left her face and drifted upward.

She motioned to the specks of white resting on his shoulders. "Is it still snowing?" When he didn't move, she propped her hands on her hips and glared. "Bill Richmond, what in the world is wrong with you?"

His mouth snapped closed. "What happened to your hair? It's blue."

"Oh. I forgot about that." She waved her hand and grabbed the pan she'd warmed the milk in to run water into it. "Never mind. It'll be fixed in a day or two. What brings you by?"

Bill shrugged and crossed his arms. "I...uh...well, I heard you weren't feeling well. I stopped by to check on you, see if there was anything you needed."

She shut off the tap and frowned. "Where did you hear that?"

"The school." Bill shoved one hand into his coat pocket and crossed to lean against the counter next to the sink. "I was contracted to handle some repairs to the concession stand at the baseball field. I was getting some measurements when I overheard the coach say you were sick. I was worried about you."

Her face warmed under his gaze. Rather than wonder why, she changed the direction of the conversation. "You know Coach Jameson?"

"Not really. I've only talked to him a couple of times before this project came along."

"Mmm." Mary dried her hands on a towel. "Listen, I appreciate you coming to see me, but this really was all just a big mistake. Wade misunderstood something I said and well..." She shrugged. "As you can see, I'm not sick."

Bill's eyebrows rose. "Wade, huh?" His face flushed, and he held up his hand. "Sorry, I didn't realize you and Coach Jameson were friends."

Suddenly, Mary felt uncomfortable. She rubbed her damp palms over her sweater. "Wade asked me out on a date. We were supposed to go out tonight until this happened." She motioned toward her head.

Bill dropped his gaze, his lips curving in a wry smile. "I see."

Did he? If she didn't know any better, she'd say he was jealous. But why would that be, since they were just good friends?

She stepped forward to rest her hand on his sleeve. "Listen, Bill, I really appreciate you stopping by to check on me."

The muscles in his arm tightened beneath her touch. "Do you still see us as just friends?" He glanced up. This time, his smile didn't reach his eyes. "I have to say, after all this time, I sorta hoped we'd be more."

Unsure how to respond, she paused to consider her words. She had always considered Bill to be good looking. In a rough sort of way, he reminded her of Harrison Ford, especially now that time and wisdom had added lines to his brow and flecks to his dark hair. But at this moment, with him staring with an intensity that sent a delicious little shiver right through her, she forgot all about Harrison Ford, or Wade Jameson, and only saw Bill.

"Of c-course we're friends," she stammered, barely able to choke the words out of a suddenly dry throat. "And our friendship means the world to me."

He said nothing. His eyes relayed more than words would have anyway. For a second, she thought he meant to kiss her, and not anything like a friend would, but then he sighed and stepped away, his hands curled up tight at his sides.

"It's getting late. I'd best be going. See you later, Mary."

He whirled and showed himself out. She wanted to call him back, ask him what was wrong, but she already knew.

He *was* jealous. Worse, there was a small part of her deep inside that was more than a little glad.

CHAPTER SEVEN

The Classens didn't work on Sundays, so Mary didn't think it fitting that Paige should either. Swallowing a bit of vanity, she fastened a scarf over her hair and headed to church with her sisters, hopeful she'd see Paige and her daughter among the attendees and disappointed when she didn't. The next day she headed to Paige's salon early, figuring they could get started on returning her hair to its natural color before Secondhand Blessings opened at ten.

Paige greeted her with a chipper smile and drew her immediately into a chair next to the window. "Come on in, Mary. I have everything ready for you."

"Thanks, Paige." She nodded toward the parking lot. "All done out there, huh? It looks good."

"Much better than before," Paige agreed.

With warm sunlight streaming over her shoulders and soft music playing on the speakers, Mary felt completely at ease as Paige fastened a black cape around her neck. She even felt a little silly for assuming that the misplaced label meant another mystery to solve. Accidents happened. Apparently, they happened to her.

She put out her hand to touch Paige's wrist. "Um, the hair color?"

"Trust me, I've checked and double-checked it." Paige held up a brown bottle like the ones Mary had seen Saturday. "This time, I know it's right."

Mary's laughter matched Paige's.

"I can't thank you enough for being such a good sport about this," Paige said, picking up a brush and a bowl to mix the color for Mary's hair. "I know I shouldn't be happy it happened to you, but another customer might not have been so understanding."

"It didn't hurt anything but my pride," Mary said, settling back in her chair and resting her elbows on the arms. She gestured to a picture of Paige's daughter fastened to the mirror. "So? How's Kailey doing? Does she like her new school?"

"It's definitely an adjustment. The classes are a lot smaller, and all of the kids already know each other." She rapped the brush against the side of the bowl angrily. "It doesn't help that her dad keeps calling and telling her that friends back home in Pittsburgh miss her. I mean, they miss her, sure, but he's only telling her that because he thinks if she's miserable enough, we'll move back."

Mary winced. "That has to be hard on Kailey."

"It is, which he would realize if he ever stopped to think about anyone but himself." She sucked in a slow breath. "Sorry. My emotions get the best of me sometimes."

Mary smiled in sympathy. "So, tell me more about your ex-husband."

"Jack?"

She nodded. "How long were the two of you married?"

"Would you believe almost twenty-five years?"

Paige went back to the cupboard for a bottle of developer and squirted some into the bowl. While she stirred, she talked about how she and Jack had met, how they had tried for years to have a child and were finally blessed with Kailey, how Paige had hoped having a baby would help their marriage, and how heartbroken she'd been when it didn't. Mary listened quietly, sometimes comparing Paige and Jack's experience with hers and Brian's, and other times thinking how different their lives had been, before and after their divorces.

"There." Paige set the bowl aside and slid her hands into a pair of latex gloves. "This should at least strip away enough of the blue to get your color back to a dark shade of blond. After that, we'll worry about adding some lowlights just to give you texture. I don't want to risk damaging your hair by adding any more bleach, which is what I would have to do if you wanted highlights."

"Right now, I'll just be glad to have my hair any color but blue," Mary said with a laugh.

The front doorbell chimed. Now that the parking lot was finished, there was no need for customers to go around to the rear. Mary watched with interest as a man—probably in his late thirties or early forties if the gray lightening the sandy-brown hair at his temples was any indication—stepped inside and then looked around the salon.

"Can I help you, sir?" Paige asked, pausing with the hair color brush hovering above Mary's head.

The man pointed to the front window. "The sign says you take walk-ins? Are you available right now? I need a trim, but I'm in a bit of a rush."

"I'm so sorry—" Paige began.

Mary cut her off. "Go ahead. I have plenty of time."

Paige looked from her, to the man, and back to Mary. "Are you sure?"

"Of course. Besides, all he wants is a trim." She angled her head to the man waiting impatiently at the door and lowered her voice to a whisper. "Go on, before he gets away."

"Thanks so much," Paige whispered back. She set the brush and mixing bowl aside and patted Mary's shoulder. "Just sit tight. This won't take long."

"I'll be fine." Mary fluffed out the cape then reached for her phone.

Paige beckoned to the man, and he climbed into the chair next to Mary's. She gave him a silent nod then studied him surreptitiously. He was a pleasant-enough looking fellow, with bronzed skin that matched his honey-colored eyes. Their gazes bumped in the mirror, and Mary realized he'd been studying her in the same curious way—prompted, no doubt, by her brilliant blue locks.

While Paige asked the man what he wanted done, Mary began checking her email.

"Now, I notice that you keep your hair cut a little closer around your ears." Paige used the foot pedal to pump the man's chair a tad higher before draping him with a black cape similar to the one Mary wore. "Is that still something you want done?"

"Yes, that's generally how I like it," the man said. "And if you could, I'd really like you to clean up my neck some. I don't like my hair brushing my collar."

"No problem. I'll take care of it for you."

Paige smiled and reached for the electric clippers she kept plugged into the wall next to her curling irons and hair dryers. Only mildly interested in what Paige was doing, Mary focused on her phone, until Paige let out a loud gasp, and the man in the chair pressed his fingers to his head, his back rigid.

"Was that...did you just...?" His expression went from disbelief to denial to outrage in the span of a second.

Paige gaped at the clippers in her hand and then at the man's head. "I don't...I have no idea how that happened."

Mary sat up straight. "What? What happened?"

Face ashen, Paige pointed with the clippers. "I was going to trim up the back, and...and..."

The man leapt up from the chair, dislodging a large clump of hair that floated silently to the floor.

"That doesn't look good."

Two sets of eyes snapped onto Mary's face. Realizing she'd spoken aloud, she sank into her seat and clapped her hand over her mouth.

Paige's head swung side to side. "Sir, I'm so sorry. I can fix it. If you'll just sit back down—"

"Sit down?" The man reached up and ripped the Velcro backing on the cape away from his neck. "Do you realize what you've done? I have a very important meeting this afternoon."

He whirled as he spoke, giving Mary an unobstructed view of the back of his head. She stifled a gasp. No wonder he was so upset. Inadvertently or not, Paige had clipped a wide swath nearly to his scalp, all the way from his nape up to his crown.

"What am I supposed to do now?" the man demanded, throwing the cape down on the chair. "It's not like I can grow it back in time for my meeting."

Seeing Paige almost in tears, Mary felt compelled to help. She clasped both arms of her chair and pushed herself forward. "Now, now, it really isn't that bad," she began, using a soothing, measured tone.

The man jammed his fist to his hip and glared at her. "Says the woman with blue hair?"

Hmm. Point taken. Mary took a deep breath. "My name is Mary Classen Baxter. My sisters and I run the Secondhand Blessings store on the other side of town."

The man gave a grunt of frustration. Obviously, he didn't want to hear about the store. He was too upset, but telling him he was overreacting would only make matters worse. Mary tugged the cape around her shoulders nervously. "Your hair looks very thick and healthy. It probably grows really fast. Until then, I'm sure Paige can do something to disguise how short it is in the back, right, Paige?"

"Of c-course," she stammered, blinking rapidly. "Just let me fetch a new pair of clippers from my storeroom. I can fade the sides a little bit—"

The man shook his head and held up one hand before she could finish. "Oh no, I'm not letting you touch my hair." He grabbed his coat and shoved his arms into the sleeves. "I should have known better than to walk into a brand-new place. I'm going to that other lady across town. Maybe she can fix this mess."

Without another word, he stormed toward the door, leaving Mary and Paige gaping behind him. The second the door closed, Paige set the clippers down, covered her face with her hands, and burst into tears.

Mary scrambled from her chair to pull her into a hug. Certainly, the man had every right to be upset, but it pained her that he'd been so harsh with her friend. Mary grabbed a clean towel, unfolded it with a flick of her wrist, and pressed it into Paige's hands.

"Here, use this."

While Paige dried her face, Mary examined the clippers. They looked normal, from what she could tell. They weren't broken or bent. So then, what explanation could there be for the mishap to the man's hair?

"Thank you," Paige said, sniffling as she wiped the last bit of dampness from her pink cheeks. "This has just been the most unbelievable week." She dropped the towel into a hamper and drew a shaky breath. "Anyway, at least Dottie will be happy."

A frown pulled at Mary's brow. "Dottie Spencer? She's Elizabeth's hairdresser. Is that who the guy was talking about?"

Paige nodded and nudged the clump of hair on the floor with her tennis shoe.

Mary set the clippers down. "I don't understand. Why would Dottie want you to lose business? Are you saying she hopes your salon closes down?"

"It's not that she wants my business to fail, exactly," Paige amended hastily. "I just mean that she'll be glad to get one of her customers back."

Mary's thoughts spun faster than a top. "You're going to have to be more specific, Paige. Are you saying Dottie has been losing business because of you?"

Paige's fingers fluttered to her throat nervously. "A little. Not any of her regular customers, but she's complained about having fewer walk-ins. That's what I heard around town, anyway."

Fewer walk-ins meant less money coming in the door. Could it be that Paige's new salon was causing a financial strain for Dottie?

Paige's hand shook as she reached up to touch Mary's hair. "I know I said I would fix your hair, but I'm terrified of anything else happening this morning." Her shoulders drooped, and she cast a forlorn glance at the door. "I almost want to cancel all my appointments and put up the Closed sign."

"Don't do that," Mary said, drawing her gaze back with a touch to her arm. "It's no big deal. I can just come back tomorrow. I'm sure you'll be feeling better by then."

Paige blew out a shuddering breath and nodded. After a moment, the red splotches on her cheeks and neck faded, and she looked more like her cheerful self.

Relieved, Mary stepped away. "So, tell me more about these rumors you've heard about Dottie. Where did you hear them?"

"The job fair. Several people were talking. At first, I didn't really pay them any mind, but then someone said they'd overheard Dottie say I was robbing her of customers." She grabbed a broom and dustpan and carried them over to sweep up the few hair clippings scattered across the floor.

"Robbery is a little strong," Mary said. "It's not like you're overtly trying to steal her business."

Paige dumped the contents of the dustpan into the garbage then rested the broom against the wall and crossed her arms. "I didn't put too much stock in it anyway. The woman who said it seemed the sort who liked to gossip. And she kept watching me, like she knew I'd overheard and wanted to see what kind of reaction she would get."

"Mmm, maybe." Mary chewed thoughtfully on her thumbnail. "But think about it. You've had two mishaps in two days. Any chance Dottie *is* responsible?"

"You probably know her better than I do," Paige said, hesitancy in her voice and in her gaze. "I've only run into her once since I moved back to town and that was while I was getting gas. Is she the type of person who would do something like this?"

Would she? Mary didn't want to think so. She pointed to the clippers. "I've never seen clippers like that before. How do they work?"

Paige picked them up and pointed to a small lever on the side. "See this? It pulls the blade up and down so you can adjust the cut." She paused, squinting at something she saw. "That's funny."

"What?" Mary leaned closer. "Are they broken? I checked earlier, but I couldn't see anything wrong."

"Not broken, but the arrow that points to where the setting should be is definitely a little cockeyed."

Mary gasped, and Paige held up her hand.

"Hold on now. I'm not suggesting that someone damaged it on purpose. Between packing and a five-hour road trip in a bouncy moving van, they could easily have gotten jarred."

"I agree, that is a possibility, but Paige, you have to at least consider for a moment that these events weren't accidents," Mary argued. "I mean, really, what are the odds?"

Paige still looked uncertain, and why wouldn't she? The idea that someone would intentionally set out to sabotage her business was disturbing.

Circling around, Mary patted one of the styling chairs then slipped into the one opposite. "Okay, let's think this through. You've been open for a couple of weeks now, right?"

"Uh-huh." Paige crossed her legs, her foot wiggling nervously. "Two and a half, to be exact."

Not even a full month. Mary bit her lip, thinking. "Have there been any more strange incidents that you can remember?"

She shook her head before Mary finished. "No, none at all."

"Think a moment," Mary urged. "It may not have been anything as extreme as blue hair color or faulty clippers. Maybe items out of place, or stock missing or mislabeled."

Paige's gaze drifted upward as she thought, but eventually she shook her head again. "Well, I mean, everything has been in boxes. I'm not sure I would even know if something was out of place. Anyway, I can't remember any one thing that's jumped out at me as being particularly out of the ordinary."

"Hmm. All right." Mary tapped her chin with her index finger. "What about customers? Can you tell me which ones have been in the salon in the last week that might have had access to your inventory?"

"You mean like the hair colors?"

"Or your clippers."

"Well, to be honest, I suppose that would have to be everyone." Paige pointed toward the back of the salon. "With the work I had done to the parking lot, everyone had to come through that door."

"Which is where you keep all of your supplies."

Paige nodded and began ticking off names on her fingers. "Right off the top of my head, there was you, Della Bradford, Kathleen from the library, Catherine Randall…goodness, quite a few. If I can find some paper, I suppose I could write you a list."

"No, that's okay." Mary waved her hand. "Della and Kathleen I know, but who is this Catherine Randall?"

"She's the lady who came in right after I colored your hair."

"Oh yes. I remember her." Mary nodded as an image of the sleek woman popped into her head. "She was the one who looked so put together."

"Yes, that's the one." Paige grimaced. "I really can't remember off the top of my head who all came in." She jumped out of the chair. "I'll get my appointment book from the office. Except for the walk-ins, I have everyone who came in written in there. Be right back."

She hurried down the short hall then turned right and disappeared. While she waited, Mary examined the lever on the side of the clippers that Paige claimed could have been jostled during the move. Using her thumb, she maneuvered the lever up and down then finagled the settings screw on the bottom of the clippers. Unlike the lever, this added tension to the blade, instead of just moving it up and down. Looking closer, Mary noted that the screw itself was unscathed, but all around it were fine scratches that feathered out like veins.

Had they always been there, or were they caused by someone in a hurry to tamper with the blade?

She lifted her head and glanced toward the office. "Hey, Paige?"

Receiving no answer, she slid out of the chair, careful to scoop the cord on the clippers out of the way so she didn't trip on it. "Paige?"

She took two steps and stopped, distracted by a glimpse of someone near the front door. It was a man, eyes slightly squinted as he peeked in through the window. Could it be the same person she'd spied loitering around the back of the salon? Mary laid the clippers down and circled around the chair. Determined to find out what he was doing, she pressed her lips together and strode toward the door. Throwing it open, she stepped out onto the sidewalk and planted her hands firmly on her hips.

"Can I help you?"

The man had seen her coming and was already backing away from the window. He stared at her, his eyes wide and his mouth a startled O. He wore an orange-and-navy coat zipped halfway. On his head was a matching cap. Sunglasses dangled from his fingers.

Mary pointed to the glass. "I saw you peeking in at us. Did you need something?"

"No. Sorry." He shook his head and pushed the sunglasses onto his nose. Whirling on his heel, the man then strode away.

"Hold on," she called. "Who are you? Didn't I see you here the other day?"

She took a step to follow and stopped. Too late she realized she was still wearing the black cape, so unless she wanted to look like a giant flapping bird as she chased him down the street, she'd not get any answers today. Bemused, Mary watched until he rounded the corner, then she pushed open the door and went back inside.

Jack Schiller. It had to be. Who else but Paige's ex-husband would hang around outside her salon looking all sneaky and suspicious?

Paige stood at the back of the salon, a strange look on her face. "Where did you go? Were you talking to someone?"

Mary yanked the Velcro tab at her neck, bunched up the cape, and dropped it into a chair. "Paige, do you remember the guy I told you about? The one I saw hanging around the back of your shop? I think I just saw him again."

"What?" She hurried to look out the door and then back at Mary. "Are you sure? Where is he?"

"He's gone. I tried to stop him, but he took off before I could ask any questions." She crossed the salon to grasp Paige's hand. "It has to be Jack. You said he wasn't happy about you moving here, right? And now there's a guy hanging around your shop both times something strange happens to one of your customers?" Mary raised her eyebrows. "That can't be a coincidence."

Paige still looked uncertain, so Mary let go of her hand and pressed on.

"Okay, I admit, I've never met him. Tell me what he looks like, and I'll tell you if the guy I saw matches his description."

Paige licked her lips and held her hand above her head. "He's taller than me. He's always said he's six-two, but that's just his vanity talking. In reality, he's probably closer to six feet and maybe a little under. And he has dark hair and a medium build. Thin lips, with a little scar on one side." She touched the right side of her mouth with the tip of her finger.

Mary frowned. Did the man she saw have a scar? She couldn't remember. And the hair she'd spotted below the cap was brown, but it was more in the line of sandy than mocha. "How dark is Jack's hair?"

"About like mine. What color did the man have that you saw?"

Mary waved dismissively. "That would have been easy enough to change. What about his eyes? Brown, right?"

"No," Paige said slowly. "Jack's eyes are blue." Her cheeks reddened, and she ducked her head. "I always thought he looked a little bit like Clive Owen. It was one of the things that first attracted me to him."

Mary drew back, perplexed. It would be a stretch to say the man she'd seen looked anything like the British actor.

"It wasn't him, was it?" Paige's hands fell to her sides, a disappointed edge in her voice.

"It doesn't sound like it," Mary admitted. "Still, he could have altered his appearance to keep from being recognized. That would explain the cap and sunglasses. And eye color can be changed with contacts." She gestured toward the office. "Any chance you've got a picture of him handy? Even an old one would help."

Paige crossed her arms with a snort. "I got rid of my pictures of Jack a long time ago. I could pull up one of his social media profiles, I suppose. The man does love to post selfies. But first…" She hitched her thumb over her shoulder. "There's something I need to show you."

More important than determining if the man behind the mishaps at the salon was Jack? Mary stumbled along after Paige as she spun and strode back to her office.

"Paige, what—?"

She broke off as Paige flung open the door and stepped aside. "Look," she said, sweeping her hand out dramatically to point at the desk.

Mary eased toward the threshold. There was a black bookshelf against one wall, sparse, except for a couple of plain cardboard boxes on the bottom shelf and a fake potted plant near the top. Next to it, light filtered through a mini blind onto a desk that wore its age in dents on the metal sides and in the grooves carved along the wooden top.

She raised her eyebrows. "What am I looking at?"

And then she saw it. Paige's head bobbed as Mary sucked in a breath. Glass glinted on one corner of the desk, presumably from the discarded shadowbox that lay splintered on the floor. And jammed into the keyhole of one of the drawers... were the antique scissors Paige had purchased from Secondhand Blessings.

CHAPTER EIGHT

T hank you for stopping by Secondhand Blessings. Please come again."

Elizabeth waved cheerfully to the mother and daughter making their way out the door. They were upward in age. The daughter was old enough to have grown children of her own.

A slow warmth filled her heart as the daughter reached around her mother to open the door. In return, her mother smiled up at her, a twinkle of love and pride in her eyes. How many times had the duo performed the exact same act over the years? Probably quite a few, judging by their gentle ease with one another. Certainly, the roles might have changed as time passed, with one bestowing the mantle of caregiver to the other. Still, their obvious affection was touching, and it struck a melancholy chord deep inside Elizabeth. She'd always dreamed of having a daughter to share shopping trips with, and going out to eat, and—

"Hey, are you okay?" Martha ducked into her line of sight, startling Elizabeth. "I've been calling your name for the last five minutes."

"What? Oh, sorry. I'm fine. I just didn't hear you." She slid the cash register drawer closed then turned her attention to a display of vintage hatpins in desperate need of arranging. "What were you saying?"

"Just that I think we're going to need to add more baked goods to our inventory as the weather warms up. We've been selling out almost every day."

Behind her, the store phone rang. Martha tipped her head toward it. "Would you mind getting that?" She lifted her hands, each holding a loaf of freshly baked bread she was stocking in the display case.

"Sure." Elizabeth stuck the last hatpin on a board covered in black velvet then hurried to pick up the handset. "Secondhand Blessings."

"Aunt Elizabeth?"

Her young niece's familiar voice was always a welcome sound. Elizabeth smiled and pressed the phone closer. "Hello, Jennifer. So good to hear your voice."

"You too, Auntie. How is everything in Bird-in-Hand?"

"Just fine. The shop keeps us busy. How are things in Indiana? Still hectic as ever?" Between a part-time job and a semester packed full of college classes, Elizabeth knew Jennifer kept a tight schedule.

"Pretty much. I've been a little stressed lately. I'm trying to get ready for midterms, and then I have finals in a couple of months. I'm in pretty good shape, though. Most of my classes are in the morning, which leaves me plenty of time to study."

Elizabeth nodded. "That's good. I'm so proud of you, sweetie. I know your mom is too."

Jennifer cleared her throat. "Thanks. Listen, speaking of my mom, is she around? I have something I'd like to talk with her about."

"No, I'm sorry, she's not here yet. She had a hair appointment this morning. Did you try her cell phone?"

"I did, but it went to voice mail, so I thought I'd try the store."

Concerned by the troubled note in her niece's voice, Elizabeth frowned. "Is it an emergency? Do I need to try to find her?"

"Oh no, it's nothing like that."

"Well, I'll certainly tell her to call you as soon as I see her."

"That'd be great. Thanks, Auntie."

"Of course." Elizabeth bit her lip and fingered the phone cord. "Jennifer, is everything all right? You sound a little upset."

There was a long pause, and then Jennifer blew out a shaky breath. Even with the distance, Elizabeth could feel the pent-up emotion. She gripped the phone and waited.

"It's Michael," she said at last. "I haven't seen or heard from him or Heidi much at all lately, not since I was there a while ago to help them with the baby. I get that it's tough having a newborn—bad sleeping schedules and all that. But every time I reach out to them, they're always too busy to get together, or the baby isn't feeling well, or…" She sighed. "I know it sounds silly. I'm a grown woman, after all, and I know Michael is determined to be the best dad ever, not like—" She sucked in a breath and switched gears. "Anyway, I feel like my brother doesn't have time for me anymore. I know he loves me, and he's not intentionally trying to cut me out, but it still hurts. I keep thinking maybe I did something wrong when I was with them, and they just don't want me around."

The angst in Jennifer's voice drove slivers through Elizabeth's heart. She rubbed her thumbnail around the numbers on the checkout register, anxious for the exact right words that would bring comfort and coming up empty. "Well, uh, have you tried talking to him about it?"

"Several times. But when I call, I get the feeling he's in a rush to hang up. I've offered to meet them a couple of times, and they sound willing, but they always end up canceling at the last minute." Pain vibrated in her voice as she continued. "I don't know what to do, Aunt Elizabeth. Am I being selfish for wanting to spend time with them? Should I try to be more understanding?"

How to answer that? Panic squeezed Elizabeth's heart, which was strange since she didn't normally find giving advice so difficult. Still, the answers Jennifer wanted eluded her.

"I…I'm sure things will get back to normal in time," she said. "Once the baby is older, I'm sure Michael and Heidi will make time to spend with you. They've just got their hands full at the moment."

It was a lame, condescending answer, and she knew it, yet she couldn't keep the words from spilling out.

"Just hang in there, okay?" she finished quietly. "And remember that we all love you."

"I will. Love you too, Aunt Elizabeth. Thanks for listening."

"You're welcome, sweetheart. And I'll be sure to tell your mom to give you a call."

"I appreciate that. Talk to you later."

They disconnected, but the disquiet in Elizabeth's heart remained. She'd never had so much trouble talking with her niece before. Where had the awkwardness come from?

"Who was that?" Martha closed the door on the bakery display case and motioned toward the phone.

"Oh, that was Jennifer." Elizabeth smoothed her hands over her skirt. "She and Michael are in a bit of a rough patch."

Martha's brows rose.

Elizabeth explained. "He and Heidi haven't had much time for anyone else since the baby was born."

"I remember those days," Martha said with a chuckle. "It's perfectly normal for the parents' world to be tossed upside down for a while. Give them a few weeks, and they'll be juggling their schedule with the baby's like pros."

The answer came so easily for Martha, and she said it with such confidence that even Elizabeth was convinced. Why couldn't she have offered the same advice?

The answer burned through her spirit like a poker. Because she'd never had children, that's why. She had no idea what it was like managing a newborn and all the responsibilities that came with it.

She lowered her head and pretended to be absorbed in straightening the area around the phone. "Anyway, I told her I would have Mary give her a call."

She ripped a sticky note off the pad and jotted the words *Call Jennifer* on it.

"Hmm, where is Mary?" Martha's gaze swung around the store. "Wasn't she supposed to be finished at the salon by now?"

Elizabeth glanced at her watch and was surprised by the lateness of the hour. "You're right, she should have been back. I wonder what could be keeping her." She frowned and stuck the note onto a small bulletin board above the phone.

Martha motioned around the shop. The store had already been open for an hour, but only a handful of customers milled the aisles. "Well, we're not busy. I suppose we could always call her if she's not back in thirty minutes or so."

"I'll keep an eye out for her," Elizabeth murmured, though inside, her feeling of disquiet intensified. Jennifer had already tried calling and said she got Mary's voice mail. "I sure hope nothing else has happened at the salon."

"What's that?" Martha lifted her hand to her ear. "I didn't catch what you said."

Elizabeth gave a wave of her hand and moved to begin straightening shelves. "Nothing. I'm sure everything is fine. She probably got caught up talking about old times with Paige and is just running a little behind."

But deep down, she worried that something else might be going on. People lurking outside the salon, hair colors gone awry...it was all too strange, and it didn't sit well. Not one little bit.

CHAPTER NINE

Mary checked the floor around their feet for nails or broken glass and then tiptoed into the office. Paige followed at her heels, one hand gripping Mary's elbow tightly.

Mary pulled up short to whisper over her shoulder. "Be careful. Try not to touch anything unless you absolutely have to."

"Okay." Paige's mouth opened, then shut, then opened again. "Why are we whispering?"

"I don't—" Mary broke off and straightened with a sigh. "I don't know. Obviously, whoever was in here is long gone."

Paige pointed toward the desk. "It's over there."

Though they'd determined that the intruder wasn't in the salon, Paige stayed close to Mary's hip as she crossed to examine the fragments of the shadowbox. "Whatever they were after, they were certainly determined." She motioned toward the desk drawer. "Did you look inside?"

Paige shook her head. "I didn't want to disturb anything."

"That's good." Mary bent closer. Except for the scissors and the glass, the rest of the desk did not look disturbed. Nor did anything else in the office.

Paige rested her hand on Mary's shoulder. "Should we call the police?"

She was back to whispering. Oddly, Mary understood why. She lifted a corner of the desk blotter. "Not yet. First, let's see if we can figure out what the person was after."

"Okay." She watched Mary curiously for a moment. "What are you looking for?"

"The key to the drawer."

"Right here." She reached into her pocket and pulled out her key ring. Separating one of the keys from the others, she then held it toward Mary.

Mary jerked a tissue from a box on the desk and carefully removed the antique scissors from the keyhole. After laying them aside, and still using the tissue, she tugged on the drawer handle. The drawer slid free without the benefit of keys.

"Well, at the very least, it looks like you'll be installing a new lock on your desk. They broke this one trying to get in." Mary handed the keys back then opened the drawer the rest of the way. Both she and Paige leaned closer to look inside. Mary took mental inventory—tape, notepad, rubber bands, thumbtacks, pens, pencils…the list went on.

"What do you think?" She twisted to look at Paige. "Notice anything missing?"

Paige craned her neck this way and that, and finally shook her head. "I don't think so."

Mary frowned and eased aside to give her a better view. "Are you sure? Why else would someone have bothered to break into your desk?"

"I have no idea. I keep office supplies in there—paper clips, a letter opener, things like that." Her eyes widened, and she pushed her hand into the drawer to feel around. "Wait, where is my appointment book?"

"You're sure it's not there?"

Paige tapped the drawer front. "I keep it right here. It's missing."

Mary scanned the area over and around the desktop. "Paige, are you sure? Maybe you moved it."

"No, no. I'm positive. I always keep it here next to the phone so I can write down—" She broke off and grabbed Mary's hand. "You're bleeding."

"I am?" Puzzled, Mary frowned and twisted her wrist around to look. She did have a smear of blood across the side of her hand, but it wasn't hers. Her gaze flew to three small red dots on the blotter. "Paige, look. Whoever broke into your desk must have cut themselves on the scissors."

"Eww. We need rubbing alcohol, stat." She strode to a cabinet, ripped open a plastic bag, and plucked out a cotton ball. She saturated it with alcohol and carried it over to Mary before wiping the blood off her hand and tossing the cotton ball in the trash. "There," she said, patting her hands dry. "Now can we call the police?"

Paige's lips thinned, and her chin trembled. At the corner of her eyes, moisture gathered. She was upset and with good reason. Mary patted her arm.

"You're right. We probably should let the authorities know there have been some strange things happening around here, just in case anything else turns up missing. My sister Elizabeth is good friends with John Marks with the East Lampeter Township Police Department. I'll give him a call later."

Paige's hands slid from her hips, and she blew out a breath. "Thank you."

"No problem."

"Good." Rubbing her hands together briskly, Paige asked, "Now what?"

"Now, let's have another look around the salon, see if we can find anything else that looks out of place. And while we're at it, we should probably try to figure out how the person got in."

Paige shuddered and rubbed her hands over her arms. "Good grief. I hadn't thought about that."

Mary pointed toward the hall. "Why don't we split up? You take the front, since you'll be more familiar with anything that might be missing out there. I'll stay back here and check the locks on the windows and doors."

Paige agreed, but even after thirty minutes of careful searching, neither of them made any headway.

"It had to be the back door," Paige said, indicating it with an exasperated sigh. "It's an old building, and the door is so warped and rusty, it really doesn't take much to force it open. I've been meaning to replace it, but I just haven't had the time." She grimaced and rubbed her palm over her forehead. "Or the money. But I won't put it off now, regardless."

"I think that's a good idea," Mary said. "If you like, I know a good contractor who could install it for you. Do you know Bill Richmond?"

Paige thought a second. "I remember the name from high school, but I never really knew him."

"He's a really nice guy." Mary's cheeks warmed thinking of him. "Anyway, I'll call him and see if he can fit you in."

"Thanks, Mary. Should I see about buying a door?"

"Check with Bill first. He does a lot of business at the hardware store, so he may be able to get you a discount."

"That would be so awesome. Any little bit helps."

It pained Mary to see the relief that such a small offer made on Paige's features. Instantly, she was jerked back in time to the days and weeks following her own divorce. Rent payments, vehicle repairs, school supplies—all were things that had taxed her suddenly single income to the limit.

Paige motioned around the salon. "What should we do now?"

"Well, for one thing, I think you should keep an eye out for anyone with a suspicious-looking wound on their hand. Judging by the drops of blood on the blotter, I'd say it's probably a pretty significant scratch."

"I can do that."

Mary's gaze drifted to the desk drawer, still hanging open. "Why do you suppose someone would take your appointment book?"

Paige's cheeks flushed pink. "It had to be because they wanted to know my schedule. What else would something like that be good for?"

"Maybe so they could plot their next hair catastrophe?" Mary reached out to clasp Paige's fingers. "I think it's safe to say now that someone is definitely trying to sabotage your business."

A shudder passed through Paige, but she agreed with a nod.

Mary offered a sympathetic smile. "We'll need to start narrowing down the list of people who might have a reason to want to do that."

"I suppose you're right," Paige said, her mouth drooping glumly. "This is so upsetting. I was really looking forward to coming back to Bird-in-Hand. Now I'm wondering if that was the right decision."

"It's one person, Paige," Mary urged, squeezing her arm in encouragement. "And it may not even be someone from here."

Surprise flickered in her eyes. "You mean Jack."

Mary nodded and dropped her hand. "You said he likes taking selfies?"

"Yes, and he posts them on social media." She patted her pockets and then her gaze swept across the desk. "Where did I leave my phone?"

"Maybe it's out front." Mary hitched her thumb toward the door and took a step.

"No, I'm sure I put it here. I was so upset after I left the salon yesterday, I didn't even think about it and left it on the desk charging." Eyes wide, she reached across the desk and picked up the white charging cord. "Mary."

Both stared wordlessly. Finally, Mary spoke.

"Paige, are you *sure* you left the phone on the charger? You couldn't have stuck it in your pocket by mistake, or left it lying around somewhere, maybe in your car?"

"I'm positive. My car has Bluetooth. Normally, it connects to my phone automatically when I start the engine. Halfway home,

I noticed a message on my dash that said there was no device connected, but I was too tired to drive all the way back here to get it." She threw up her hands in exasperation. "A phone and an appointment book. And it's not even a very expensive phone. It's one of those cheap phones you buy data for on a monthly plan. Why in the world would anyone steal it?"

The bell on the front door chimed before she could answer. Paige glanced at her watch and groaned. "That's Eloise Parkhurst. She's my next appointment."

"Who is Eloise Parkhurst?"

"She's chair of the Chamber of Commerce. Have you met her?"

"The name doesn't sound familiar," Mary said.

"Trust me, you'd remember her. She's sharp as a tack, but she's a little pushy, and very particular about her appearance. Today she's coming in for a cut *and* a perm." She wrung her hands nervously. "I knew I should have canceled."

"Don't be silly," Mary urged. "You'll do fine."

"I don't think so. Seriously." She held out her hand to prove how it shook. "See? I can't do it. I'm going to ask her to reschedule."

"Paige, stop." Mary pushed her hand down and grabbed her by the shoulders. "You can't afford to lose any more customers. You and Kailey need the money."

After a moment, Paige puffed out a breath. "Okay. But just in case, would you mind saying a prayer for me?" She said it jokingly, but with a gleam of fear in her eyes that said she could use the fortification of knowing someone was praying.

"Of course I will." Mary locked gazes with her until Paige nodded, and then she took out her keys and motioned with them toward the back door. "I'll go out this way."

"Okay."

Before she could move away, Paige pulled her in for a hug. "Thanks for being here, Mary. I'm not sure what I'd do if I had to face all this alone."

"Well, you don't," Mary assured her, holding her tight. "I'm here, and I'm going to help you figure out what's going on, okay?"

Paige stepped back and rubbed her palms down her pant legs. "All right, I'll go and see to Eloise."

Mary smiled. "I know it's hard, but try not to fret."

Paige's chin lifted. "Not sure I can promise that, but at the very least, I'll try not to let it show."

"That's good enough."

Mary laughed, and though Paige didn't join in, she did smile. That was something. But then Paige's gaze slid to Mary's hair, and just as quickly as it had appeared, her smile faded.

"Your hair."

"Don't worry about it." Mary gave a toss of her head and thrust out her chin. "I'm actually starting to like it."

"No you're not."

"No, I'm not."

The two stared at each other, and then burst into laughter.

"Mary, you're a hoot," Paige said as she crossed to the door. "And I bless you for it, but now I'd better go check on Eloise before she thinks I've forgotten about her and leaves."

"You're right. Go." Mary shooed her away.

As soon as Paige was out of sight, Mary gathered up her things and slipped out the back door. This time, no suspicious character lingered near the dumpster or around the front. She hurried to her car, already creating a mental list of the things she would do when she got home, including a call to John Marks and, more importantly, an internet search for a picture of the infamous Jack Schiller.

CHAPTER TEN

Mary shivered as the door to Secondhand Blessings whooshed closed behind her, creating a wintry gust that ruffled the fur trim on the coats of the women huddled in front of the cash register.

Elizabeth tore off a cash register receipt and handed it to one of them along with her bags. "There you go, ladies. Thank you all for coming in."

Catching sight of Mary, Elizabeth's eyes rounded. She closed the cash drawer with a snap and circled the counter to her. "Your hair is still blue. I thought you were going to the salon to get it fixed."

"Never mind that." She shrugged out of her coat and tossed it over the counter. "Where is Martha? We need to talk."

Elizabeth glanced over her shoulder. "She's in the back, I think, putting up a box of consignments that came in on Saturday. Should I go get her?"

"We'll both go." Mary grabbed her hand and pulled her down one of the aisles.

Elizabeth stumbled, caught herself, then quickened her steps to match her sister's. "Mary, slow down. What is going on?"

"I'll tell you in a minute."

Spying Martha, Mary swerved into another aisle and lifted her hand to catch her attention. When their gazes met, she signaled for her to go toward the back and then pulled Elizabeth along behind her to the storeroom.

"Hey, what happened?" Martha asked as Mary ushered her inside and closed the door. "You were supposed to be getting your hair done. It looks exactly the same as it did this morning."

"I know," Mary said. "That's why I wanted to talk to you both."

Elizabeth pointed to the door. "We can't just leave our customers like that, can we?"

"This will only take a minute," she insisted, and then plunged into an abbreviated account of everything that had transpired at the salon.

"My goodness," Elizabeth said, her eyes wide as Mary finished. "It really does sound like someone is trying to drive her business under."

A worried frown creased Martha's brow. "What did Paige have to say?"

"She's understandably upset, and worried for herself and her daughter, Kailey." Mary turned to Elizabeth. "I told her we would give John a call and fill him in on what's been going on."

She nodded. "Of course. I'll do that right away."

"Thank you. And one more thing." She sucked in a breath and plunged in. "Would you mind talking to Dottie Spencer?"

"Dottie?" Elizabeth's gaze darkened, and she folded her arms over her chest. "Whatever for?"

"Now, hear me out," Mary began, holding her hand up. "I know she's your friend, but there've been rumors circulating that she's lost business since Paige moved back to town."

"That's no reason to think she would do something underhanded," Elizabeth protested. She stood with her chest puffed out and her chin angled defensively. "She's not that kind of person."

"Maybe you could just ask her if the rumors are true," Martha interrupted gently. "And if she says yes, then we could do a little more digging."

A bit of the stiffness trickled from Elizabeth's spine, and she relaxed her shoulders so they no longer reached toward her ears. "I guess that wouldn't hurt anything," she grumbled at last.

Mary nodded her thanks and then turned to Martha. "Do you think you could help me keep an eye out in case anyone comes in with a suspicious-looking wound on their hand?"

"Absolutely." She tapped her finger against her lip. "Does Paige have any idea who else might have this kind of vendetta against her?"

"We have some theories." Mary scowled, a burning in her stomach that had nothing to do with hunger. "Her ex-husband tops the list. He wasn't happy about them moving back here." She gave them a description of the man she'd seen loitering about outside the salon, adding that though he didn't fit Paige's description, she still wasn't convinced he hadn't altered his appearance. When she finished, Martha nodded.

"He would be a likely candidate. Who else?"

Mary didn't like to think there would be anyone else, especially since in her mind, it had to be Jack. Even so, she knew better than to let her emotions rule her head. Martha would say she had to approach things logically, and so she would try.

"We did talk about who might have had access to her supplies," Mary said. "We figure it could have been any of her customers. That's why she was looking for her appointment book, except it was gone. And then there's a girl she just hired, and another lady. An old school rival."

Martha frowned. "It doesn't seem likely that a woman hoping for a job would try to put her employer out of business."

"Unless she was only applying for the job so she could get access to Paige's supplies," Elizabeth said.

Martha thought a minute and then conceded with a shrug. "Maybe. As for Paige's customers, maybe she could just write down the names of the people she remembers and email it to you."

"I'll call the salon and ask her to do that." Mary took out her phone and pulled up Paige's contact info.

"And what about that other woman…not a customer…the old school rival," Martha continued. "What do you know about her?"

"Not much. Just her name, Vanessa Bancroft."

"Wait." Elizabeth's eyes widened. "Her name didn't used to be Wyland, did it? The girl who always wore her hair in a ponytail."

Mary looked up from her phone. "That's her."

Martha pressed her lips together. "Hmm. I'll see what I can dig up. In the meantime, I'd better get back out there." She poked her finger toward the door and paused, her hand on the knob. "Mary, when you contact Paige, please tell her we're all praying this gets resolved quickly."

At Elizabeth's answering nod, gratitude flooded Mary's heart. Her story and Paige's were similar, but she had one thing

Paige didn't following her divorce, and that was the support of two strong, godly sisters. Even the menial things like packing and relocating had been easier with family to support you. Never mind the peace she'd been granted knowing she could turn to them whenever her children were in trouble. Who did Paige have to fill that gap?

The question strengthened Mary's resolve to help her friend in whatever way she could. She left a message at the salon then grabbed a sheet of paper and a pen from a stack of office supplies. She scribbled Jack Schiller's name down next to Della Bradford, Kathleen from the library, and Catherine Randall, the three people Paige said had come into the salon in the last week. She also added Vanessa Bancroft to the list, and Eloise Parkhurst, though she mentally discounted any involvement from her since she had only come in that morning. Nibbling the end of her pen, she studied the list.

"Not Della," she muttered, scratching a line through her name. "Or Kathleen." Both women were close friends of the Classens. Plus, Della was in Europe on vacation, and Kathleen, well, she was simply incapable of doing something as mean-spirited as forcing someone out of business.

That left only Jack, Vanessa, Catherine, and Eloise. Was it intentional that she listed them in order of suspicion? She frowned and wrote down Chelsea White. True, there were easier ways of gaining access to the salon than applying for a job, but they still needed to keep her on the radar.

She wrote down Dottie Spencer's name. That certainly wouldn't make Elizabeth happy, but she owed it to Paige to ask. She wrestled for anyone else who might be within the scope of suspects. Finding no one, she folded up the list and tucked it into her pocket to ponder later, then pushed open the storeroom door.

"Oh, Mary, you startled me." Rachel Fischer put her hand to her chest and blew out a breath. "I was not expecting anyone to come out from there."

She spoke softly and properly, in the way so typical of the Amish people who lived in and around Bird-in-Hand. Mary reached out to take her hand.

"I'm so sorry, Rachel. I didn't mean to scare you."

Rachel smiled and motioned toward the door. "Where were you going in such a hurry?"

"Would you believe I was going to solve a mystery?"

Rachel's eyes twinkled, and Mary laughed.

"Of course you would." She pulled her list out of her pocket and showed it to her. "Do you know any of these people?"

Rachel scanned the list and pointed to Vanessa's name. "This one is familiar. She owns the big house just outside of town with all the beautiful landscaping. I know several Amish women who sell their plants and flowers to her for a little extra income."

Mary nodded eagerly. "What else can you tell me about her?"

Rachel lifted her hands apologetically. "I am sorry, Mary. I do not know her well. What is it you think she has done?"

"Well, not her, specifically." Mary shared the same information she'd given to her sisters, then folded the list and replaced it in her pocket. "These are just a few of the people I thought might be worth checking out."

"I see." Rachel shook her head sadly. "I am sorry to hear about your friend. I will pray for her, and wisdom for you."

"Thanks, Rachel."

She nodded and pointed to Mary's pocket. "Add Ellen Yoder to your list of people to speak to. She has a very large garden and sells a lot of her flowers either at the markets or to the local florists. If anyone can tell you something about Vanessa Bancroft, it will be her."

"Ellen Yoder. Got it. I'll let Martha know. She was going to see what she could find out."

"Excuse me, ma'am. Do you work here?" A portly gentleman with a scruffy beard and bad comb-over peered at Mary from behind a brass table lamp.

Mary nodded and held up one finger. "Be right with you." She leaned toward Rachel. "I should go. Thank you for your help," she whispered and then turned to the man. "Yes, sir, what can I do for you?"

The man held up the lamp. "I don't see a price tag on this. Can you tell me how much it is?"

Mary eyed the lamp and frowned. She'd priced that item herself, just a couple of days ago. If the tag was missing, likely the man had removed it himself, hoping for a better deal.

"That's a Felix table lamp by Frederick Cooper," she said, measuring her words in even tones. "Brand-new, they run anywhere from four to six hundred dollars."

His brows rose. "Oh?"

"We're selling that one for one hundred fifty," Mary continued, pasting a pleasant smile on her face. "Can I wrap it up for you?"

The man sniffed and shrugged his shoulder. "To be honest, I didn't want to pay more than seventy-five."

"We have several other lamps that are in that price range. If you'd like, I'd be happy to show them to you."

His jaw hardened, but Mary met his glare without flinching. Finally, he shook his head and shoved the lamp at her with a scowl. "No thanks. I'll check back with you in a couple of days."

Mary sighed as she took the lamp and carried it up front to write a new tag. Just like Paige's clients, not all their customers were sweet and kind. On the other hand, some were more than customers—they'd become lifelong friends.

She smiled, thinking of Rachel Fischer. She was so gentle and steadfast, always willing to lend a helping hand. She showed kindness and accepted people without judgment. She didn't ask questions or poke fun.

Even when her friends had blue hair.

CHAPTER ELEVEN

It was too cold to sit on the porch, so Elizabeth brewed a cup of tea and relaxed in front of a cozy fire instead. At her feet, Pal snored softly, his furry head resting comfortably on his paws. Elizabeth sighed deeply. This was always her favorite part of the day, when the supper dishes were done and a blanket of stillness draped the house in quiet comfort.

Tink's nails on the wood floor broke the silence, and she trotted into the living room with Mary close behind, a mug cradled in her hands as well.

Elizabeth perked up from her place on the couch. "So? How did your talk go with Jennifer?"

Mary had called her daughter after Elizabeth told her of their conversation earlier that day. Though she'd tried not to listen, she couldn't help but overhear bits and pieces. Apparently, her concern that something wasn't quite right had been spot on.

Mary reached for one of the throw pillows and sank onto the couch next to Elizabeth. "Poor Jennifer. I think she's really just homesick."

Elizabeth dropped her gaze and took a sip from her cup. "Really? Is that all?"

"Oh, you know how it is," Mary said, sweeping her blue locks back from her face. "Her classes are really stressful. Between that and her job, I think she just needs a break."

"Hmm." Elizabeth turned her gaze to the crackling fire. "Did she happen to mention Michael at all?"

"Michael?" Mary's gaze turned questioning. "Not really. She said he's been really busy. Why?"

Elizabeth bit her lip. Surely Mary would sense if something was wrong with one of her own children. More so than, say, an aunt. She shrugged. "Just wondering."

Mary craned her neck to glance behind them at the stairs. "Did Martha go to bed?"

"She was going to take a hot bath first. Hopefully that will help her relax."

"She still having trouble sleeping?"

Elizabeth fingered the handle on her cup. "Yeah. I sure wish we could figure out what's troubling her." She sighed and set her cup down. "Did you hear back from Paige?"

Hugging the pillow, Mary swallowed a sip of her tea then rubbed a drop from her lip with her thumb. "Yeah. Poor thing. She's devastated over this whole mess, and who can blame her? Elizabeth, we just have to figure out what's going on, and soon. Otherwise…" She blew out a breath and shook her head. "I'm just not sure what Paige and Kailey are going to do."

Elizabeth agreed with a nod.

Shortly after the shop closed, Mary had received a phone call from an overwrought Paige telling her there had been a *third* incident at the salon.

Mary's nails clicked against the side of her cup. "It's so hard to believe she had a perm go awry, especially since she was being so careful."

She set her cup next to Elizabeth's on the coffee table. "Paige said someone switched the waving lotion with the neutralizer. You can't tell me that was an accident. Thank goodness Paige realized something was wrong before there was any real damage to the customer's hair. She tried to explain what happened, but I don't think Eloise cared one way or the other. Paige said she just stormed out of the salon in a huff."

"Well, I can't say as I blame her. I know it wasn't Paige's fault," Elizabeth went on quickly when Mary snorted, "but Eloise is somewhat of a public figure and so tends to be very conscious of her appearance."

"Public figure?" Mary protested. "It's not like she's the mayor."

"Now, Mary."

Mary grimaced and blew a strand of blue hair from her face. "I know, I know." Tink whined from the floor. She shoved the pillow aside and reached down to scoop the little dog into her lap. "I can't help it. I'm feeling a little protective. Paige is worried this latest fiasco will ruin her, since Eloise chairs the Chamber of Commerce."

"That's perfectly normal. She's your friend," Elizabeth said.

"It's not just that. I feel bad for her because of our shared circumstances." Mary reached over to grasp Elizabeth's hand. "I at least had my sisters supporting me after Brian left. Paige only has me."

"And me," Elizabeth said. "And I'm sure Martha too."

Mary's chin trembled, and she blinked back sudden tears. She always had been the most sensitive of the three Classen girls, Elizabeth thought. Despite all her quirks, she was the kind of friend everyone wanted—the kind you could count on.

Elizabeth let go of Mary's hand and got up to throw another log onto the dwindling fire. "So, what about your hair? Didn't you say you rescheduled your date with Wade for tomorrow night?"

"I did, but after what happened today, I didn't have the heart to bring it up again. Poor Paige. She was so upset, she's not taking any appointments or walk-ins tomorrow, but she can't afford to stay closed long. With moving expenses and buying inventory for the salon, she admitted to me that her savings are just about gone." Mary reached for her cup and drank down the last of her tea.

Sympathy pressed heavily on Elizabeth's heart. "Anything we can do to help?"

"I don't know. I'm planning on going by her place to check on her. I'll ask her tomorrow when I see her."

Mary rose and took her mug with her to the door. Tink jumped to her feet and followed, her little tail wagging furiously. Pal's eyes opened, but too lazy to actually leave his spot on the rug, he merely let out a sigh and closed them again.

"I think I'll turn in," Mary said. "Do you want me to shut off the lights?"

Elizabeth stirred the coals in the fireplace to life then replaced the poker in the stand and straightened. "Don't worry about it. I'll get them."

"All right, then, good night. Come on, Tink."

"Good night."

Alone with her thoughts again, Elizabeth swept her hands free of ash and settled onto the couch. It was funny how different the three of them were, especially considering they'd been raised by the same parents.

Dottie's name came to mind, and Elizabeth rethought her earlier conclusion. Maybe she and her sisters weren't all that different. She'd read compassion and loyalty in Mary's gaze when she spoke of Paige. It was the same thing Elizabeth felt whenever she thought of having to approach Dottie.

"It can't be helped, I suppose. Right, Pal?"

The dog moaned and rolled to his other side.

Elizabeth chuckled and reached for her cup. Obviously, Pal agreed. The sooner she cleared Dottie's name, the better.

CHAPTER TWELVE

Mary wound a brightly colored scarf around her head then pulled the ends of it to the side of her neck and knotted them just below her ear. Tied in this way, most of her hair was covered, although several blue strands still poked out around her face and next to her chin. A pair of silver hoop earrings completed the look.

She dragged her gaze from the mirror and peered at the dachshund curled at her feet. "At least my hair matches the scarf, right, Tink? That's something."

In fact, the style gave her an almost contemporary, Bohemian look. Hopefully, Wade would think so too. She scooted away from her vanity and reached for a wool sweater before heading for the door.

The shop closed at two on Tuesdays, so rather than ask her sisters to cover for her again, she decided to wait until then to check on Paige. And Elizabeth would run over to visit with Dottie while Martha investigated Vanessa. A busy day for all of them. Fortunately, traffic in the store was slow, so right at two o'clock, the three of them locked the doors and headed off in different directions.

As usual, Mary found Paige at the salon. Unusual was the CLOSED sign hanging in the door window. Mary peeked around the sign and knocked. From the back of the salon, Paige poked her head out of the hall. Spying Mary, she hurried to unlock the door.

"Hey, Paige."

"Hi, Mary. I didn't expect to see you today." Paige stepped aside to let her in, then closed and locked the door behind her. Her face was devoid of makeup, her hair pulled into a messy bun that suggested she hadn't washed it. And beneath her eyes were smudges that hinted at the kind of night she'd had.

Mary swallowed a swell of compassion and pasted a bright smile on her face. "I came to see what you were up to." She glanced around the salon at the boxes piled on the floor next to the empty chairs. "What's all this?"

"I'm sorting through all of my supplies." Paige shuffled toward a plastic laundry basket and sank down next to it. "These are all the things that have a broken seal or that look unusual in any way."

Mary eyed the basket in surprise. "That's a lot of stuff. What are you going to do with it all?"

"Throw it away. I can't risk using anything that looks like it might have been tampered with."

Mary swallowed a sudden lump in her throat. How much money did the stuff in the basket represent? Too much. It was money Paige couldn't afford to lose and inventory she couldn't afford to replace.

"So, what can I do to help?" Mary asked. She took off her coat and pushed up the sleeves on her sweater, then startled when she saw a familiar black-and-white blur dart out from the pile of boxes.

"Where? H-how?" she stammered, one hand on her chest to slow her racing heart.

Paige laughed, and she instantly looked ten years younger. "That's Figaro. I found him outside my door this morning. When I came inside, he decided he needed to come too."

"You've already named him?" Mary watched Figaro dart around the room, finally coming to a stop in Paige's lap.

"Yup, I have." Paige stroked the little cat, and Mary could hear his answering purr. "He's a tuxedo cat—just like Figaro in *Pinocchio.* He can't be more than five or six months old. I think little Figgy's just what the doctor ordered."

"You're going to keep him, then? In here?"

Paige lowered Figaro to the floor and stood. "I am," she said. "I'll go out later today and get a litter box and food for him, and I'll get him neutered ASAP."

Mary bent and rubbed Figgy's head. "Well, he's as cute as a bug, and your customers will love him." She straightened. "And he's obviously chosen you."

Paige glanced at the clock hanging high on the wall. Instead of hands, a pair of slender shears indicated the hour. "What about the store? Aren't you working today?"

"Business is always slow on Tuesdays. We close early." She pointed toward the back. "How about I get the boxes and pull them out here while you sort through them?"

Paige nodded eagerly, her eyes a little brighter and a little less watery than when Mary had first come in. "That's a good plan. Don't grab any from the metal shelves on the right side of the hall, though. I've already sorted those."

"Okeydoke."

Mary strode to the back and hauled out the first box. After a few more, she peeled off her sweater. Before long, her face was hot, and she was ready for a break.

Paige folded the flaps on a carton of conditioner and pushed the box aside. "I need something to drink. How about you?"

"Water would be great," Mary said. "Or a Diet Coke, if you have it."

"Back here." Paige pushed to her feet and headed toward her office. "I keep some in the mini-fridge next to my desk."

After taking two diet sodas out of the refrigerator, Paige pushed one to Mary, then popped the top on the other and took a long swallow before flopping into a leather desk chair.

"Oh, that's good." She propped her feet up on a crate and tipped the can up for another long drink. "I was really thirsty." Figaro hopped up on her lap and settled down for some serious ear scratching.

"Me too," Mary said after swallowing a drink of her own soda. "Thanks for this." She lifted the can to Paige, who dismissed her thanks with a small nod.

"It's the least I can do."

"So." Mary wiped away a bead of sweat from the side of the can with her finger then dug in her pocket for a tissue. "Did you get the message I left last night?"

Paige nodded and handed her a napkin from a local fast food restaurant. Mary took it and laid it on the desk before setting her soda can on top of it.

"I did. Honestly, Mary, I lay awake for hours last night wracking my brain for anybody who might have a vendetta against me, but aside from the people you mentioned, I really don't have anyone to add." Her feet thumped to the floor, and she reached into the drawer with the broken lock and pulled out a steno pad. "I wrote down the names of everyone who has come in anyway, just in case. Well, the ones I could remember."

"Good. That'll help."

Paige leaned back in her chair. "It's so weird, thinking someone could hate me that much."

"Hate is a pretty strong word. How about we concentrate on figuring out who might have cause to dislike you."

"Dislike." She snorted but tipped her head in agreement.

Mary clicked the tab on her soda can. "So, I've been thinking. What can you tell me about Chelsea White?"

Surprise flickered in Paige's eyes. "The girl I hired as a nail tech?" At Mary's nod, she continued. "Not a whole lot. She's a local gal. Her family owns a dairy farm outside of town. Why?"

Mary rubbed her chin and met Paige's gaze hesitantly. "I added her to our list of suspects."

Paige's eyelashes fluttered. "I don't understand. Why would you do that? What has she done?"

"Well, she was here, which meant she had opportunity."

"But only once," Paige said, "and I was with her the whole time. Wouldn't that mean she didn't have a chance to mess with anything? I would have seen her."

"You only *saw* her once," Mary corrected gently. "She could have come in through the back door other times."

Paige leaned forward, and Figgy spilled out of her lap. "You're right, I suppose, even though I don't like it. Who else?"

"Jack is the obvious choice," Mary said, tapping the note-pad, "but what about the others on the list? You mentioned you and Vanessa have a history. Tell me more about that. What happened between the two of you?"

Paige drew in a long breath. "Goodness, that was all so long ago." Her gaze drifted to the ceiling, and her face took on the faraway look of someone who was revisiting old memories. "I guess I would have to say it wasn't one thing. More like a bunch of little things."

"Such as?" Mary pressed.

Paige cupped her hands over her knees. "Boyfriends, teen-age angst, you name it. We were always at odds over something, though I would have to say it all came to a head our senior year."

"I remember that year. You were on the homecoming court."

Paige nodded. "We both were. Vanessa was really upset that I was chosen as homecoming queen. She was gorgeous and popular, and as head cheerleader, everyone pretty much assumed she was a shoo-in." She dropped her gaze. "That was also the year I first started dating Jack."

Mary's eyes rounded. "What? How did I not know this?"

"I didn't talk much about him. He was a senior from New Holland. We met at a school track meet."

"Let me guess." Mary narrowed her eyes, and Paige nodded.

"He was dating Vanessa at the time. They broke up a little while after he and I met."

"And she wasn't happy about that."

"Not even a little bit. She confronted me in the hall at school and accused me of stealing him from her." Paige rolled her eyes. "If only I'd known then what I do now. Jack didn't need to be stolen. He was the type to go looking for someone new whenever he got bored. Which happened a lot, believe me." A bitter note crept into her voice. "Sorry. I shouldn't speak poorly of Kailey's dad. I try not to do it in front of her, but every now and then, stuff pops out."

She grabbed her Diet Coke and took another drink. Several seconds ticked by, and Mary used the time to think. Could it be that her own wounds made her more suspicious of Jack than she should be? Vanessa was a married woman now, but was it possible that her past with Paige was reason enough for her to want revenge after so many years? It seemed petty, yet there had been far greater crimes committed for much less.

Paige clicked the tab on her soda can with her thumbnail. "Anyway, Vanessa and I were young and stupid, and we both said things to each other that were pretty hurtful. But then we graduated, and a couple of years later, I heard she got married. I figured it was all in the past. Now, I'm not so sure."

"Me neither," Mary bit out grudgingly, after a long moment. Much as she hated to admit it, Jack wasn't the only likely suspect. He wasn't even the *likeliest*. If Vanessa still nursed a grudge, she could very well be the person behind all the mishaps at the salon, and only careful investigation would prove otherwise.

Mary lifted her chin as an idea took root. Careful investigation. That was the key. And she knew just where to start.

CHAPTER THIRTEEN

Elizabeth pulled into the driveway outside Dottie Spencer's home, which also doubled as her salon. Her hands shook slightly as she switched off the ignition and slid her keys into her purse. She shouldn't feel nervous, and yet here she was.

She pushed the car door open and stepped out onto the crunchy grass poking up in brown tufts through the smattering of snow along the driveway. Farther back, a large maple shook woody fingers at a dog barking from a fence behind the garage. Elizabeth glanced over to see a golden lab with his nose pressed to the gate. A low whine rose from his throat.

The screen door screeched as Dottie pushed it open to welcome her. "Hey, Elizabeth! Come on in. Don't mind Laddie. He's curious but harmless."

Elizabeth climbed the steps leading to Dottie's porch. "I didn't know you had a dog."

Dottie's lips stretched in an exaggerated grimace. "I don't. I'm dog sitting for my neighbor, who's out of town." She pointed across the street to a cute little ranch-style home with black shutters.

Once Elizabeth was inside, Dottie held out her hands. "Can I take your coat?"

Elizabeth wiggled out of it and stuffed her scarf into one of the pockets before delivering it into Dottie's waiting grasp.

While Dottie hung it on a peg, Elizabeth glanced around the salon at the many empty chairs. "Thanks for fitting me in so fast. I have to say, I was kinda surprised when you said you had an opening today. Usually, your schedule is pretty full."

Dottie gave a lighthearted laugh and shrugged. "What can I say? Lucky for you, business is slow."

"Lucky. Yes." The sound that emerged from Elizabeth's mouth was more like a titter than a laugh—too high and definitely too loud to be natural. It had to be her conscience that put her so on edge. She and Dottie were friends, after all, and she didn't like the feeling of disloyalty this visit inspired.

Of course, that was her own fault, she mentally scolded herself as she eased over to slide into one of the stylist chairs. She should have been up front about her reason for scheduling the appointment in the first place. She opened her mouth to set things right, but Dottie cut in before she could utter a sound.

"So, how's business? Everything going okay at the store?" She shook out a cape and draped it around Elizabeth's shoulders. "I keep meaning to get over there again."

"Oh yes, we're doing fine. I missed you coming in last week. Martha said you found some dishes you like?"

Dottie's eyes gleamed as she pulled a comb and a pair of scissors from a drawer. "Yes. I found a blue and white Currier & Ives sugar bowl and a soup tureen with the lid. I'm so excited. I have plenty of the everyday pieces, things like plates, coffee cups, saucers, and the like, but very few irregular pieces. These will round out my collection nicely."

"I'm so glad." Elizabeth lifted her chin so Dottie could secure the cape around her neck. "Say, Dottie—"

She held up the comb, halting Elizabeth's speech. "Sorry, what did you say you wanted done today? Is it just a trim?"

Elizabeth froze, her eyes riveted to a long scratch that ran down one of Dottie's fingers. "Um, yes, that's all."

"Perfect." She grabbed a spray bottle and gave it shake. "Rats. Give me just a second to go fill this, okay?"

Elizabeth nodded. She could use a minute to gather her thoughts anyway. "Sure."

"I'll be right back."

She drew a deep breath as Dottie scooted through the doorway to the kitchen, her sneakers swishing lightly against the tiled floor.

"Hey, did you happen to stop by the job fair last week?" Dottie called above the sound of water rushing from the faucet.

"Only for a minute," Elizabeth called back.

"I heard there was a really good turnout. I'm glad. With summer coming, we really are going to need a few kids to help out the businesses around town."

She continued chatting, but her words were lost on Elizabeth, whose gaze was drawn to the appointment book lying open on Dottie's worktable. Was she a bad friend for taking a peek? Anyone could look at the book. It was just lying there, after all.

She hesitated, torn by indecision. Wasn't this why she'd come? Maybe she could avoid embarrassing herself and Dottie just by taking a quick glance.

Her mind made up, she leaned forward. Her breath caught at the number of open spaces lining the calendar. No wonder she'd been able to get right in. There were only two appointments scheduled for later that day, and the next was wide open.

In the kitchen, the water shut off. Elizabeth slumped back into her seat just as Dottie emerged through the doorway.

"It'll be funny to see how all that plays out, don't you think?"

Elizbeth blinked, guilt sweeping over her. "Um, sorry, I didn't quite catch what you said."

Dottie waved her hand, and once again, Elizabeth's gaze was drawn to her finger. "Anyway, it's all just gossip. I probably shouldn't even be talking about it." She elbowed Elizabeth's shoulder playfully then scooped up her hair and began spraying it down with water from the bottle.

"That's, um, a pretty bad scratch on your finger," Elizabeth said. "What did you do?"

"This?" Dottie turned her hand this way and that, and then chuckled. "This is nothing. I cut myself sometimes when I get in too big a rush with the scissors."

If she noticed the silence that fell over Elizabeth, she didn't let it show. Dottie chatted cheerfully about everything from the latest television show she'd gotten hooked on to the complaints filed on the local message board about a pack of strays wandering the neighborhood.

"I don't know if it's bad as everyone says," she said, sweeping the last few hair clippings from Elizabeth's shoulders onto the floor. "But those dogs sure drive Laddie nuts. He hasn't stopped barking since he got dropped off three days ago." She chuckled and reached for the Velcro tab on the cape. "The things we do for friends, right?"

A stone settled in Elizabeth's stomach at the words. "You're awfully sweet to take care of him. How long will you have him?"

"Just a couple more days. His owners are in San Diego visiting relatives." Dottie rolled up the cape and dropped it into a laundry hamper while Elizabeth took out her checkbook. She paid for the haircut then went to retrieve her coat.

"Thanks again for fitting me in."

"It was no trouble at all," Dottie said, reaching for a broom. "I always appreciate your business."

Elizabeth licked her lips. "Say, Dottie, is everything okay, here at the salon, I mean?"

Dottie tilted her head, one hand resting on the top of the broom handle. "Sure. Why do you ask?"

"I just..." She gave her head a small shake and then pressed her lips together. "No reason. I'll see you in a few weeks."

"You bet. See you later, Elizabeth. Say hello to your sisters for me."

"Will do." She turned to go.

"Oh, Elizabeth."

She froze with one hand on the knob and gulped down a breath. "Yes?"

"If you happen to get any more of those dishes, would you hold them for me? You know the ones I mean? The blue and white winter scene?"

"Yes, I know the ones."

"Great. Thank you." She waved goodbye and went back to sweeping.

Elizabeth watched a moment and then let herself out the door. She wouldn't have believed it if she hadn't seen the scratch on Dottie's hand and the appointment book. Didn't *want* to believe it, despite the evidence. Still, there was no doubting it. Dottie's business was in trouble. The question was, how far would she go to save it?

CHAPTER FOURTEEN

The hollow feeling in Elizabeth's gut lingered as she backed out from Dottie's driveway and headed toward town. Was it possible? Could her friend really be trying to drive Paige Schiller out of business?

She drummed her fingers against the steering wheel. Granted, she and Dottie hadn't been friends since high school like Mary and Paige, but she still considered herself a pretty good judge of character, and the Dottie she knew was hard-working and kind. She brought casseroles to the church pot-lucks and baked cookies for children's church. She even helped organize clothing drives for the area's homeless population. A woman like that wouldn't stoop to sabotaging another person's business. Or would she?

Elizabeth groaned and flipped on her blinker to signal her next turn. No matter what her personal feelings were, she had to tell Mary and Martha what she'd learned. Hopefully, they would have something even more incriminating that pointed at someone else, because Elizabeth really did not want to believe the culprit they were looking for was Dottie.

Behind her, a car honked, and Elizabeth realized the light had turned green. She lifted her hand in apology and rounded the corner. Crossing into town, she passed the gas station and the library and was just coming up to the Two Bird Café when a figure caused her to pull her foot off the accelerator and apply the brake.

Elizabeth craned her neck to see out her window as she rolled slowly past the café. A man was entering the restaurant. He was tall, possibly six one or two, with a medium build under an orange-and-navy blue parka, and sandy-brown hair. Orange-and-navy...the same color coat Mary said the man loitering outside the salon wore. Could this be Jack Schiller?

She jerked the steering wheel to her left and angled her car into a narrow parking spot between two other vehicles. The truck on her left sat perilously close to the line, and Elizabeth was forced to wiggle her way out to keep from banging her door into the side. Once she was out, however, she wasted no time scurrying into the café.

The man she'd spotted ducked into a booth not far from the cash register. His back was to her, but that gave Elizabeth a clear view of the person sitting across from him.

Her breath caught. *Vanessa Bancroft?* If this was Jack, what was she doing sitting down with him?

"Good afternoon, and welcome to the Two Bird Café."

Elizabeth startled at the voice. From behind the counter, a young blond with freckles splashed across her nose smiled at her and held out a menu.

"Would you like a seat?" she asked, gesturing toward the tables.

Elizabeth shot another glance at Vanessa's table. She and the man with her were deep in conversation. Much as she would have liked to hear what they were discussing, the restaurant was far too small to hide in. Vanessa was sure to spot her, and then she might want to talk to her.

Elizabeth shook her head at the young waitress. "No thanks. I've changed my mind. I'll just be going."

The girl's smile slipped, but she nodded and replaced the menu atop the stack. "Okay. Well, come again."

"I will. Thank you." She shot one last glance at Vanessa before ducking out the door.

Maybe the man she was having dinner with was Jack Schiller, and maybe he wasn't, but Elizabeth couldn't help but feel cheered as she hurried back to her car. She'd grasp anything that might take the heat off Dottie, even something as tenuous as this.

Except for the pets, the house was empty when she got home. Elizabeth hung her coat and purse near the door then went to the kitchen to fix a cup of tea. While she waited for the water to boil, she struggled to pinpoint what the connection could be between Vanessa and Jack. How did they know each other? What reason could they have for meeting? The questions circled endlessly inside her head.

Finally, the kettle began to whistle, and Elizabeth took a cup from the cupboard and dropped a bag of Earl Grey into it. She wasn't hungry, but she grabbed a box of shortbread cookies out of the pantry and carried it, along with the cup and the kettle, over to the table. Instantly, Butterscotch appeared, his golden eyes glowing as he eyed the cookies. Right behind him was Tinkerbelle, her black nose twitching as she hunkered at Elizabeth's feet.

"These aren't for pets," Elizabeth scolded as she filled her teacup.

Butterscotch stared, unblinking, the tip of his tail twitching. Tink let out a soft whine. Elizabeth sighed and reached for the cookie box. "Fine. But if either of you tell Martha or Mary…"

Tink took the cookie eagerly from Elizabeth's fingers. In two gulps, it was gone. Butterscotch simply eyed the cookie Elizabeth laid at his feet.

"Take it or leave it," she said, brushing the crumbs from her fingers with a smile. She removed the teabag from her cup then stirred in a spoonful of sugar and a dollop of cream. Afterward, she dipped a cookie into her tea, let it soak a second, and took a bite. Hopefully Mary and Martha wouldn't be long. Otherwise, she was likely to devour the entire box of cookies out of nervous energy.

Outside, a car door slammed, and Tink scampered across the kitchen, her long nails clicking on the wood floor. Mary entered on a gust of cold air, her cheeks rosy red against the blue paisley scarf tied over her hair.

"You're back. I figured I would be the first one home," she puffed, bending to give Tink a scratch behind the ears. "Did you have any luck?"

Elizabeth stood, her hands clasped in front of her. "I did. Come sit down, and I'll tell you all about it."

Briefly, she touched on her visit with Dottie and the open slots she'd noticed in her appointment book, but then quickly switched gears to the scene she'd witnessed at the café.

"Let's assume the man with Vanessa was Jack Schiller. That's way more intriguing, don't you think?"

Martha entered through the back door, a bag of kitty food under one arm. "What's more intriguing?" Her brows lifted with curiosity as she dropped the food on the counter and tugged off her gloves.

While Martha took off her coat, Elizabeth related what she'd seen at the café, this time adding that she hadn't quite been able to figure out what the connection could be between Vanessa and Jack, though she sensed deep down there was something there.

"I think I can answer that," Mary said, holding up one finger.

Both Elizabeth and Martha swung their gazes to peer at her. Mary gestured toward an empty chair, and Martha moved to claim it.

"So?" Elizabeth cupped her hands around her cooling tea. "What is it? How do Vanessa and Jack know each other?"

"Would you believe they dated in high school?" Mary took one of the shortbread cookies out of the box. "Paige said they were actually going out when she and Jack first met."

"I guess that explains the history Paige said existed between her and Vanessa," Elizabeth said as Mary took a bite.

Martha frowned. "But does she really think that's the reason Vanessa still holds a grudge?"

"How else would you explain the fact that Vanessa and Jack were together?" Mary asked, wiping a crumb from her lip. Her eyes sparked with excitement. "They have to be in cahoots. All we have to do now is prove it."

"Not so fast," Martha said, holding up her hand in warning. "I may have learned something today that throws a monkey wrench into that theory."

"What?" Mary blinked and lowered her half-eaten cookie to the table. "What do you mean?"

"You asked me to find out what I could about Vanessa Bancroft. Rachel suggested we talk to Ellen Yoder."

"Yes, I remember. And?" Mary motioned with the cookie for her to go on.

"Turns out Vanessa's husband sells farm equipment. A large portion of his customers are Amish, including the Yoders. Ellen was very complimentary of Mr. Bancroft. She says he has always dealt honestly with them and other Amish families she knows."

Elizabeth shook her head in confusion. "I don't understand. What does any of this have to do with Vanessa meeting Jack at the café?"

"Nothing, except it may not have been Jack. What did this man look like?"

Elizabeth gave them a brief description, and Martha shook her head.

"The Yoders have known Mr. Bancroft a long time. From what she told me, he sounds a lot like the person you saw earlier today."

"So, you're saying the man with Vanessa was her husband?" Mary sounded almost disappointed.

Martha shrugged. "I think we have to consider the possibility."

Mary rubbed her fingers over her eyes, then froze. "Wait." She thought a moment, then placed her hand on her head, a look of amazement creeping over her face.

Elizabeth pointed at her. "I know that look. What are you thinking?"

Mary sat up closer to the table. "Okay, suppose the man you saw with Vanessa really was her husband."

"Yeah?"

"Who's to say she's not still behind the incidents at the salon? Maybe she was afraid to sabotage Paige's supplies herself because she knew she'd be recognized if Paige caught her in the salon. That doesn't mean she didn't find someone else to do it."

Elizabeth frowned. "You're saying maybe she got her husband to help?"

Mary looked from Martha to Elizabeth. "Well? Couldn't she?"

"Hold on now, I'm not sure that fits," Martha said. "Ellen seemed pretty adamant about Mr. Bancroft's integrity."

"Hmm. Well, that would seem to rule him out as an accomplice. Still, there's an easy way to find out if the man with Vanessa was her husband." Elizabeth turned to Mary. "All we need is a picture of either Jack or Mr. Bancroft."

Mary slapped her hand to her forehead. "I forgot. Paige told me Jack likes posting pictures of himself on social media. I was supposed to see if I could pull one up the other night, but then Elizabeth told me Jennifer called, and I got distracted."

"Do you think you could look now?" Martha asked. "It sure would help if we could clear some of this up."

Mary started to rise, but Elizabeth reached out a hand to stop her. "Aren't you supposed to be meeting Wade tonight?"

"Oh." Her eyes widened, and she glanced at the clock on the microwave. "I forgot all about it."

"You still have time," Elizabeth said. "You go get changed, and Martha and I will see what we can dig up."

"But how will you know if it's him?"

"We'll look for pictures of both men. Plus, I got a look at the guy at the café, remember? If it wasn't Jack, I'll know."

Finally, Mary gave a reluctant nod and pushed up from the table. "Okay, but will you text me copies so I can see if either one is the same man I saw outside the salon?"

"No problem," Elizabeth said.

Mary muttered her thanks, but Elizabeth couldn't help but think she didn't seem nearly as enthusiastic about her date with Wade as she had a couple of days ago. Had she lost interest in him already, or could it be that her acceptance of his offer of dinner had simply been a case of flattery going to her head?

That was a question that only Mary could answer.

CHAPTER FIFTEEN

Mary spritzed on a light perfume then took one last look in the mirror before walking out her bedroom door. Wade would be arriving at any moment, and though she'd had plenty of time to freshen up and dress, she couldn't help but fuss with the scarf on her head as she crossed to get her coat. Fortunately, Jennie's was a casual place, so the scarf, her red-and-gold sweater, and dark denims would fit right in.

The bell rang just as she pushed her arms through the sleeves. Mary called goodbye to her sisters and opened the door to greet Wade. Her heart hammered a bit at the sight of him. Dressed in dark khakis and a North Face ski jacket with silver trim, he might have just hopped off a ski lift or the cover of a magazine. Perhaps that was exactly the look he was going for. The aviator sunglasses didn't hurt.

Wade smiled when he saw her and toyed with the keys in his hand. "Hey, Mary. You ready to go?"

"Almost."

She lifted her purse from a hook in the closet and slung it over her shoulder then pasted a smile to her face as she turned to Wade. "All set."

Taking her elbow, he led her to his car, a smoky-gray Dodge Challenger with bucket seats and alloy rims.

"Nice car," she said as he settled into the seat beside her.

Wade grinned and reached for the seat belt. "I like it."

The car was a standard, so his hand came very close to her knee when he reached over to back out of the drive. Mary felt her stomach flutter nervously, then scolded herself for being silly.

"So, I hope you're hungry," Wade said, reaching up to remove the sunglasses and drop them into a cup holder next to the gearshift.

"Starving. I was so busy helping Paige today, I didn't have time to eat lunch."

"Paige?" His eyebrows rose.

Grateful to have something to discuss, Mary told him all about her friend and how she'd moved back to Bird-in-Hand from Pittsburgh, and everything that had befallen her since. Midway through, she realized she was talking too much, but filling the silence felt better than fumbling to make small talk, so she kept going until they turned onto Route 30, and the metal diner with its bright red stripes came into view.

"Here we are," Wade said, slipping into a parking space. He shut off the engine and leaned over to flash her a grin. "Reservations are for seven. What do you want to do until then?"

She was caught off guard for a moment. Then, realizing he was joking, she returned his smile and reached for her door handle.

"Uh-uh." He wagged his finger at her. "Allow me."

He jumped out, circled the car, and pulled her door open with a flourish.

"Uh, thank you," she said, blushing a little at the production he made of stepping forward to offer his arm.

Across the parking lot, a couple of people glanced their way, and Mary couldn't help but wonder if the chivalry was for her benefit or for theirs as Wade smiled at them and ducked his head.

Thankfully, he was much more reserved when they went inside, though he did offer to help with her coat and then proceeded to hold her chair.

"Thank you, Wade. You're very much a gentleman," Mary said as she took her seat.

Wade rounded the corner of the table to sit in the chair closest to her and flashed a smile that was particularly bright against his tanned skin. "Can't help it, Mary. I've lived in Pennsylvania for several years, but I was raised in the South. People have a different way of doing things down there. Paying attention to your manners is one of them."

That certainly explained the charm he exuded. On him, it seemed as natural as breathing. Mary reached for a menu. Once they'd ordered, Wade leaned forward to touch a lock of hair peeking out from beneath her scarf.

"So, still blue, huh?"

She shrugged self-consciously. "I was supposed to make an appointment so Paige could fix it for me, but with everything else that's been going on, we just haven't had time."

A sparkle lit his eyes. "I actually kinda like it." His gaze lingered, and then he let his hand fall away.

Mary swallowed a sudden knot. She liked Wade, but did she like that he was already so comfortable touching her? She cleared her throat. "So, how is school going? Have you started spring training?"

The look in his eyes changed to something like excitement. For the next several minutes, she had only to interject the occasional "oh" and "uh-huh" as Wade talked about everything from the players trying out to the new concession stand. At last their food arrived, and Mary dug into her chicken potpie with gusto.

Not that Wade was boring. Far from it. He smiled a lot, was easy to talk to, and he asked questions about her with a genuine gleam of interest in his eyes. So?

Mary's gaze drifted to the door. As if on cue, it swung open, and Bill Richmond walked through. Only he wasn't alone. Nettie Walters was on his arm. Beautiful Nettie Walters, who was as slender and colorful as the flowers she sold in her shop. And she was staring up at Bill with something like adoration in her gorgeous almond eyes.

Mary choked on a suddenly dry bite of chicken potpie.

"Hey, are you all right?" Wade handed her a napkin and reached over to pat her on the back.

"Yes. Sorry." Still coughing, she grabbed her water glass and took a sip, then used the napkin to wipe the tears from her eyes.

Keep walking. Don't stop here, she begged silently, to no avail. Bill and Nettie seemed to notice her plight and paused as they passed their table.

Bill's steady gaze fell to her and then Wade. "Hey, Mary. Wade."

Wade returned his nod then went right back to peering into Mary's face. "You okay now?"

"Better, yes." Mary could only hope her face wasn't as red as her sweater as she smiled up at Nettie. Bill's gaze, she avoided entirely. "Hi."

"Hi, Mary. Date night, huh?" She sidled closer to Bill. "Bill and I were just grabbing a bite to eat."

"Wade and I too. Grabbing a bite to eat," Mary said, stumbling over her words like she had something to hide. Which was silly. She'd already told Bill that Wade had asked her out. She snapped her mouth shut and fiddled with her straw.

"Well, we won't keep you," Bill said, laying his hand on Nettie's back. "Bye, Mary. Good seeing you, Coach."

"Bye," she mumbled, her gaze riveted to Bill's strong hand as they walked away. She knew exactly what it felt like to have the steady pressure of his hand guiding her, protecting her, and it was nothing like Wade's touch.

"Hey."

She ripped her gaze away and looked at him.

His mouth lifted in a grin. "You okay?"

"Yes. Yeah. Of course." She fumbled to an embarrassed stop. Hearing her phone buzz, she snatched it up. "Sorry. I'll just be a minute."

"That's not what I think it is, is it?"

She stared. "Sorry?"

"You didn't ask one of your sisters to call you with an emergency so you could end our date early?"

Her eyes widened. "No! I would never...I mean..."

He grabbed her hand. "Mary, I'm kidding. Go ahead and take the call. Do what you need to do."

Cheeks flaming, she pulled her hand free and pushed out of the booth. "Thanks. I'll be right back."

"Take your time."

She smiled, but it felt empty. Hurrying toward the bathroom, she jabbed the ANSWER button and pressed the phone to her ear. "Hello?"

"Mary, it's Martha. Did you see the text I sent?"

"Not yet." She pulled the phone away and swiped up. Martha's text appeared. In it was a picture of a handsome man with dark hair and one brow that winged upward in a sort of imitation of Dwayne Johnson. Mary laid the phone to her ear again. "Who is that?"

"Apparently, it's Jack Schiller."

"What? This looks nothing like the guy I saw outside the salon."

"Are you sure?"

"Positive."

Martha's sigh rang heavy over the line. "Well then, I'm afraid we're back to square one."

Mary's fingers tightened on the phone. "You mean Elizabeth didn't recognize him either?"

"Nope. Afraid not."

"So then, who was the guy with Vanessa?"

"Best guess, her husband. Elizabeth has been searching for a while, but so far we can't find any pictures of Mr. Bancroft."

Mary thought a second then frowned. "Tell you what, you guys keep looking for a picture on your end, and I'll see what I can find out here."

"I'll text you if we find something."

"Okay. Thanks, Martha. I'll talk to you later." She hung up and made her way back to the table.

Wade glanced up as she sat down. "Everything okay?"

"Everything's fine. No emergencies here." She smiled and took a sip from her glass.

While Wade finished his supper, Mary pushed a piece of flaky crust around her plate. "Say, Wade, you've lived in Bird-in-Hand a while, right? You know a lot of the people?"

"Some." He shrugged and wiped his napkin across his mouth. "Most of the people I know are affiliated with the school in some way, either as parents or other staff. Why?"

"Do you know a family by the name of Bancroft? Specifically, Vanessa Bancroft and her husband?"

He thought a moment, then shook his head. "Sorry, that name isn't familiar."

"That's all right. I was just wondering." She hid her disappointment behind a bite of her now cold potpie.

Wade took up the conversation, chatting about the people he'd met while in Bird-in-Hand. Mary had to admit, there were no awkward silences with him. He handled small talk easily, and was always quick to change the subject when he sensed she was getting bored. But later that night, when she was back in her bedroom with the covers pulled up to her chin, she couldn't help but feel that the potpie had been the best part of their date.

Wade was handsome enough, and charming, but she'd caught him looking at other women several times throughout the night. Or rather, she'd caught him admiring the fact that other women were looking at him. Did it really matter to him that other people found him attractive? Was he so conscious of his appearance that he saw his own worth reflected in other people's eyes?

The thought bothered her as she flipped onto her side to stare into the gloom. If she was honest, she might even say the same thing about herself, which was funny, considering how she'd struggled with self-esteem following her divorce. But what other explanation could there be for the way she'd felt when she'd looked into the mirror and seen blue hair? Had she subconsciously let the pendulum swing so far in the other direction that she was now one of those self-centered women who worried constantly about her appearance?

Growling, Mary jerked the covers off and rolled onto her back to glare at the ceiling. "I'm trying to find the balance, Lord," she said quietly.

Tink lifted her head from her bed, and her floppy ears pricked.

"Sorry, girl. Go back to sleep," Mary said.

As if she understood, Tink sighed and snuggled back into her bed. Mary closed her eyes and tried to shut out thoughts of Wade and Paige and anything else but the words of a humble prayer. Oddly, when she finished, it wasn't Wade's face she had to fight to keep from swimming before her eyes.

It was Bill's.

CHAPTER SIXTEEN

Mary woke to the tantalizing odor of frying bacon the next morning. Though it had cooled overnight and there was a frosty nip in the air, she couldn't help but be drawn out of her comfy covers by the smell. Spying Tink's empty bed, she grinned. Obviously, the little dog had also been tempted. The bedroom door was open a crack where she'd scampered through.

Mary hurried to the bathroom, washed up, put on her makeup, and donned a fluffy crew-neck sweater and snug-fitting jeans. As a finishing touch, she tugged on a pair of thick socks then jammed her feet into a pair of stylish boots before heading downstairs. As she suspected, Tink sat doe-eyed and quietly begging for scraps at Martha's feet as she scrambled some eggs.

Martha looked up from the frying pan as Mary entered. "Good morning. Would you like some coffee?"

"Coffee sounds wonderful." Mary rubbed her hands over her arms. "What's the weather like? It feels chilly in here."

"The furnace is acting up. I called the repairman. He's meeting me here in a little bit."

Mary grunted and grabbed the coffeepot and a cup from the counter. "I didn't know we were having furnace troubles."

Martha shrugged and added the eggs to a plate next to a slice of toast and a couple of pieces of bacon. "I didn't either. Hopefully it's nothing major."

She handed the plate to Mary then fixed another for herself and walked over to the table. "So...um...how was your date with Wade?"

"It was fine. We went to Jennie's." She joined Martha at the table and told her all about her night. Though she didn't press, Mary sensed that Martha had something on her mind. She sat down and took a sip from her coffee cup. "How'd you sleep?"

At her heavy sigh, Mary pushed her cup away and laid her hand on Martha's arm. "Won't you tell me what's been bothering you?"

Martha looked up and just as quickly looked away. "It's actually a couple of things, but I'm not sure it's my place to say anything," she said hesitantly.

A picture of Martha's troubled face when she heard about her date with Wade flashed into Mary's mind. "Does one of the things have anything to do with me?"

Martha's silence spoke volumes.

"You don't have to worry about me, you know," Mary said, touched by the concern twisting her sister's features.

"I know. It's just, sometimes I wonder if you realize you're a lot stronger than you think. Smarter too."

"But?" Mary prompted, sensing one was coming.

Martha took hold of her hand and squeezed. "You never used to care so much what other people thought about you. I didn't always understand it, but I admired you for it."

"Really?"

Martha nodded. "All of that changed after Brian. It took you awhile to get your confidence back, but you did it."

"And now?"

She sighed. "I'm worried about this thing with you and Wade. Is he really the man you want to date? You told Bill you weren't ready for a relationship when you first moved back to Bird-in-Hand. You insisted on just being friends. But it bothered you seeing him with Nettie. Do you think, possibly, what you're feeling is jealousy? And if that's the case, aren't you being a little oblivious to his feelings by going out with Wade? Maybe you need to sort out your feelings where both men are concerned."

Mary snorted.

"What?" Small furrows formed between Martha's brows as she pulled her hand away.

"I had the same realization last night."

Martha's eyes widened, and Mary smiled. "Don't you fret, sister dear. It might be taking longer than it should, but I'm figuring things out."

"I know you will."

Tears rose to Mary's eyes at the confidence in her sister's tone. She cleared her throat. "So? What's the other thing?" At her blank look, Mary tipped her head and offered a wily smile. "You said there were a *couple* of things bothering you."

Martha dropped her gaze and fingered the handle of her coffee cup. "It's Jared," she said finally. "I'm worried about him."

"*Trish's* Jared?" Mary sat up straight. "He and Trish aren't having problems, are they?"

Martha put up her hand. "No, no, he and Trish are fine."

"Well then, is everything okay with the kids?"

A patient smile curved Martha's lips, and Mary took a deep breath and forced herself to slow down.

"Sorry. Go ahead." She motioned with her hand.

Martha sucked in a breath and blew it out slowly. "It's Jared's job. You know he's been working in the IT department for the state bank commissioner."

I thought he loved his job, rose to Mary's lips, but she swallowed the words and nodded.

"He's very happy with his job, but now that the kids are getting older, that hour-long commute has really become a problem. Trish says he's never around when she needs to run the kids to Little League practice or dance classes and, well"—a tremor shook her hand as she reached up to smooth her hair behind her ear—"she told me the other day she's starting to feel like a single parent."

"Uh-oh."

"Exactly."

"Has she told Jared how she feels?"

Martha picked crumbs off her slice of toast. "She tried. They ended up getting in a big fight."

"I'm sorry, Martha. No wonder you've been having trouble sleeping. You've probably been worrying yourself sick."

Martha dropped her toast onto her plate and reached for her coffee. "Not very mature of me, considering that the scriptures are pretty clear about worry. Specifically, not to do it." She gave a soft snort and brought her cup to her lips.

"Then again, I've never known you to worry about your-self," Mary said, patting her arm gently. "When you do it, it's always for someone else."

Martha's gaze clouded, and she reached for a napkin to press to her nose. "Kids. No matter how old they are, they'll always be our babies, eh?"

A floorboard creaked in the hall, and Elizabeth swept into the kitchen and made straight for the coffeepot. She was already dressed, her hair done and light makeup in place.

"You're up late," Mary said, since normally she was the one bringing up the rear.

"Yeah. I thought I'd get over to the store to do some rear-ranging." She waved her hand. "No big deal. You two having a nice talk?"

Mary shot a curious glance at Martha. Elizabeth obviously had something else on her mind. Did Martha think Elizabeth was acting a little odd too?

"Mary and I are just working through some things," Martha said. She motioned to the stove. "Would you like some breakfast? I can scramble up another egg."

Elizabeth plucked a slice of bacon from the plate and held it up. "Don't worry about me. This will do just fine." She grabbed a travel mug from the cabinet and filled it with coffee. "I'll see you guys over at the store, okay? I'm going to go ahead and get started."

Mary glanced at the clock. "But it's only seven thirty."

Elizabeth's light chuckle sounded forced as she angled toward the door. "You know what they say. No sense burning perfectly good daylight."

She grabbed her coat then fluttered her fingers and slipped out the door before either of them could protest.

Mouth open, Mary blinked in bemusement. "Was that weird to you?"

"I'll say. Did you notice what she did?"

She looked at Martha, who gestured toward the coffeepot. "Black coffee is my thing, not Elizabeth's."

Mary's gaze drifted over to the untouched cream and sugar bowls. "I wonder why she was in such a rush."

Martha dropped her gaze and reached for her fork, but not before Mary caught the knowing glimmer shining there.

"What?"

Martha looked up, her wide eyes the picture of innocence. "Hmm?"

"You know something." Mary leaned forward to rest her elbows on the table. "What have I missed?"

Martha toyed with her eggs, then set her fork aside. "It's just a hunch."

"Your hunches are usually spot on. Come on, out with it." She picked up a slice of bacon and gestured to her with it, then took a bite.

Martha's face twisted sadly. "Elizabeth seemed a little off the other day after she talked to Jennifer."

Mary put her hand to her chest and lifted her brows in question.

"Uh-huh. Your Jennifer. She wanted advice, and Elizabeth was a little hesitant giving it to her."

Mary chewed slowly and swallowed. "Sorry, I'm not following. What's so odd about that?"

Martha's hands encircled her cup, and she pulled it close. "Elizabeth's not the type to keep what she thinks inside. But last night, after you and Wade left for your date, she acted all uncomfortable when I told her about Jared and Trish."

"Well, we're their parents. Maybe she doesn't want to overstep."

"Maybe." Martha bit her lip. "But I suspect it's more than that. I think there's something she's not telling us."

Mary glanced toward the door and then out the window toward the barn. "You think something happened between her and Jennifer?"

"Maybe." Martha picked up her fork again. "It would certainly explain why she was in such a rush to head out this morning."

Mary bit her lip. "I should go and talk to her."

"Hold on there," Martha said, grabbing her hand before Mary could push back from the table. "If she hasn't said anything, it may be she doesn't want to mention it, and us rushing out there will only embarrass her."

Mary settled back against her chair. "You're right. So then what should we do? Act like nothing's wrong?"

"I think if the situation were reversed, Elizabeth would find a way to let us know she's there for us."

They fell silent, thinking, and then Martha's eyes lit with excitement. "I know. I'll make something special for supper. All of her favorites."

Mary perked up in her seat. "Italian cream cake?"

"And homemade lasagna," Martha said, laughing as Mary rubbed her hands together.

"My mouth is watering. I'll pick up some ice cream after work."

"That'll be good." Martha scowled down at her plate. "Ugh. These are cold by now. Do you want me to warm yours up in the microwave?"

Mary stuffed in a quick bite and followed it with a swallow from her coffee cup. "No thanks. Cold or not, you're still the best cook in Lancaster County." She drained her cup and then carried it to the dishwasher along with her dish. "Hey, I'd like to swing over to see Paige before the store opens this morning. I don't think I'll be long, but just in case, would you mind covering for me a little bit?"

"Of course not." Martha opened the microwave door and set her plate inside, then punched the buttons on the timer. "Hey, before you leave, did we tell you about Vanessa?"

Mary froze with one arm in the sleeve of her coat. "What about her?"

"No big mystery behind the person Elizabeth saw her with the other day, I'm afraid. We pulled up the website where Ellen said Mr. Bancroft works and looked through the staff directory."

Mary nodded.

"The man in the restaurant? It was her husband."

Disappointment welled in Mary's chest—not because Vanessa and her husband met for lunch. That was nice. Sweet even. No, what bothered her was the fact that suddenly, they were right back where they started.

CHAPTER SEVENTEEN

All the way across town, images of Jack Schiller and the picture of Miles Bancroft Martha had shown her flashed through Mary's mind. Miles. That was Vanessa's husband's name, and neither he nor Jack looked anything like the man she'd seen outside Paige's salon.

Frustration vibrated through her as she turned into the parking lot of the Bird-in-Hand Bakery for one more cup of coffee. On a day like today, she had the feeling she was going to need the extra caffeine.

Inside the bakery, the music of the morning played out on the ring of the cash register, the hum of many conversations, and the tinkle of spoons in coffee cups. Mary glided to the counter and pulled out her billfold.

"Good morning," the woman behind the cash register sang out cheerily. "What can I get for you?"

"Coffee to go, please." She laid a five-dollar bill on the counter. "Leave room for cream?"

"Will do."

As the woman shuffled off to get her coffee, Mary took in the bakery. This time of day, there weren't many empty tables. And everywhere the scent of coffee, vanilla, sausage, eggs, and cheese wafted. Another waitress walked by, a plate with a large, buttery croissant balanced in one hand. If she hadn't already stuffed herself with Martha's breakfast, Mary would have been tempted to order one of the croissants for herself.

She cast an admiring glance at the customer to whom the plate was delivered. The woman's face drew her up short. She looked familiar but...

Mary narrowed her eyes. Catherine Randall? The picture in her mind solidified. Yes, this was the same woman who'd been in the salon the day Paige dyed Mary's hair blue.

Mary smiled at her. Catherine's gaze fluttered up to her hair, and then she glanced away, her cheeks pink.

"Ma'am? Here's your coffee." The waitress held out a paper cup in a brown sleeve.

"Thank you." She took it and removed the lid to add cream and sugar later on. "Say, that woman in the corner?"

The waitress flicked a glance over her shoulder. "Yeah?"

"Is her name by any chance Catherine Randall?"

The waitress nodded. "That's her. She comes in here about once a week. Always orders the same thing, one plain croissant and a cup of English Breakfast."

"Hmm. What does...um...do you know anything about her? I mean, does she live here in Bird-in-Hand?"

"Sorry." The waitress pushed her hands into her apron pockets, felt around, then pulled out a pen. "I don't know her all that well. I think maybe she runs a little specialty shop."

Mary angled her head questioningly. "What kind of specialty? Like, clothing?"

"Not clothing. Coffee." She snorted and marked something on a piece of paper, then handed it to the cook. "I think she just comes in here to scope us out. You know, since we're the competition."

"Interesting. Do you happen to know the name of her store?"

She stuck the pen behind her ear and slid the pad of paper into her apron pocket. "No, but I can ask her if you'd like."

Mary shook her head and pushed the five across the counter. "Don't worry about it. Thank you. You've been very helpful." She nodded to the money. "Keep the change."

The waitress quickly rang up the sale and dropped the change into a cup on the counter. Mary crossed to a small coffee stand stacked with several metal baskets containing sweetener and flavored creamer cups, as well as several slim metal carafes of milk, half-and-half, and heavy cream. While she doctored her coffee, she peeked at Catherine Randall. Just as before, she was perfectly coiffed, her hair and makeup flawless, clothes stylish and refined. Of course, that made sense now that Mary knew she owned her own business.

She stirred some sugar into her coffee and refastened the lid then reached for a napkin. Would it be too forward to go over and speak to her? Maybe she could subtly ask how her appointment with Paige had gone.

She'd just made up her mind to speak with her when Catherine rose and headed for the door. She had a magazine tucked under one arm, and by the determined look on her face, she was a woman with places to be.

Mary sighed and dropped her coffee stirrer into the trash. Perhaps another time. She thought a moment then returned to the counter. She could at least pick up another coffee for Paige.

The remainder of the drive over to the salon passed without incident. The sign on the door read OPEN, but Paige's car was the only one in the lot.

Mary gripped both coffee cups as she walked toward the door. Hopefully, that wasn't a bad omen. After all, it was still early yet.

The salon looked especially neat when she entered. No more boxes lined the hall, and a new display of hair care products had been set up near the window. Obviously, Paige had used the time she was closed to get other work done. She emerged from the back room, and Mary crossed to her and stuck out one of the coffee cups.

"Here. I brought you something. It's black, so if you take cream and sugar, you'll need to doctor it."

"Today, black works." Paige tipped up the cup and took a long sip. "Mmm. Thanks, Mary."

Mary looked around. "Where's Figgy?"

"He's sleeping in his bed in the back," said Paige. "The vet had an opening for him yesterday afternoon, and he's still sleeping it off."

"Good for you," Mary said. She set her cup down so she could slip out of her coat. "So? Anything else happen yesterday after I left?"

"Nope. Then again, I was closed." She shuddered and ran her fingers through her dark hair. "I spent half the morning praying everything would go smoothly today, and the other half working up the courage to actually flip the sign on the door."

Mary laughed, but deep down, she knew Paige was only half joking. "What do you need me to do? Anything I can help with?"

Paige shrugged and held out her hands. "Not unless you want to break down some boxes and pile them in the recycle bin."

"I can do that."

Paige waved Mary forward. "This way. I've got them all stacked up by the back door."

"The place looks really good, Paige," Mary said as they passed the office. "You got a lot done."

"Well, if I'm honest, it was mostly nervous energy." She laughed and pushed open the back door. "I had to do something, or I was gonna drive myself crazy."

Outside, it was still cool, but most of the snow had melted and the sun shone brightly overhead. Mary set her coffee down and pushed up her sleeves. Several boxes had been piled one atop the other against the wall, and she knew it wouldn't take long to work up a sweat. While Paige attacked one pile, Mary grabbed a box from another. They worked silently for several minutes, and then Mary held up one of the smaller boxes stamped with the words MEANINGFUL BEAUTY SUPPLIES, in bold, swirling script.

"Say, Paige, what is this?"

She looked at Mary over her shoulder. "The box?"

"The business." Mary pointed to the name, and Paige shrugged.

"That's the company I order most of my supplies from."

"Like a warehouse?"

"I suppose there's a warehouse somewhere. To be honest, I don't really know where. I order my supplies online, and they're delivered once a month." She arched a brow. "Why?"

Mary ripped the tape off the bottom then folded the box flat and added it to the stack she'd started. "Just puzzling through some stuff. Did I tell you my sisters and I found a picture of Jack?"

She shook her head and stomped down another box. "Rats. I meant to do that for you. I forgot all about it."

"It was no problem. Like you said, he does like to post those selfies." She raised her eyebrows and added an eye roll for effect.

Paige snorted a laugh. "What'd you think?"

"I think you're right. He does look like Clive Owen. And he definitely wasn't the guy I saw outside your salon."

Paige looked surprised and then sad. "I didn't figure so. Jack is a lot of things, but I can't say he was ever vengeful. So then, we're back to square one?"

"I suppose we are."

Mary picked up another box and stared at the name stamped on the front. Maybe this would be a good place to start. She tucked the name away for later.

"So, does Kailey seem to be adjusting any better at school?"

Paige ripped a piece of tape off the bottom of the last box in her stack. "I think she's made a new friend. That should help."

"Really?"

Paige tossed her flattened box into the recycle bin. "Uh-huh. Kelly Wallace. Do you know her?"

"Not well. I know her mother, Eleanor Wallace."

Paige nodded. "That's her. I understand Kelly is ill?"

"That's right. Leukemia." Mary tsked with compassion. "She's in remission now, I believe, but it was hard on her and her family for a while there."

Paige straightened and swiped the back of her hand over her brow. "I can't even imagine."

"Me neither."

Hitching her thumb toward the door, Paige said, "Well, that's it. Thanks so much for your help, Mary. Do you want to come inside for a little bit?"

"Actually, I need to head back," she said, checking her watch. "The store will be opening in a little bit. I did want to ask you though, besides the people you mentioned, were you able to remember any other customers who might have come into the salon?"

"A few." Paige nodded. "When I get a chance today, I'll email you a list."

"Okay. And what about Catherine Randall?"

"Catherine?"

"Yeah. I saw her in the bakery this morning. How much do you know about her?"

"Well, other than the fact that she is very particular about her looks, not a whole lot." Paige waved toward the door. "But I don't think she has anything to do with this. Why would she? I don't even know her."

"Okay. Well, then I guess I'll just see what other leads I can come up with. I'll see you later, Paige."

"Sounds good. And thank you." Paige folded her into a hug. When she pulled away, her eyes were wet. "I'm glad I call you friend."

"Me too, Paige." Mary wished her goodbye and then headed toward the front of the salon and her car. Paige was putting up a good front, but it was obvious that the stress was wearing on her. For her sake, Mary needed to figure out who was trying to sabotage her business. And she needed to do it fast.

CHAPTER EIGHTEEN

Elizabeth put the final polish on a silver teapot and set it on a tray alongside the rest of the service. It was an elegant set. Likely they wouldn't have any trouble selling it, even with the lid missing on the sugar bowl.

She frowned and angled the tray on the shelf to better reflect the light streaming from the windows, then grabbed a delicate, spoon-shaped infuser and laid it on the tray next to the pot. There. Perhaps that would make up for the missing piece.

"That's beautiful."

Elizabeth looked over her shoulder for the voice. A tall woman, pretty but with a very bad perm, nodded toward the tea service.

"How much are you asking?"

"We have three hundred and fifty on this set." She moved aside to give the woman a better view.

The woman's eyes widened, and interest sparked in her gaze. "Is that all? It's very lovely. German, isn't it?"

Elizabeth nodded appreciatively. "You have a good eye. But it is missing a lid, and it's silver plated, not sterling. Still, it's a very nice collection overall. Are you looking for a tea service?"

The woman offered a pleasant smile and shook her head. "Actually, I have one that my grandmother passed down to me several years ago." She inched her purse strap higher onto her shoulder. "No, I just was passing by on my way into town and thought I would check out your shop." She stuck out her hand and shook Elizabeth's. "I'm Eloise Parkhurst. I chair the Chamber of Commerce. This is a nice little business you have here."

Parkhurst. The bad perm. Suddenly, the two things clicked in Elizabeth's brain. This was the woman Mary had told her about. Somehow, Elizabeth managed to keep her gaze from drifting upward to the woman's hair. "Why, thank you. It's a pleasure to meet you, Ms. Parkhurst. I'm Elizabeth Classen."

"I know. I met your sister, Martha." She smiled and pointed toward the front of the shop where Martha was busy assisting customers with baked goods. Then she swept her hand to her chest. "And please, call me Eloise."

"Thank you. I will. And you can call me Elizabeth."

Eloise motioned around her. "This is a really neat place. I love the atmosphere you've created. Very homey."

"That's because it is home. I grew up here. My sisters and I inherited this farm from our parents."

"Sisters? You have another besides Martha?"

"Yes. Mary. She'll be here a little later. Right now, she's running errands, or I would introduce you."

"I'm sorry I missed her." She inclined her head. "So, Elizabeth, have you and your sisters thought about becoming members of the chamber?"

Elizabeth smiled and ducked her head. "I'm sorry to say I don't know much about the chamber. If I may ask, what is it you do?"

"Oh, don't feel bad. It's not unusual for people to be unfamiliar with us, though since I took over as chair, I've tried to remedy that by introducing myself to all the local business owners."

Eloise's chin lifted, and she drew her shoulders back proudly. She took a card from her purse and held it out for Elizabeth. "We work with local businesses to help them expand, attract new employees, and navigate any issues that may come up. Plus, it's a great way to engage with other local business owners, create network opportunities, that sort of thing." Her hands fluttered in the air. "But all of that is on our website. You should check us out. And if you're interested in learning more, we're having a meeting tomorrow night to discuss a few upcoming events we'd like to add to our calendar. We'd love to have you join us."

Elizabeth looked down at the card in her hand and smiled. "I'll certainly mention it to my sisters. Thank you so much for the information."

"You're welcome. Nice meeting you, Elizabeth." She wagged her fingers. "Bye now."

"Goodbye."

Eloise sauntered off, a cloud of perfume wafting in her wake. Watching her go, Elizabeth fingered the card thoughtfully. It wouldn't hurt to consider becoming a member of the chamber, and Eloise seemed nice enough. Her hair was unfortunate, but in the end, that was neither here nor there. Shaking free of her thoughts, Elizabeth slid the card into her pocket and went in search of a broom. Soon she forgot all about Eloise.

Several chores and customers later, a rumble in her stomach reminded Elizabeth that it was almost time for lunch. Mary offered to take her break last, and Elizabeth was only too happy to agree since the bacon had long since worn off. She headed up to the house, intent on grabbing something fast and easy, and was surprised when Martha joined her in the kitchen not long after, two large grocery bags clutched in her arms.

"What is all of that?" Elizabeth asked, eyeing her over her half-eaten turkey sandwich. "And when did you have time to run to the grocery store?"

"Oh, I just thought I'd pick up a few things for supper." The bags rustled as Martha set them down on the counter. "I hope you haven't made any plans."

"Nope, I haven't." Elizabeth wiped the sweat from her glass with a napkin and then took a sip of her cola. "What are we having?"

Hearing what Martha had planned, Elizabeth's brows rose. "What's going on? Those are all my favorites. Do I have some sickness I don't know about or something?"

"Can't a gal treat her favorite sister?" Martha's eyes twinkled merrily as she began pulling items out of the bag.

Elizabeth chuckled wryly. "Right. I heard you tell Mary she was your favorite just last week."

"But that was last week. Today, I want you to know that you're pretty special too."

A lump rose in Elizabeth's throat at the sincerity in her sister's voice. She stood and gave Martha's arm a squeeze. "Thank you. I admit, it's nice hearing things like that now and again. We don't say them often enough."

"Agreed," Martha said, squeezing back.

Elizabeth went back to her seat at the table and took another bite of her sandwich.

"So, I showed Mary the picture we found of Miles Bancroft," Martha said. She opened the fridge and set a bowl of ricotta cheese inside then closed the door and leaned against it thoughtfully. "I have to say, I'm a little at a loss. If the man outside the salon wasn't Jack, and he's not Miles, who could he be? Mary saw him twice. His presence there can't be a coincidence."

Elizabeth swallowed her bite with a frown. "I agree. It would help if we at least had a picture. Maybe he'll come back. Do you suppose one of us should try hanging around to see if we can catch him outside of the salon?"

"Do we have a choice?" Martha asked, pushing away from the fridge to set a box of lasagna noodles on the counter. "What other leads do we have?"

Elizabeth snapped her fingers. "I should have asked Mary if she got any more names from Paige." She pushed her plate away. "I'll do that now."

"What about your lunch?" Martha pointed to the half-eaten sandwich. "I'll do it. You go ahead and finish eating."

"Too late. I'm done." Elizabeth grabbed her plate and carried it to the door. "Wynken, Blynken, and Nod will be happy."

Martha chuckled as she took a mixing bowl out of the cupboard. "I'm sure they will. Those goats are pretty spoiled. Let me know what Mary says."

"Will do."

After feeding the goats the remainder of her lunch, Elizabeth hurried back to the store to find Mary. Paige had emailed the list of names to Mary, so the two of them hunched over Mary's phone to study them together.

"Well?" Mary pulled back to look into Elizabeth's face. "Any of these look familiar?"

Elizabeth shook her head helplessly. "Where do we even start? I don't know, Mary. I'm a little at a loss on this one. What if we can't figure out who's behind all of these incidents?"

Mary sucked in a deep breath. "There has to be something we're missing. We just have to keep looking until we find it."

Her phone chimed, and Elizabeth looked down at it the same time as Mary.

"Oh, that's Jennifer." Mary bit her lip and glanced at Elizabeth. "I can text her later."

"Don't be silly. Go ahead. See what she wants."

Mary swiped up, read silently a moment, then typed a quick message and slid her phone into her pocket.

"Everything okay?" Elizabeth asked, surprised she had to force a light note into her voice.

"Jennifer and Michael aren't talking," Mary said with a sigh. "Jennifer's feelings are hurt, and Michael is annoyed because he feels like Jennifer is being unreasonable. At this point, I'm not even sure what I can do or say that will help."

She looked at Elizabeth hopefully. Elizabeth tore her gaze away and gestured toward a couple at the cash register. "Looks like those people are just about ready to cash out. I'd better go check."

She hurried away before Mary could question her. Martha was right. Something was bothering Elizabeth. Why hadn't she told them about it?

CHAPTER NINETEEN

The sweet, vanilla scent of a cooling Italian cream cake teased Mary's nose as she walked into the house for her lunch break. Later, that scent would be mingled with the tangy garlic scent of baking lasagna. Her mouth watered just thinking about it. For now, she'd make do with leftover beef stew.

She pulled it from the refrigerator, poured some into a pot, and set it on the stove to warm. While she waited, she poured herself a glass of tea and carried it to the table, setting it next to her laptop.

"Now, how about we see what we can find out about this Meaningful Beauty Supplies place, eh, Tink?" The dog merely blinked at her.

"No? What about you, Pal? Think it's worth checking out?"

The border collie showed even less interest than Tink. He let out a sigh from his place next to the door but didn't bother raising his head.

She scowled at them both and raised the lid on her laptop. "Well, I think I'm onto something."

At any rate, it was worth a try. Every lead so far had been a dead end. That meant going back further, digging deeper, and hoping something would turn up. She typed "Meaningful Beauty Supplies" into the search bar and hit ENTER. In less than a second, several links pulled up. Mary clicked on IMAGES and kept scrolling until she spied a logo with the same swirling script she'd seen on the box at the salon. She clicked on it and waited while the web page loaded.

"'Wholesale, professional beauty supplies,'" Mary read aloud. "Hmm."

She swiped her finger across the touchpad. "Hair, skin, nails, appliances, and equipment. Guess they carry a little bit of everything." She clicked one of the tabs and waited for the page to load. "There's the hair color Paige uses."

She glanced down at Tink, who had stopped listening and lay with her eyes closed, her soft snores filling the silence. Mary clicked on another page. This one showed an assortment of clippers, trimmers, brush irons, and other appliances, none of which were of any interest.

She frowned and took a drink of her tea. "Maybe this is a waste of time," she muttered. Her eyes drifted upward to a phone number listed at the very top of the page. A Pennsylvania area code? That would make sense. Paige probably ordered from them because the delivery time was quicker. So, then, where were they located?

Mary clicked through several pages before remembering that oftentimes, contact information was listed at the bottom of web pages. Scrolling down, she found a "Contact Us" link and smiled.

"Here it is." While the page loaded, she took the steaming stew off the stove and poured it into a bowl. Instantly, Tink perked up and scampered over to sit at Mary's feet.

"Oh, now you want attention, huh?"

Hearing the commotion, Pal also trotted over to sit next to Tink.

"Wow, you two are really something. And I suppose Butterscotch will be joining us any minute?"

As if summoned, the cat rounded the door, rubbing his side against the jamb and purring as he entered.

"Forget it, guys. This is mine, and I only have about forty-five minutes left before my lunch is over. Go on, scoot."

All three animals remained rooted. Mary sighed and carried her stew to the table. After saying a quick blessing, she took a cautious bite then leaned over to study the web page she'd opened. Next to the phone number, an email address was listed, along with a mailing address. Seeing it, Mary nearly dropped her spoon.

The address was a PO box, but the town was Bird-in-Hand.

She pressed closer to the screen. Could that be right? She looked at the phone number. This one was toll-free, which meant it could be from anywhere. Her stew forgotten, she reached for her phone and punched in the number. After several rings, a recording came on with a lengthy directory of choices for ordering, checking on an existing order, requesting help with an invoice—

She hung up and bit her lip. She still had over thirty minutes left on her lunch break. Maybe she could find out something at the post office.

Her mind made up, Mary carried her bowl to the sink then grabbed her purse and keys. After scribbling a hurried message on a scrap of paper, she stuck it to the fridge and swept out the door.

The post office was a red brick building located on the Old Philadelphia Pike, near the Bird-in-Hand Bakery. Mary parked and hurried inside. Only one customer stood at the counter, an older gentleman with a large box supported in both hands.

"So, if I send this priority, will it get there by next week?" he asked. His low, raspy voice indicated a lengthy habit of smoking. He hefted the box onto the counter and rested his elbow on top of it. "I really need it to get there by next week. It's my granddaughter's birthday, and I bought her a coffeemaker for her dorm room." He glanced over his shoulder at Mary. "She's going to Penn State. First one in our family to go to a major university."

Hearing the pride in his voice, Mary smiled. He swung his gaze back to the woman at the counter.

"I understand. Let me check for you, sir," the postal worker behind the counter said. Her nails clicked noisily on the keyboard as she inputted the address, the glowing screen reflected in the lenses of her black-framed eyeglasses. She nodded. "Yes, I show that package being delivered by Friday, or possibly Monday."

"And how much did you say priority would cost?"

The postal worker repeated the amount and then looked at the man expectantly. "Would you like to go ahead and send it?"

The man frowned and rubbed his fingers over his chin, his knuckles rasping loudly against his graying whiskers. "What are the other options? Any of 'em a little cheaper?"

"Yes, sir."

The woman quoted him several options and waited patiently while he talked about how high the price of postage had become. As he launched into a tale about the cost of stamps when he was a boy, Mary glanced at her watch nervously. Maybe she should have told Martha and Elizabeth where she was going before she left instead of just leaving a note. She sent them a quick text then crossed her arms, her fingers tapping against her coat.

Was there anyone else working in the post office she could ask? She craned her neck to peer around the counter toward the back of the mail room. Catching the eye of tall gentleman in a blue USPS sweater, she raised her hand. The man nodded to her and approached the counter.

"Yes, ma'am. Can I help you?"

Mary eased around the man with the box, who had abandoned his rant over the price of stamps and had moved on to the cost of college.

"I hope so," Mary said. "Thank you for helping me. I'm on my lunch break, and I don't have a lot of time." She gestured toward the post office boxes lined up against the wall. "I'm interested in your post office boxes. Could you tell me a little about them?"

"Of course. Are you interested in renting a box?"

"Actually, no. But I do have some questions. Do you have to live in Bird-in-Hand to have one of them?"

He smiled pleasantly and shook his head. "Technically, no, but living farther out would defeat the purpose of having a box here. Most people rent a box at a post office that is near to them to make it easier to collect their mail." He eyed her a moment then reached under the counter for a piece of paper and slid it across to her. "Are you interested in the price of renting a box?"

"Not today, but thank you." Mary scanned the paper and slid it into her purse. "Could you possibly help me with one more thing?" At his nod, she went on. "I was researching an online company earlier today, and in their contact information was the address of a PO box here in Bird-in-Hand. Is there any way you could tell me who it belongs to?"

His posture stiffened. "Is this a legal matter?"

"Oh no, it's nothing like that. I was just curious and hoping you could help me."

He was shaking his head before she finished. "I'm sorry, ma'am. We are not allowed to give out that kind of information. Not without a subpoena."

Next to him, the female postal worker also gazed curiously at Mary. Butterflies fluttered in her stomach. She laid her hand, palm down, on the counter.

"I'm afraid I've given the wrong impression. This isn't a professional request. I'm not in law enforcement or anything. I really am just curious if there is a way to get this kind of information."

"Well, there is a Boxholder Request Format form you could fill out." He riffled through a stack of forms, found the one he wanted, and laid it on the counter. "If this were a legal matter, you would need all the names of the parties involved in the litigation, along with other pertinent info." He indicated a couple of spaces on the lengthy form.

Mary shook her head. "I'm afraid this won't help me. Thank you anyway."

"You're very welcome. Sorry there wasn't more I could do."

Mary smiled and turned for the door. It opened just as she got there, and Vanessa Bancroft stepped through. Swallowing her surprise, Mary froze where she stood and mumbled a hello.

Vanessa acknowledged her with the barest of smiles. In her hand were several letters. She hurried over to deposit them into the mail slot then crossed to the wall of post office boxes. For a long moment, she fumbled to tug her keys from her purse. Finally, she pulled them free, only to drop them on the floor. Heaving a sigh, she retrieved them, sorted through until she found the one she wanted, and poked it into the lock on one of the boxes. The door swung open, and she pulled out a sizable pile of letters, plus one newspaper flyer that she tossed into a nearby trash can.

She riffled through the letters one at a time, slipping each one to the back with just a cursory glance. When she finished, she closed the box door and locked it, then hurried on her way.

It was purely coincidental that Vanessa had come in when Mary did. Or not. Lots of people ran errands on their lunch break. Still, the odds of them passing made Mary think that perhaps there was a larger hand at work. Someone who was pointing toward a clue she needed to find. Nudging her to see something she'd missed before.

She eased toward the boxes, her eyes glued to the one she'd seen Vanessa open. Could it be? Her eyes confirmed what her head was already thinking. The number on the PO box Vanessa opened was the same number she'd seen on the contact page for Meaningful Beauty Supplies. It was the break she'd been hoping for.

Meaningful Beauty Supplies and Vanessa Bancroft were the same person.

CHAPTER TWENTY

The post office door swung open again, only this time, it was Wade who sauntered through. Spying Mary, a grin spread over his face, and he walked over to greet her.

"Hey, Mary. Fancy meeting you here."

"Hi, Wade."

"Whatcha up to?"

Mary glanced toward the door. More than anything, she wanted to call her sisters and Paige and let them know what she'd discovered, but running off would be rude. She pasted a smile to her face. "Oh, just running a few errands."

He waved a letter in his hand. "Me too. I'm on my lunch break. Figured I'd get some stuff done. So, listen"—he stepped away to push the letter through the mail slot, then eased to her side and slid both hands into his back pockets—"I sure had a great time last night."

She blinked in confusion, her mind grinding as she struggled to switch gears. Oh. Their date. She nodded. "Yes, I did too. Thanks again for dinner, Wade. Jennie's is one of my favorites."

His grin broadened, and he rocked back on his heels. "Glad to hear it. I'm really glad I ran into you. Maybe we could go out again? Actually, I was going to call you this afternoon, see if you're available on Friday."

"Friday. I…hmm." She thought a moment and then sighed. "I'm not really sure. Can I call you when I get back to the store? I need to check my schedule."

He narrowed his eyes playfully. "Busy woman, huh?"

"Nothing like that. I just…there's this thing…"

"Mary, relax." He reached for her arm and ducked his head to look into her face. "I was joking."

Her heart sank. What was it about Wade that always made her feel awkward? He was nice, after all, and she liked him. "I'm sorry. I just have a lot on my mind."

He let go of her arm and straightened. "No problem. How about I call you this afternoon? Maybe we can get together."

"Yes. That would be nice. Thanks, Wade."

His smile returned, and with it, a slight glimmer in his gaze that she read as appreciation. "Bye, Mary. Talk to you later."

She made for the door, giving one last wave before she slipped through. Outside, she put all thoughts of Wade aside. Vanessa owned Meaningful Beauty Supplies. That had to be how she'd managed to tamper with Paige's products without stepping foot into the salon. She'd switched the labels before they'd ever gotten to her.

Driving back to the shop, Mary had another thought. The clippers weren't new. Paige said she'd packed them when she moved from Pittsburgh. So, maybe they *had* gotten damaged during the trip. Maybe it was just the hair color and perm that Vanessa had meddled with in her attempt to get back at Paige.

She thrummed her fingers against the steering wheel. But what about the appointment book and Paige's cell phone?

Why would Vanessa have taken them? Were those thefts also an attempt to cripple her business? Make her look inept when she had to call everyone to reschedule?

Thinking back, Mary wished she'd thought to study Vanessa's hands. She couldn't remember seeing a wound when Vanessa had fumbled with her keys, but maybe that was just because she hadn't been looking for it.

She was only five minutes late when she pulled into the driveway at home. Mary scrambled from her car and hurried to the store to find Elizabeth and Martha. Both were wrapped up with customers, and Mary fidgeted from foot to foot while she waited for them to finish.

"Mary, you look a sight. What has you so riled up?" Martha asked, wiping her hands on her apron as she walked over to join Mary and Elizabeth.

Her sisters listened, wide-eyed, as Mary relayed what she'd learned.

"It was Vanessa who tampered with the hair products. It had to be," Mary said, urgency making her voice thin. "I need to call Paige and warn her not to use any of the Meaningful Beauty Supplies products."

"Hold on, you said you *didn't* see a scratch on Vanessa's hand?" Martha asked.

"That's true, but I wasn't looking for one."

Martha sucked in a breath through gritted teeth. "I admit, it all looks pretty damaging, but maybe we should try to get a look at her before we jump to any conclusions."

"How would we do that?" Mary asked.

Elizabeth lifted her hand. "I might have an idea."

Both sisters turned their gaze to her.

Elizabeth rummaged in her pocket until she found the card she'd placed there and held it up proudly. "The Chamber of Commerce meeting tomorrow night. Eloise Parkhurst was here earlier today and gave this to me. She said she was driving by and thought she would invite us to come, see if we were interested in joining."

Martha grabbed the card from her hand and smiled. "This is perfect. Surely Vanessa is a member of the chamber."

"But that's not until tomorrow night. What about Paige?" Mary asked. "She can't take a chance of something else happening to one of her customers."

"You're right, Mary." Elizabeth pinched her lip, thinking. "Maybe you should call and warn her."

"Better yet, why don't you head on over there and see if there is anything more she can tell you about Vanessa and her husband?" Martha asked.

Elizabeth's brows rose. "Her husband?"

"Someone was hanging around outside the salon. We can't rule him out, even if it wasn't him. He may have hired someone to help."

Hired someone? Mary froze. It hadn't occurred to her before, but yes, the man she'd spotted could have been hired by Vanessa or Miles, even Jack.

"It just doesn't make sense." Mary threw her hands out to her sides and tapped her foot in frustration. "Why would Vanessa's *husband* help her get back at the woman who stole her *boyfriend* in high school? It had to have been someone else."

"Unless there's more we don't know." Martha gave Mary's shoulder a push. "And that's what you need to find out."

Elizabeth nodded her agreement, and Mary blew out a sigh. "Okay. I'll go. I'll be back as soon as I can."

Both of them waved her off, and Mary hustled back to her car to head over to the salon. When she got there, Paige was bent over one of the sinks, giving a young lady a shampoo. In her hand, she held a large bottle poised over the woman's head.

"Paige, stop!" Mary held her breath as she hurried over to check which bottle she was using.

Paige jerked her hand back and stared, wide-eyed, at Mary. "What? What's wrong?"

"What's going on?" The young woman in the chair looked up at Mary, her eyes dark with curiosity and worry. "Who are you?"

"I…uh…sorry." Mary grabbed the bottle of shampoo and turned her back to the chair so only Paige could see. She held up the shampoo. "Paige, where did you get this?"

Her mouth hung open in bewilderment. "I ordered it online. Why?"

Mary grabbed another bottle from the shelf above the young woman's head. "What about this one?"

"I got it from a sales rep who was trying to get me to sample his products."

Mary shoved it toward her. "Use this one. Don't ask. I'll tell you later." She smiled down at the young woman. "Sorry. Didn't mean to scare you." She wiggled the bottle. "This one isn't for color-treated hair."

The young woman glanced from Mary to Paige. "My hair isn't color treated. I'm a natural blond."

"My mistake," Mary said, backing away sheepishly. She met Paige's gaze and tipped her head toward her office. *I need to talk to you*, she mouthed, then spun for the office.

While she waited for Paige, Mary paced the floor. How many products had Vanessa ruined? Was there any way to tell? Surely the products had seals? But what if they didn't? Could Paige afford to replace them all again? If she didn't, she'd likely lose the salon anyway.

Hearing the door rattle, Mary turned in time to see it swoosh open. Paige's face was white, her lips pressed into a thin line.

"I only have a few minutes while my customer is under the dryer. Talk to me. What's going on? What did you find out?"

Mary held up the shampoo bottle. "It's this, Paige. Meaningful Beauty Supplies. Vanessa Bancroft owns it. My sisters and I think she's the one behind the tampering of your products."

Paige's gaze dropped to the bottle. When she looked up, there was fright in her gaze. "How do you know?"

Mary explained about the website and her trip to the post office. She also explained about the coming chamber meeting and that she and her sisters planned to attend so they could get a better look at Vanessa's hand.

Paige's jaw firmed, and she crossed her arms. "I knew it. Vanessa always hated me." She narrowed her eyes. "What time is this meeting?"

Mary held her hand up. "Hold on now. It may not be a good idea for you to be there."

A flush crept over Paige's face. "Why not? This woman is trying to ruin my business. I have every right to confront her."

"Except we're not certain it's her. Granted, the clues are all pointing to it being Vanessa but—"

"But what? You said you and your sisters think Vanessa *is* the one behind all of this."

"We do."

"Well then?"

Mary placed a light touch on her arm. "What about the man outside your salon? And your phone and appointment book? There are still a lot of unanswered questions here. It wouldn't be good for us rush headlong to confront Vanessa and then find out we were wrong."

Paige wiped angry tears from her eyes. After a long moment, she spoke. "You're right. But I can't just sit back and let you handle everything. I have to be there, Mary. I have to see for myself if Vanessa is the one trying to ruin me."

"We will, Paige. I promise. It'll just take a little more time—"

"No. You don't understand."

She circled the desk, took out a long manila envelope, and handed it to Mary, who eyed it curiously.

"It's from Jack. He's taking me back to court, trying to force me to live within a certain radius so that he has easier access to Kailey. Of course, he said he'd drop the case if I agreed to let her live with him, but I can't do that to Kailey. She was having such a hard time at her old school. It scared me. She was depressed, anxious all the time. That's the whole reason we moved in the first place."

This time, the tears that trickled down her cheeks had nothing to do with anger.

"What am I going to do? I can't afford more lawyer fees. Rent is due, I need new supplies, and unless business picks up..."

She grabbed a tissue and blew her nose.

Mary's heart pounded. "What are you saying, Paige?"

Eyes red, she stared at Mary. "I have a week. Maybe two. After that, I'm going to have to close the salon."

"Paige, no."

"I don't have a choice, Mary." She took the envelope and slid it into the drawer. "I can't afford to pay a lawyer *and* run the salon. If I want to keep Kailey, I'm either going to have to close the salon or move closer to Pittsburgh. Either way, the business is done."

A weight pressed on Mary's chest, filling her with despair. "So that's why you're so determined to confront Vanessa?"

Paige's jaw firmed, and she nodded.

Though she resisted, Mary knew Paige was right. She had every right to be at the chamber meeting, and whether Mary liked it or not, nothing was going to stop her. She lifted her chin and looked Paige in the eyes.

"Paige, you're a grown woman, and whether you go to the chamber meeting is your decision. But first, there's something I need to ask."

Paige threw the tissue in the trash and crossed her arms, her expression shuttered. "Okay. What is it?"

Mary studied her friend carefully. Paige half turned from her gaze, her dark eyes hooded, her hands restless and fidgety.

Even before she asked the question bubbling on her tongue, Mary knew. Paige hadn't been honest with her, and whatever she was hiding, it wasn't good.

She let out a breath, bracing for an answer she wasn't sure she was ready to hear. "What haven't you told me about you and Vanessa?"

CHAPTER TWENTY-ONE

Mary stepped out from the Wednesday night prayer service, her mind whirling not with thoughts of God but of Vanessa and Paige and everything she had told her earlier at the salon.

"Hey, you!"

Bill's voice snapped the endless circle her thoughts were trapped in. Mary lifted her head to look for him. A few cars over, he wound toward her, a cautious smile on his face.

"Hey, Mary. How's it going?"

Mary hugged her Bible close to her chest and lifted one shoulder in a shrug. "It's a long story."

A dimple appeared on his cheek as he smiled. "I have time. You in the mood for some ice cream?"

Mary bit the inside of her cheek. After Martha's rich lasagna and a healthy slice of Italian cream cake, the last thing she needed was more calories. Bill's expression instantly iced like the snow crystals crunching under their feet.

"Hey, it's no problem if you're busy. I'll catch you another time."

Mary put out her hand to stop him. "Bill, wait. Actually, ice cream sounds really good."

He stopped, and the muscles in his jaw twitched. "Really?"

She made a face and jabbed her thumb toward his truck. "You driving?"

He hesitated, and then his whole body relaxed as he gave her a warm smile. "Yeah. I'm driving."

Bill's old pickup was as familiar to Mary as a cozy sweater. Inside, it always smelled of wood shavings and fresh paint. She climbed up onto the seat and tucked her legs inside then waited while Bill closed the door and circled around to join her.

"You know, it's a little chilly for ice cream," she said, angling her head toward the frosty gray clouds outside her window. "The weatherman said we might be in for a light snow."

He smiled sidelong at her as he jammed the key into the ignition and rolled the engine. "You're right. Should we make it coffee and pie instead?"

"Coffee yes. I'll split the pie with you."

"Greta's Coffeehouse?"

Mary raised her eyebrows. Bill laughed. Mary hadn't felt so relaxed in a week.

Once they were settled in a booth with their food in front of them, Bill picked up his fork and gestured to her with it. "So? You never did tell me. What's this about a long story keeping you too busy to see your friends?"

Mary took a hasty swallow from her coffee cup. The last time she'd used that word to describe them, Bill had left in a huff. In fact, she did notice a telltale tightening around his eyes, but nothing more.

She put her cup down, and beginning with their friendship in high school, told him all about Paige, concluding with all her recent troubles.

Bill chewed a bite of his apple pie thoughtfully. "Sounds rough. And you're certain Vanessa Bancroft is somehow involved in all of this?"

"Pretty sure, especially after today." Mary sighed and sank against the back of the booth. "Paige told me our senior year, she and Vanessa went out to a party at the old Simmons Mill."

"Where the kids used to hang out after ball games."

She nodded. "There was a lot of stuff going on, drinking and drugs and so on. Paige saw Vanessa smoking pot and reported her for it."

"Uh-oh."

Mary grimaced. "Paige swears when she went to the principal, she didn't realize how much would come of it."

"What do you mean?"

"Vanessa was kicked out of the Honor Society. And the pep squad. She had a really good shot at a cheerleading scholarship before all this happened, but when she couldn't list those things on her college resume…"

"I think I see where this is going."

Mary dropped her gaze to the coffee swirling in her cup. "Paige said she's wanted to apologize many times over the years, but she just couldn't work up the courage."

"And now she thinks it's too late."

"Yes. She's certain all of this is a result of Vanessa trying to get back at her, but unless we can prove it, we're pretty much at a dead end."

Bill set his fork down and laced his fingers. Mary watched him as she took a small bite of the pie.

Finally, she swallowed and narrowed her eyes at him. "What?"

He blinked and snapped his gaze to her. "Hmm?"

"I know that look. What are you thinking?"

He cleared his throat and pushed up to rest his elbows on the table. "It's just that I had a chance to meet the Bancrofts at a fund-raiser a couple of years ago. They both seemed nice, and they were very generous with their giving."

"Bill—"

"I know, looks can be deceiving, but I like to think I'm a pretty good judge of character."

"And?"

He shook his head. "This just doesn't seem like something either of the Bancrofts would do."

Mary sighed and pushed the pie toward him. "Well, much as I hate to admit it, you may be right. That's why Martha, Elizabeth, and I decided to go to the meeting of the chamber tomorrow night."

Bill picked up his coffee cup and pushed Mary's toward her. "Here's to square one?"

She sighed. "If you only knew how many times I've been there the last few days."

He held his cup steady.

She laughed at the grin on his face and clinked her cup against his. "Fine. To square one."

They each took a sip and then Mary signaled to Bill. "What about you? Did you finish the concession stand at the baseball field?"

"Yep. All done," he said, wiping a napkin over his mouth. "Now I'm just waiting for some cabinets to come in so I can finish up another job I've been working on."

"Glad to hear you're keeping busy. I know things can slow down a lot for you in the winter."

"I'm hanging in there."

His grin carried up to his eyes, and Mary had to catch her breath. Bill wasn't dashing or handsome in the same way as Wade, but he still made her heart go pitter-patter when he looked at her like that. She dropped her gaze and concentrated on scooping up a bite of pie. Did he affect Nettie Walters the same way?

Thinking of them together brought a bitterness to Mary's tongue that contrasted sharply with the pie.

Bill lowered his cup. "What's wrong? Still worried about Paige?"

She met his gaze. How easy it would be to lie, but somehow, she didn't want to. She wanted him to know what was on her mind.

"Actually, I was thinking about you and Nettie."

He dropped his gaze and pushed a slice of apple around on the plate. "Oh."

"That's new, eh? I didn't realize you two were a thing."

He swallowed, and a blush crawled up his neck. "Not necessarily a thing. We hang out now and then."

"Like us?"

His eyes locked with hers, and there was a sharpness to his gaze she wasn't used to seeing from him.

"Never mind," she said, backpedaling quickly. "I'm sorry I asked."

"Nettie is not like you. She never will be," he ground out.

Mary's heart slammed against her chest at the ache she heard in his voice. "Bill—"

"Don't say it. Not again. I'm not sure I'll be able to get over it if you tell me again that we're just friends."

His knuckles shone white around his fork, but that was the only clue to what he was feeling inside. Mary wanted to reach out to him, wanted to take his hand and smooth away the tension. But would that be fair? No, not until she understood her own feelings where he was concerned. Instead, she lowered her head and concentrated on the pie. Only now, instead of cinnamon and sweetness, it scraped down her throat like sandpaper. When she finished, she laid her fork down and signaled to the waitress for a refill of her coffee. Bill didn't have to ask. He slid the creamer to her and handed her two packets of sugar.

"So, about the chamber, are you a member?" she asked, stirring the sugar into her coffee.

Bill seemed to have recovered his good humor. He slumped sideways a little to rest one arm atop the back of the booth. "Yeah, I joined up a few years ago."

"Really. And what do you do at these meetings?"

"Talk mostly." He shrugged. "It's a lot of planning, tossing ideas around. You'll probably know a lot of the members. It's all local business owners and such."

"Hmm. I was just planning on going so I could talk to Vanessa. I guess we should seriously consider joining."

"You should. It'll be good for business."

He wasn't joking. But neither was he angry or tense. Mary pushed her hair behind her ear and tilted her head to study him. "How do you do that?"

"Do what?"

"Be so nice."

His lips curved in a wry smile. "I want the best for your family, Mary. And I try my best to live a Christ-filled life. I hope you know that by now."

Yes, she did. She could vouch for that. As long as she'd known him, Bill had always tried to lead a life that would please his heavenly Father.

And right then, she understood the biggest difference between Bill and Wade.

CHAPTER TWENTY-TWO

The Chamber of Commerce met in an old red brick building on the outskirts of town. Clustered around the building was a stand of thick white oaks, yearning to don their spring attire. Mary could just imagine the shade those trees would offer once their broad leafy cap was in place. For now, their woody arms reached skyward, barren except for a thin coat of ice and snow.

"Well, this is it." Mary shut off the car and tossed the key ring into her purse. "Are we all clear about what we need to do?"

"I'll talk to some of the local business owners and try to get a feel for the Bancrofts," Martha said.

"And all of us will keep an eye out for Vanessa," Elizabeth added. "If we see any unusual scratches on her hands, we'll meet up and decide what to do next."

"Okay, that's good." Mary put her hand to the door. "One more thing. We should also try to keep an eye out for the guy I saw outside the salon. It's a long shot, I know, but just in case, if you see anyone that could possibly fit the description I gave you, point him out to me. Hopefully he'll be wearing that same blue-and-orange coat."

They exited the car, and all three went inside. A blast of warm, coffee-scented air hit them as soon as they entered.

Mary peeled off her coat and hung it next to Elizabeth's and Martha's. As Bill had said, there were several faces Mary recognized, and several more she did not. Vanessa's was not among them.

"Where is she?" Elizabeth whispered, huddling close. "Do you see her?"

"Not yet, but it's still early," Martha whispered back.

"Uh-oh, who is that?" Mary pointed to a tall woman striding toward them, a determined look on her face.

"That's Eloise Parkhurst," Elizabeth said. "She's the one who invited us."

Mary raised her chin and peered at her. "So, *she's* the one who got the bad perm at the beauty salon."

But there was no sign of a bad perm tonight. Her blond hair—almost identical in shade to Mary's—was smoothed into a tight chignon, and she was elegantly dressed in khaki-colored slacks and a navy cardigan, a strand of pearls gleaming at her throat. Mary pasted a bright smile on her face as Eloise approached. Next to her, her sisters did likewise.

"Elizabeth, Martha, so glad you could make it. And you must be Mary." She extended her hand, but her gaze stayed pinned to Mary's hair, which right up to that moment, she'd forgotten was still blue. "Such a pleasure. I just love your store. So quaint."

Mary shook Eloise's hand. "Thank you. And thanks again for inviting us here tonight."

"Oh, it's my pleasure. We're always looking for reputable new members." Her bright laugh was almost musical as she motioned toward a table stacked with drinks and light refreshments. "Please, help yourselves to a snack. The meeting will begin shortly."

"Thank you. We will," Mary said.

Eloise shot one final glance at Mary's hair, her displeasure expressed in her tightly pressed lips. Giving a wave, she flitted off to join several others clustered near the door.

"She sure seems to have gotten over her perm," Martha remarked dryly.

"Yes, well, Elizabeth was right when she said she was very conscious of appearance. Did you see the way she looked at my hair?"

"Now, now, don't take offense," Elizabeth soothed. "She may have just been wondering if Paige did your hair too."

"Actually, I don't think you're helping things, Lizzie," Martha said with a snort. She motioned to the refreshments. "I'm going to grab something to drink. Either of you want anything?"

Elizabeth shook her head and pointed. "I see Dottie over there. I'm going to go talk to her."

Mary caught her arm. "Be careful. We don't know for sure Vanessa is the one we're after."

"Don't worry. I'll watch what I say to her," Elizabeth said, but by the dismay in her eyes, Mary knew she didn't like it.

Martha tsked. "Poor thing. I sure hope Dottie is innocent, for Elizabeth's sake."

"Me too," Mary admitted. "Fortunately, it's starting to look like she is." She shooed Martha toward the table. "Go on. See what you can find out. I'll stay here and keep an eye out for Vanessa."

Martha glanced at her watch. "All right. We still have fifteen minutes or so. Sure hope she shows up."

She ambled off, taking the long way as she wove around groups of people milling about and chatting. Mary bit her lip. In this big room, with gleaming wood floors, it would be hard to sort through all the conversations. Martha had a difficult task ahead.

The door opened, and a blast of cold air blew in, riffling the edge of Mary's skirt. Eagerly, she looked to see who entered. It wasn't Vanessa, but her heart rate sped up anyway.

"Bill."

Their eyes locked, but only for a moment, because directly on his heels, Wade entered. He smiled when he saw her, and cut around Bill to walk toward her.

"Hey, Mary. I didn't know you were a member of the chamber."

Mary's gaze darted over his shoulder to Bill, who was hanging up his coat. "I'm not. My sisters and I are…"

She didn't want Wade or anyone else to know the real reason they'd come. She forced a weak smile. "We're thinking about joining."

"That's awesome."

She gestured to him. "What about you?"

"I come as a representative of the school." He slid off his coat and draped it over his arm, then held out a hand toward the chairs lined up in rows. "Would you like to have a seat?"

She glanced at the door. Vanessa still had not arrived. She shook her head and gave a small wave. "Not yet. I'll head over there in a little bit. I'm waiting for…um…"

"Your sisters?"

She motioned toward the refreshment table. "Martha is getting something to drink."

True. Not entirely, but somewhat.

"Okay, well, I'll save you a seat."

"Oh, you don't have to do that."

"It's no problem." He angled his head close to whisper. "Otherwise, I might end up sitting next to some old biddy."

He chuckled, but Mary couldn't find it in herself to join in. She breathed a sigh of relief when he moved off.

She couldn't help it. She looked around the room for Bill. He had also moved to join a small cluster of people. Among them was Nettie Walters.

Mary fought not to growl. Why shouldn't Nettie be here? She owned a flower shop. Still, Mary could almost feel her claws come out.

"Hey." Martha sidled next to her.

Mary jumped. "Don't do that."

"Do what?"

She shrugged and adjusted her sweater.

"See anything?" Martha brought a Styrofoam coffee cup to her lips but she didn't drink. She just peered over the edge around the room.

"Nothing." Mary humphed. "Wouldn't you know we'd pick the one meeting that Vanessa and her husband didn't show up to?"

"Not so fast."

Martha angled her head toward the door just as it blew open, and the very couple they'd been waiting to see stepped through.

Mary grabbed her arm. "It's them."

"Good evening, folks." All heads turned as Eloise stepped up to a small podium and raised her hand. "Thank you all so much for coming out tonight. It's great hearing all the lively chatter, but at this point, if you wouldn't mind finding a seat, we'd like to get started."

"Are you kidding me?" Mary groaned and shot a quick glance at Vanessa and her husband. Both wore heavy coats. Vanessa also wore gloves. Instead of removing them, they walked over to claim a couple of chairs in the back row.

"Maybe we can sit next to them," Elizabeth whispered as she joined her sisters, except right then, Wade stood and waved to all three of them before pointing down at three empty chairs beside him.

Elizabeth quirked an eyebrow. "Isn't that—?"

"Yes." Mary clenched her jaw. "Come on. We'll try to catch Vanessa and her husband after the meeting."

Wade had chosen seats very near the front, the absolute worst location for keeping an eye on the Bancrofts at the rear of the room. Mary hesitated to sit, and caught Bill's gaze. He was seated closer to the Bancrofts and on the opposite row. He tilted his head toward Vanessa, a question in his eyes. Mary nodded. She could use some help keeping an eye on them. He shifted his chair. Not much, but enough so he could keep them in clear view.

Mary let out a sigh of relief. She could always count on Bill.

"What are we going to do?" Elizabeth whispered urgently. "The meeting is about to start."

"It's okay. Bill is watching them," Mary whispered back. Wade was looking at them curiously. Mary smiled at him and shook her head.

"All right, ladies and gentlemen, once again, thank you all for coming. We've got several items on the agenda tonight."

Mary turned her gaze to where Eloise stood speaking. A long table was spread out behind her, dotted with tall tabletop displays and posters. For the next forty-five minutes, Eloise gave reports on events the chamber had participated in, and several more that were coming up, but Mary couldn't listen. Her attention was divided between Wade on her right, whose knee she kept inadvertently bumping in an attempt to see over her left shoulder, and Bill, whose face she could just barely see from the corner of her eye.

"A-and th-that's about it."

Mary's gaze snapped to Eloise. She stuttered? Until now, she'd been very smooth in her delivery. Eloise's face had gotten particularly pale against her navy sweater, and her gaze seemed locked on something going on behind Mary's head.

"Excuse me, don't we have any new business to discuss?" a voice asked from the back of the room.

Mary craned her neck with everyone else to see who had spoken.

"Who is that?" Martha spoke in a loud stage whisper to be heard above the mumbling.

"I believe that's Catherine Randall. She's one of Paige's clients," Mary said. Curiosity filled her at Eloise's reaction to Catherine's words. If she'd seemed uneasy before, she looked downright uncomfortable now. She raised her hand and cleared her throat.

"I'm so sorry, new business can only be introduced by members of the chamber," Eloise said.

Like observers at a tennis match, heads swung to Catherine for her response. Her eyes narrowed, but she said nothing.

"What in the world is going on?" Elizabeth asked.

Mary shrugged and looked at Wade, but he pecked at his phone like a teenager, oblivious to the sudden tension in the room.

A smug smile creased Eloise's lips. "All right then, if there is nothing else, we are adjourned. Please feel free to enjoy the refreshments on the back table. Good night, everyone, and please be careful driving home."

Mary lingered at the edge of her seat, expecting the bang of a gavel. When none came, she rose with the rest of the crowd and stretched up on her tiptoes, hoping to spot Vanessa before she could leave.

"Well, that was fun." Wade reached out to touch her elbow. "Say, listen, I meant to tell you, I'm sorry about not calling."

Mary blinked in confusion.

He held up his hand. "Yesterday at the post office? I said I would call about getting together on Friday?"

"Oh." She waved her hand. "Don't worry about it. I forgot all about it."

"You forgot." Disappointment clouded his gaze, but he got over it quickly and cleared his throat. "Anyway, you gonna stick around for a while?"

Vanessa and her husband were moving toward the door. Mary stifled a growl of frustration.

"How about some coffee? I could get us a cup," Wade offered.

"Mary," Martha urged, pressing close.

"I know." She turned to Wade. "I would love some coffee. Could you check and see if they have some of those little flavored creamer cups? My favorite is Amaretto."

Honestly, she wasn't picky, but maybe he'd be occupied for a bit looking.

He nodded. "Oh, okay. I'll check."

He eased into the line heading for the refreshments. Mary grabbed Martha's hand and motioned to Elizabeth. "Come on."

By now, most of the crowd had filtered into the aisles, and Mary found her way blocked. Worse, Vanessa was making a clear beeline for the exit.

"Maybe we should try to go around," Elizabeth said, a worried frown wrinkling her brow.

Martha grunted in agreement. "You go that way, Lizzie. Mary and I will try to swing around the other way."

They split up, and Mary couldn't help but be reminded of two small chipmunks as she and Martha sang out "pardon me" and "excuse me" on their way toward the door.

Just a few feet from it, Mary saw Vanessa's husband reach for the knob.

"We're too late," Martha moaned. "They're getting away."

Suddenly, Bill appeared at Mr. Bancroft's side. "Excuse me, Miles? Have you got a minute? I need to ask you about something."

Mary blew out a sigh of relief. Once again, Bill had saved the day. He drew Miles aside, leaving Vanessa standing idly near the door while she waited.

"Now's our chance." Mary tugged Martha around the last few people separating them and approached Vanessa with a smile on her face.

"Hello. Do you remember me? I'm Mary Baxter. You and I went to school together."

Vanessa's face registered her confusion. "Baxter?"

"Actually, my maiden name is Classen." She needed to see her hands, but how to accomplish that? She pulled Martha forward. "This is my sister."

Martha stuck her hand out awkwardly. "Martha Watts. Pleased to meet you."

Mary watched eagle-eyed as Vanessa shook Martha's hand. No scratches. But in her other hand, she clutched her gloves. Was that the one she'd injured trying to break into Paige's desk?

Vanessa blinked, and a sudden spark of recognition lit her gaze. "Wait...Classen? Weren't there three of you sisters?"

Mary nodded eagerly. "That's right. My other sister, Elizabeth, is over there." She pointed her out from the people drifting by.

"Yeah, I remember." Vanessa shifted her gloves to her right hand. With her left, she swept a lock of hair behind her ear. "You used to do a lot sports and stuff."

"Basketball, mostly," Mary said, her gaze locked on Vanessa's smooth skin. Not a mark or a scratch on her. But how could that be? She'd been so certain when they got here that Vanessa was their culprit.

Behind them, the door swung open, and another chilly breeze snaked across the floor to wrap around Mary's ankles. Next to her, Martha gasped. Mary couldn't help it. She did the same. A split second before Paige strode through the door.

CHAPTER TWENTY-THREE

Paige glared at Vanessa, her face flushed and indignant. "You."

Mary stepped between them, her voice lowered to a whisper. "Paige, wait."

Paige ignored her and sidestepped so she and Vanessa stood face to face. "You're trying to ruin my salon."

"What?" Vanessa's bewildered gaze jumped from Paige to Mary. "What is she talking about?"

"Don't pretend you don't know," Paige said, her voice rising. "You own Meaningful Beauty Supplies. You tampered with the products I bought before they ever got to me."

By now, several gazes had swung their way. Martha circled around to push the door closed and then gave Mary a gentle nudge toward Paige. "I think I saw an empty room near the bathroom. Take Paige and Vanessa over there to talk."

Mary cleared her throat and grabbed Paige's hand. "You heard her. Let's go. Now." She glanced apologetically at Vanessa. "Please? I promise, I'll explain everything."

By now, Vanessa's husband had dislodged from Bill and made his way back to his wife. He cast a wary glance at Paige and laid his hand against Vanessa's back—his injury-free hand. Mary shot a glance at his other hand. That one too was devoid of scratches. That meant the Bancrofts were innocent, unless they'd hired the man outside the salon to do their dirty work, and that was only a very slim possibility.

Miles frowned. "Honey? Is everything okay?"

"Everything's fine." Vanessa held Mary's gaze, and though she had no reason to, she agreed to talk. "We'll be just a minute."

"Thank you," Mary breathed.

"Hold on a sec," Paige said, resisting the pull of Mary's hand. "Mary, what are you doing? You said—"

"I know what I said, and I was wrong." Mary tilted her head close to Paige's ear. "It's not her, Paige. I'm almost certain."

With those words, the steam seemed to leave Paige's body. She allowed herself to be pulled toward the hall, her steps dragging over the wood floor.

When they reached the room Martha had pointed out, Mary dropped Paige's hand and clicked on the light. "First"— she turned to Vanessa—"Paige and I owe you an apology."

Vanessa shook her head in confusion. "I don't understand. What is it she thinks I've done?"

Mary shrugged miserably. "I know this is going to sound crazy, but would you mind showing Paige your hands?"

Vanessa's mouth dropped open, but seeing Mary wasn't kidding, she snapped it shut and stuck out her hands. "One more time, could I ask what all this is about?"

Mary looked at Paige. "See?" When Paige said nothing, Mary touched her shoulder. "It's not her. She wasn't the one who broke into your desk."

"Okay." Vanessa crossed her arms. "That's it. One of you needs to explain what's going on here."

Beginning with her foiled hair color, Mary explained everything that had been going on at the salon, including the clues that led them to believe Vanessa might be involved.

"I'm so sorry, Vanessa," Paige mumbled when she finished.

Vanessa dragged her fingers through her hair. "So you actually thought I was involved…because I was holding a thirty-year-old grudge? What kind of person do you take me for?"

"You have every reason to be angry," Mary said quickly.

"Well, that's good. Because I am. And I don't need your permission to feel that way."

Properly chastised, Mary fell silent.

"Don't blame Mary," Paige said. "It's my own guilty conscience that made me suspect you. I never apologized for turning you in after that party our senior year."

"Paige." Vanessa dropped her hands to her sides and shook her head sadly. "That was my doing. I never blamed anyone but myself for losing that scholarship. And trust me, after all these years, I'm over it."

Tears welled in Paige's eyes. "You are?"

Vanessa blew out a breath and spun to pace the floor. "Okay, so I admit, I was pretty angry at first. I wanted someone to blame, and you were an easy target. But after a while, I couldn't do it anymore. I knew I had to acknowledge my part in the mistakes of my past or let bitterness consume me."

She cast an apologetic glance at them both. "And if I'm being honest, some of those old feelings were dredged up when I heard Paige was back in town. That's why I stayed away and why I helped spread some of those rumors about Dottie losing business when you moved in."

Paige's mouth fell open. "You did that?"

Shame bathed Vanessa's face in color. "I'm really sorry, Paige. I know it probably won't mean much now, but I really am glad you're back. Maybe it will give us a chance to put old wounds behind us. Start fresh."

"I...I think I'd like that," Paige said hesitantly.

Mary raised her finger in the air. "If I could?"

Both Paige and Vanessa turned to look at her.

"What about your beauty supply company? Is there a possibility that someone else could have tampered with the products Paige ordered before they got to her?"

"I don't see how." Vanessa held up both hands. "I never see the products. You see, I'm not a supplier. I don't purchase products and ship them out of a warehouse or anything like that. I'm more like the middleman. I go out and search for the best prices on wholesale products and offer links to them on my website."

"So there's no way anyone could know where those products were coming from?" Mary asked.

Vanessa shook her head. "I'm afraid not."

A soft knock interrupted their conversation. Thinking it was Martha, Mary opened the door and was surprised to see Eloise standing on the threshold.

"Pardon me, ladies. I'm sorry to break in like this." Her gaze shifted to Vanessa. "I wanted you to know, we have several new member applications we need to review."

Vanessa nodded. "Oops. Sorry. I didn't realize. I'll be right there."

Eloise excused herself, and Vanessa turned to look at Paige. "Ugh. I'm so sorry. I'm on the board, and Eloise doesn't like to be kept waiting. She insists we look over all of the applications before we bring them to the membership for a vote. Maybe we can finish this another time?"

"I'd like that," Paige said quietly.

Mary frowned. "Vanessa, do you know the woman who spoke at the end of the meeting tonight?"

"Catherine Randall?" She nodded. "Sure do. She runs a little coffee shop on the outskirts of town."

Mary rubbed her chin, thinking. "So, if she owns a business, why isn't she a member of the chamber?" She waved her hand. "Eloise said only members could introduce new business."

Vanessa snorted. "Yes, that's right. Catherine did apply for membership, but Eloise stopped it because Catherine refused to give her a part in the play the Bird-in-Hand Stage is doing later this spring."

Mary held up her hand in confusion. "Wait, you lost me. I thought you said Catherine ran a coffee shop."

"She does, but she also directs plays. Eloise has been a longstanding member of the community players, so she was pretty upset when Catherine stepped in after the old theater director retired." She laid her hand beside her mouth and lowered her voice. "Don't tell Eloise I said this, but she can be pretty spiteful. A couple of others and I think she abused her power as chair of the chamber to get back at Catherine, but what could we do? She influenced enough of the board members to have Catherine's application voted down."

"That's really sad," Mary said.

Vanessa shrugged. "Anyway, I'd better get going before she makes me her next target." She stopped to take Paige's hand.

"And I'm really sorry about the stuff that's been happening at your salon. I hope you can figure out who's behind it."

"Me too," Paige said. "Bye, Vanessa."

"Bye." She gave a nod to Mary and then slipped out the door.

Groaning, Paige rubbed her hand over her face. "Wow. I just made a complete fool of myself. Worse, half the business owners in Lancaster County saw me do it."

"Don't beat yourself up," Mary said, draping her arm over Paige's shoulders. "It's my fault you suspected her in the first place."

"And we're still no closer to knowing who really is behind all this." Paige blew her hair from her eyes, her shoulders drooping wearily. "I'm tired, Mary. At this point, I'm just about ready to give up."

"I'm afraid I can't let you do that," Mary said, more cheerfully than she felt. "You and Kailey are just getting settled. Besides, Martha, Elizabeth, and I are still very determined to figure out exactly who has a thing against you and force them to stop."

"But—"

Mary held up one finger. "No buts. Tomorrow you go back to work like nothing's happened and let us handle the rest."

"And my supplies?" She peered at Mary hopefully.

"You've already cleaned out anything that was open or looked suspicious. And now that we know where the Meaningful Beauty Supplies stuff comes from, I think they will be okay to use."

"Then I'll use them on you first." Paige picked up a lock of blue hair from Mary's shoulder. "Come by the salon tomorrow so I can get you fixed up."

"It's a deal." Mary gave Paige a hug then set her back and smiled encouragingly. "Try to hang in there. We'll figure this out. We just need a little more time."

"Unfortunately, time is the one thing I don't have. Well, that, and money." Paige craned her neck to look over Mary's shoulder. "Think there's a back door out of this place? Sneaking out sounds so much better than parading past all those people out there."

"Come on," Mary said, chuckling. "I'll walk you to your car."

Afterward, Mary stood, shivering, as she watched the taillights of Paige's car disappear.

"Hey. You forgot this."

She turned. Bill held up her coat. "You'd better put it on before you freeze to death."

Mary willingly obliged. Bill held her coat for her while she slid her arms in. "Thank you."

"So? Did you find out anything?" He tilted his head toward the door. "In there?"

"Not really. Not what we'd hoped anyway." Mary sighed, her breath rising in the air like a smoky white cloud. "Of course, we might not have learned anything if you hadn't stopped Vanessa and her husband from leaving. Thank you for that."

He glanced away. "It was nothing."

She stepped closer. "No, it wasn't. You're always helping me. Us. My sisters and me." She fumbled to a stop, her face warm.

He gazed at her a long moment, the glow of the parking lot lights revealing a hint of sadness in his eyes. "That's what friends do, right? They help each other."

"Bill."

He shook his head and pulled back a step. "It's okay, Mary. I've accepted it."

Her breath hitched. "Accepted what?"

Deep down, she already knew, but she needed to hear him say the words.

"We're friends. That's all we'll ever be. And if there's to be any hope of hanging on to even that, I need to accept it and move on."

"With Nettie?" Mary couldn't help the edge of bitterness that crept into her voice.

"Maybe, or maybe someone else." He shrugged. "Nettie's a sweet gal. You'd like her if you gave her a chance."

Not likely. Not if she stole Bill's heart. Then again, his heart couldn't be stolen if it wasn't hers to begin with. She pointed, mouth dry, toward the chamber building.

"I should get back inside. Martha and Elizabeth are probably wondering where I am."

He reached for her arm. "I can walk you."

She stopped him before he could touch her. "That's okay. Thanks anyway. And thanks again for your help tonight."

She whirled, her boots crunching on the icy rocks and patches of snow, and didn't stop until she'd walked through the chamber door and closed it behind her. Even then, she knew, sensed somehow, that Bill was still there, that he'd watched every step she took away from him. And that if she'd looked at him, if she'd seen the look in his eyes as he watched her go, that she'd have run back to him, as fast as she could, straight into his arms.

CHAPTER TWENTY-FOUR

There you are." Elizabeth hurried over to Mary and clasped her arm. "Are you all right? What happened?" She straightened to her full height to throw a glance around the room. "Where's Paige?"

Mary looked around. Several people still milled about, chatting and plucking food off the refreshment table, but Wade wasn't one of them. At some point, he must have given up waiting for her and left. Maybe that was for the best, though she certainly owed him an apology. She focused on Elizabeth and started with the easiest question. "Paige and I got things straightened out with Vanessa, and then Paige went home."

As she spoke, Martha walked up, the concern on her face matching Elizabeth's. "Was she all right?"

Mary shook her head. "She was upset, of course, and a little disappointed that it wasn't Vanessa who tampered with her supplies. Not that she has anything against Vanessa. I think she just wants all of this to be over, for Kailey's sake as well as her own."

"Of course she does. That's understandable." Elizabeth bent closer. "We all do."

"There's one more thing." She told them about the court papers Jack had filed and then sighed. "We're running out of time. If we don't figure out who is sabotaging Paige's business soon, it'll be too late."

Martha cooed soothingly and then motioned toward the parking lot. "I saw Bill leaving. I didn't get a chance to thank him for his help tonight."

"I did. I thanked him and told him I was glad he was here," Mary said, but with a sadness to her tone that belied her words.

"I saw the two of you talking." Martha frowned. "Everything okay there?"

"Yes, of course," Mary said.

Martha shrugged. "I'm only asking because I noticed Wade was here too."

"Wade *and* Bill are just friends," Mary insisted firmly. "My relationship with both of them is purely platonic."

Mary's voice had begun to rise, as had the heat in her cheeks. She knew Martha was concerned for her. She knew Martha didn't want Mary to care too much about what others thought of her, but that wasn't the case with Wade and Bill. At least, it wasn't anymore.

She raised her chin and crossed her arms defensively. "Okay, if I'm being honest, it may not have started out that way. I was flattered by Wade's attention."

"Of course you were. Anyone would be. Wade is a very handsome man," Elizabeth said.

Mary shot her a grateful look. "But I need to figure things out on my own," she continued, with a glance at both of her sisters. "And I'm going to need a little time to do that."

Martha was slower to nod than Elizabeth, but then she stepped forward and caught hold of Mary's hand.

"You'll do it. I know you will. And we'll be praying for you."

"Thank you, Martha."

"Good. Now that's behind us."

Mary drew in a deep breath and went on to tell her sisters about the conversation with Vanessa and Paige.

"Was Paige convinced by her story?" Martha asked, doubt creeping into her voice.

"Vanessa doesn't see the products before they ship out. Plus, there were no scratches on her hands or her husband's," Mary pointed out. "So unless evidence turns up that proves she or her husband hired someone to sabotage Paige, we need to cross them off our list of suspects."

Martha folded her arms over her chest. "So, we're back to square one."

"Not exactly." Elizabeth's face darkened in a troubled glower. "Something happened that I probably should have told you about earlier."

Both Mary and Martha squared to look at her. "What is it?" Martha asked. "What haven't you told us?"

"It's about Dottie." Elizabeth's mouth worked, and then she shook her head. "I'm sure it's nothing, but…"

"Lizzie, what is it?" Mary urged gently. Whatever it was, Elizabeth was having a hard time voicing it.

Her shoulders slumped. "It's about the day I went to talk to her at her salon."

"The same day you saw Vanessa and her husband going into the restaurant together," Martha said.

Elizabeth nodded. "I'm so sorry. I intentionally focused more on that point than what I saw at the salon, but it was because I was so sure Dottie couldn't be guilty. I'm still sure, except…" She winced and lowered her gaze. "I left out one detail."

Mary's jaw dropped. Inside, irritation and disbelief bubbled in her throat. "Elizabeth, why on earth would you do that?"

"Maybe we should let her explain," Martha said, giving a nod to Elizabeth. "Go on. Tell us."

Elizabeth's chest rose and fell, and then she ran her fingers over the back of her other hand. "It was while Dottie was cutting my hair. I noticed a large scratch on her finger. She said she cuts herself with the scissors sometimes when she gets in a hurry. It wasn't very deep," she added quickly, "but I didn't say anything about it, and I should have." She groaned and rubbed her palms over her eyes. "I'm so sorry I didn't mention something sooner."

Though she wanted to be upset, deep down, Mary knew she couldn't blame her. She placed a soothing hand on Elizabeth's shoulder. "It's all right. We understand."

She looked at Martha, who murmured in agreement.

"But maybe we need to take another look at Dottie and at least consider that she may be involved," Mary said.

Elizabeth nodded, misery making her lips droop. "I'll talk to her again tomorrow, maybe in the morning before things get too busy at the store."

"I'll go with you," Martha said. "It might be easier if I ask the questions." She looked at Mary. "Plus, I think we need to also consider the man you saw outside the salon." She slid her arm around Elizabeth's waist. "Dottie isn't the only one on our list of suspects."

"Thank you," Elizabeth whispered, patting Martha's hand on her waist.

Martha smiled.

"While you two do that, I'll manage the store," Mary said.

Elizabeth's gaze lifted. "Will you be okay by yourself?"

"It'll keep my mind off other things, at least until I go see Paige." Mary waved a lock of her hair. "I'm finally going to get this fixed."

Martha sniffed. "That's too bad."

Both Mary and Elizabeth stared at her. She shrugged, an impish smile playing on her lips.

"After all this time, it was finally starting to grow on me."

CHAPTER TWENTY-FIVE

Elizabeth fidgeted on the passenger seat of Martha's car, nervousness making it hard to sit still the closer they drew to Dottie's salon. She folded her gloves carefully in her lap, then snatched them up again and shoved them into her coat pocket.

Martha glanced at her. "You okay?"

Elizabeth trapped a sigh behind clenched lips. "I will be, once this is done. Thanks again for offering to come with me."

"Glad to do it." Martha paused and sent another long glance in her direction. "Do you want to go over what we're going to say when we get there?"

Elizabeth mulled the thought, then pushed it away. "It probably wouldn't hurt, but to be honest, I think I'd better just focus on making sure I don't let my feelings get in the way of sound judgment where Dottie is concerned."

"Wise words," Martha said. After flipping on her blinker, she turned down Dottie's street and slowed almost to a stop. "Did you let her know we were coming?"

"I know I should have, but every time I picked up the phone to call, I just couldn't sort out enough words that didn't sound accusatory."

"In that case, it's possible she'll have customers," Martha said.

Elizabeth pressed her hands together to stop them from shaking. "I didn't think about that."

"Don't worry," Martha said. "If there's a car in the drive, we'll just come back later."

Elizabeth nodded, the churning in her stomach growing stronger as Martha made the last few maneuvers before turning in to Dottie's drive.

"No cars." Martha shut off the engine and held up the keys. "Ready?"

"I suppose." Elizabeth fumbled with the door handle and finally managed to push it open and climb out. When they reached the door, Dottie was waiting. She swung it open, a bright smile on her face.

"Elizabeth, Martha, what a nice surprise."

Each word was an arrow to Elizabeth's heart.

"I didn't know you were stopping by. Have you had coffee? If not, I can put on a pot."

More stabbing wounds, each one deeper than the last. Elizabeth shot a look of pleading at Martha.

"Actually, Dottie, Elizabeth and I have something we'd like to discuss with you. Do you have a minute?"

Dottie's face grew puzzled, but she nodded and held the door wide for them to enter. "Come on in, ladies."

Once they were inside, Dottie put out her hands for their coats and led them to the kitchen table. She laid the coats over the back of one of the chairs, her gaze more than a little confused as she eyed first Elizabeth, and then Martha. "Goodness, you two certainly look somber. Is everything okay out at the farm?"

"The farm is fine," Elizabeth said.

"This is about Paige Schiller," Martha added.

Dottie's eyes narrowed, but she motioned them toward the chairs before claiming one of them herself. "So, how is Paige? I've heard she's had more than a little trouble lately."

Elizabeth startled, then fought to keep it from showing on her face. "You know about the things that have happened at her salon?"

Dottie chuckled. "This is a very close-knit community. For better or worse, it doesn't take long for word to spread. And I've had one of her customers. A man came in who had a spot shaved on the back of his head." Slowly, her smile faded, and she waved her finger from Martha to Elizabeth. "Wait. Is that why you two... Did you drive out her because you think that I...?"

When neither answered, she sat back in her chair. "I see."

"Dottie—" Martha began, but Elizabeth put out her hand to stop her.

She trained her gaze on Dottie's face, ignoring the small, throbbing ache that had taken root at the back of her head and was now spreading downward toward her chest. She'd thought of at least a hundred different ways to start this conversation on the ride over, but now that the time had arrived, none of them came to her mind.

God, give me the words, she prayed, then sucked in a breath and opened her mouth.

"Dottie, we're here because we have questions. You don't have to answer them. In fact, I would understand if you tossed us out right now and never spoke to us again. But I hope you won't do that. I hope you'll hear what we have to say, and maybe understand a little better why we felt we had to come."

Dottie listened. And then she nodded for Elizabeth to continue. So, beginning with Mary's botched hair color, Elizabeth explained all that had happened, and which clues had led them back to Dottie.

She held up her hands, the scratch still evident on her finger. "But I told you how I got this. Sometimes I just get in too much of a hurry."

"Yes, but you do understand why we wanted to check with you again, after hearing about the scissors?" Martha asked.

Dottie sighed and dropped her hands to her lap. "I suppose I do."

"And there's also the matter of your appointment book," Elizabeth said, her voice low.

Dottie's mouth fell open. "What about my appointment book?"

"It was open on your stand," Elizabeth said. "I couldn't help but see it."

Dottie thought a moment, then waved her hand through the air. "You're right. I do have a habit of leaving it lying around." She blew out a breath and laced her hands together on the tabletop. "Well, I'm not even sure what to say right now, except that I didn't tamper with Paige's supplies. Further, I have no idea who did."

"I'm glad to hear that, Dottie," Martha said. "And you should also know that Elizabeth has been adamant this entire time that you had nothing to do with what's been happening over at Paige's place."

Dottie looked at Elizabeth gratefully.

"Thank you so much for talking with us," Elizabeth said to her. "You surely didn't have to."

"No, I didn't." She paused for a long moment, until finally a slow smile came to her lips. "I guess I'm at least glad that you spoke to me instead of asking around town."

"Of course," Elizabeth said.

"And you did give me the benefit of the doubt by filling me in on your concerns."

Elizabeth and Martha both nodded.

From the salon, a bell chimed, and Dottie craned her neck to see who had come in. "Oh, that's Matt. I forgot he was making a delivery. Would you gals excuse me for a minute?"

"Sure."

"No problem."

Dottie smiled as their words overlapped. "I'll be right back."

She moved away from the table, and Elizabeth blew out a nervous, and somewhat relieved, breath. "That went better than I expected."

"I agree." Martha scratched her cheek. "I have to say, Elizabeth, I agree with you about Dottie. I don't think she's the person we're looking for."

"I'm glad to hear it, though I don't think that will be the news Mary is hoping for."

Sympathy made Martha's eyes bright. "Mary is worried about her friend, just like you."

"I know." From her place at the table, Elizabeth could get a view of the salon if she leaned back a bit. From this vantage point she was able to glimpse the delivery man's profile. Tall and good-looking were two descriptions that jumped to mind, but also—

"Is Dottie still with the delivery guy?"

Elizabeth nodded. While she watched, he handed Dottie a clipboard and a pen. "She's signing for her stuff now. They must be almost finished."

"Great. Thank you," the man said, taking the clipboard back and slipping the pen into his shirt pocket. "Okay if I leave your stuff by the door?"

"That will be perfect." Dottie smiled and pointed to a bare space along the wall. "Right there."

"Okeydoke."

He reached for the knob, turning just enough as he opened the door to give Elizabeth a better view of his profile.

She grabbed Martha's hand. Beneath her touch, she felt Martha startle.

"What?"

"Look at the delivery guy. Quick, move over here by me before he comes back."

Rising, Martha scooted to an empty chair next to Elizabeth. Both waited silently until the door swung open again, and the delivery man appeared pushing a dolly. This time, they got a clear view of his face.

"Thanks," he said, shooting a smile toward Dottie as she held the door open.

Wide-eyed, Elizabeth looked at Martha. "Well? He fits the general description Mary gave us, don't you think?" She motioned toward the dolly. "And it would make sense that he'd be outside Paige's salon."

Martha plucked at her bottom lip. "It could be him, I suppose. Should we take a picture?"

Elizabeth hesitated. Both Dottie and the delivery man were facing them. They'd surely notice if they tried to get a picture. She shook her head. "Let's wait until Dottie gets back. Maybe she can tell us more about him."

Martha nodded and then slid back into the chair she'd vacated. After a moment, they heard the salon door close, and Dottie walked back into the kitchen.

"Sorry about that."

"No problem at all," Elizabeth said. Across the table, Martha tipped her head toward the salon. Elizabeth cleared her throat. "Say, Dottie, I don't think I've ever seen that delivery man before. Is he new?"

"Him?" Dottie gestured toward the door. "Yes, that's Matt Zoch. He's new. The guy he replaced retired a couple of months ago."

Martha motioned toward the stack of boxes. "Meaningful Beauty Supplies? You must buy a lot of stuff from them."

Dottie chuckled. "Yes, well, their prices are good. And I get it fast, usually just a few days after I place the order."

"You've never had any trouble with anything you bought?" Elizabeth asked.

Dottie shook her head and braced both hands on her hips. "Not at all. Just the opposite, in fact. I've never had to return a single thing. Plus, I really like Matt. He's pretty quiet, but I think that's just because he's shy. He seems really sweet, and more importantly, he's always on time." She tapped her watch. "And, now that I think about it, I'd better get moving.

I have a lady coming in for a cut and color in about fifteen minutes."

Elizabeth and Martha pushed to their feet.

"We certainly won't keep you," Martha said. "Thanks again for chatting with us."

"No problem." One side of Dottie's mouth lifted in a grimace. "I only wish there was more..." She stopped, and her eyes widened, her gaze bouncing from Elizabeth to Martha.

"Hold on a minute. I have an idea. It's a long shot, but I think I may have just come up with something I can do to help."

CHAPTER TWENTY-SIX

It was after lunch by the time Mary made it to the salon. Inside her head, the idea Dottie had come up with swirled like a tornado—staking out the Valentine's Dance hosted by the Bird-in-Hand Stage. Most of the town would be there. It was the perfect opportunity. Dottie even volunteered to work the sign-in table, so she'd be able to keep an eye out for anyone with a suspicious-looking wound.

Mary still marveled at the generous offer Dottie had made, even after Elizabeth and Martha had explained the reason for their visit. And she had to admit, the idea was perfect.

Almost.

Valentine's Day wasn't until next week, but the dance was being held on Saturday—tomorrow—to try to take advantage of the weekend crowd. That meant Mary needed to find a date, and fast.

She stepped out her car and made her way into the salon.

Paige waited, cape in hand, Figaro sleeping in an empty chair. "All right, this time, we fix it for real."

Relief filled Mary at the playful note in her friend's voice.

"So, *you're* feeling better," she said as she took off her coat and set it on a chair next to her purse.

Paige shook out the cape with a smile. "Actually, I am feeling better. Especially after you told me what Dottie had to say when you called. And...I spoke to Jack."

"What?"

Paige nodded. "It's the first civil conversation we've had in months."

"I'm glad to hear that, Paige."

"Well, we're a long way from having things settled, but we both want what's best for Kailey, so...we're willing to work on it."

"That's good news."

Paige sniffled and patted the chair. "Shall we?"

Mary bent and pulled a folded piece of paper from her purse. "Before we get started, would you mind taking a look at something?"

Paige's brows furrowed, but she nodded. "Sure. What is it?"

Mary unfolded the paper and held up the photo Elizabeth had printed from their computer at home. "Earlier today, Elizabeth and Martha went over to see Dottie. While they were there, this guy showed up with a delivery from Meaningful Beauty Supplies. Elizabeth found his picture on their website. Do you recognize him?"

Paige tapped the photo with her finger. "Yeah, I know that guy. He's the one who replaced the old delivery driver. His name is..." She snapped her fingers, thinking.

"Matt Zoch?"

"That's him." Her eyes narrowed as she peered up at Mary. "What about him?"

Mary folded the paper and pushed it back inside her purse. "That's the guy I saw hanging around outside your salon. Remember?"

Paige considered this a moment, and then shook her head. "He was probably just making a delivery."

"I didn't see him with any boxes." Mary rested her hand on the arm of the chair. "Paige, can you think of any reason why this guy might tamper with your supplies?"

She shook her head in confusion. "Wait, I thought you said Vanessa had nothing to do with—"

"Not Vanessa." Mary held up the picture again. "He had access to them, and probably plenty of opportunities."

Paige's fingers tightened around the cape, and she turned to pace the floor. "I don't think so, Mary. I mean, except for the few times we've talked here at the salon, I don't even know the guy all that well."

"What about family members? Friends? Anyone you can think of who might know who he might be working with or... for?"

She stopped and stared at Mary. "You mean Jack."

"Maybe. Or someone else."

She lifted her hands helplessly. "I have no way of knowing that. How could I?"

Mary patted her arm. "Okay. Well, we'll put him on the back burner for now. But if you think of something, be sure to let me know."

"Okay." Paige rubbed her index finger over her bottom lip. "You know, this is Matt's normal delivery day. He's usually here around three or three thirty."

Mary glanced at the clock on the wall. It was only two, but by the time they finished with her hair, it would be just around the time he showed up. She nodded. "I'll wait here with you. Maybe it'll give us a chance to talk to him."

Paige drew in a breath and nodded.

Mary sat in the stylist chair, and Paige leaned forward to meet her gaze in the mirror. "Do you really think we'll be able to figure out who's been messing with my supplies?"

"I do," Mary said, reaching up to pat her hand.

She didn't want to give Paige false hope, but neither did she want to throw a damper on her mood. She lifted her hair from her neck while Paige fastened the cape, then settled back in the chair to let her work.

"So about the dance," Mary said. "Dottie said it starts at seven thirty, but a lot of people start showing up before that so they can have their picture taken on the stage."

Paige nodded and grabbed a paper towel to wipe up a bit of color dripping down Mary's temple. "Yes. Catherine, the theater director, told me about that. Apparently, this is their biggest fund-raiser, so they go all out. They have a special set built with flowers and cupids and a Valentine's arbor with twinkly lights all over it." She stopped dabbing on color long enough to sigh. "Almost makes me wish I had a date."

"You and me both."

Paige's eyebrows rose, and she went back to brushing color on Mary's hair. "What about Wade? Couldn't you ask him? I'm sure he'd like to take you." She chuckled and gave a knowing wink in the mirror.

Wade. Mary bit her lip. "Yes, I suppose I could see if he's free, although at this late hour, he more than likely already has a date."

"Would that bother you?"

Would it? Mary quirked an eyebrow. "My pride, maybe. Not sure about anything else. Although..." She thought back to the meeting at the chamber and winced. "You know, I could hardly blame him after the way I've treated him the past few days. I've been so caught up trying to solve this mystery, I haven't paid him much attention."

"Well, all I can say is, I'm very thankful." Paige added the last little bit of hair color to the loose strands around Mary's forehead and above her ears and then patted her shoulder. "There. You'll be good as new in"—she turned her wrist to look at her watch and pretended to count on her fingers—"exactly forty minutes. Follow me. I'm going to sit you where I can see you. And I'm going to check your hair several times to make sure the color is developing properly."

While they waited, Mary asked about Paige's ex-husband. "So he called. Did he say what he wanted?"

Paige carried two bottles of water from a mini-fridge and handed one to Mary. "You're never going to believe it," she said, twisting the cap off her water. "Jack is getting married."

Mary rested the ice-cold bottle against her thigh. "You're kidding. Isn't that kind of soon?"

Paige downed a quick gulp and wiped her hand over her mouth. "That's not even the best part. He asked what I thought about him and his new bride moving to Bird-in-Hand to be closer to Kailey."

Mary's mouth fell open.

Paige shrugged. "What could I say? We're going to try and work it so that he and Kailey can spend more time together." She rolled her eyes as she took another swallow from the water bottle. "Anyway, I guess I should be glad that he cares enough to want to see her. He never spent time with her when we were married, but that's neither here nor there. Who knows? Maybe he's a different man."

She put the bottle down and rose to check Mary's hair.

"What did Kailey have to say about her dad moving closer?" Mary asked, removing the cap from her own bottle and taking a drink.

Paige sighed and wiped her fingers on a tissue, then balled it up and tossed it into the trash. "To be honest, I haven't told her yet. I'm waiting to see if Jack actually follows through."

"You think he won't?"

"I think he used to be the kind of guy who thought nothing of going back on his word. Call me cynical, but I'll believe he's actually dropping the lawsuit and moving to Bird-in-Hand when I see it."

A soft ping interrupted their conversation, not once, or twice, but three times, before Paige jumped up with a small, "Oh." She patted the pockets of her apron and pulled out a cell phone. "That's my new phone. I'm still not used to the ringtone."

Swiping her finger over the screen, she turned slightly and spoke into the phone. After a moment, she disconnected.

"That was Kailey calling from school. She's staying after to get some extra help with her math class."

"Is she having trouble?"

Paige shrugged. "Not really. Her new teacher doesn't spend a lot of time on each lesson, and Kailey's worried about keeping up. But she works hard, and she's a smart girl. She'll get used to the pace."

Mary nodded and pointed to Paige's hand. "So what kind of phone did you get? Do you like it?"

Paige showed her, and then pressed the HOME key and brought up a program. "This app is a lifesaver," she said, wiggling the phone. "I use it whenever I'm not at the salon to keep track of my appointments. That was the worst part of having my old phone stolen. I lost all of my info when my phone was stolen and couldn't even call my clients to reschedule, because I didn't have their numbers."

She ran through the program, showing Mary how it worked, and also how she plugged the info into the calendar on her desktop. When she finished, it was time for Mary to rinse, so Paige put the phone away and walked her to the sink. After a trim and a blow-dry, Mary sat with her back to the mirror, her palms sweating profusely under the cape.

"Okay, tell me what you think." Obviously feeling as nervous as Mary felt, Paige blew out a breath and spun the chair around.

Mary fingered her hair, once again its normal soft shade of blond. "Oh, thank goodness." She turned to the sleeping cat. "What do you think, Figgy?"

Figgy opened one eye and closed it again, obviously unimpressed.

Both laughed at that, and Paige reached up to loosen the Velcro tab at Mary's neck. She folded the cape over her forearm and grabbed a small handheld mirror. She gave it to Mary to check her hair from every angle. "I have to say, I was tempted to leave in a lock of blue, just for grins," she said, her cheeks ripening to the color of a tomato.

Mary laughed. "One lock, I could handle. It was the whole hardware store that had me bothered."

A chime from the back interrupted their banter. Wide-eyed, they stared at one another, then Paige rolled up the cape and set it on her station table.

"I'll go and see if that's Matt."

"I'll come with you."

Together they walked toward the back of the salon, though Mary accomplished it on wobbly knees. At the door stood the man she'd confronted at the window, his face tanned, but with lines at his temples that suggested he often wore the dark sunglasses he'd had with him last time. Today, he wore a navy blue coat, his name embroidered on a white patch trimmed with red.

"Hey, Paige, I have your—" He drew up short at the sight of Mary, a clipboard frozen in his hand. "Uh…"

"Matt, this is my friend, Mary Baxter." Paige extended her hand for the clipboard. Matt dragged his gaze back to Paige and gave it to her.

Mary stepped forward. "Matt, is it? Pleasure to meet you. Officially, I mean."

She poked out her hand. Matt shook it nervously.

"You too, Miss Baxter."

Mary bit the inside of her lip. This guy didn't look danger-ous. If anything, he seemed sweet and...bashful. She threw a glance at Paige, who watched them both, the clipboard pressed to her chest.

"So, tell me, Matt, have you been a delivery driver long?"

His face reddened a little, and he pushed his hands into the pockets of his coat. "Actually, I've only been doing this a few months."

His gaze slid to Paige, and he dragged in a breath as though being near her made him nervous, or shy. Maybe both. Understanding dawned.

"Um, Paige, why don't you go ahead and check your inven-tory while I have a word with Matt?"

Paige opened her mouth to speak, but Mary ignored her and motioned Matt into the hall, away from the door. They weren't quite out of earshot, but almost.

Mary lowered her voice. "It was you, wasn't it? You were the guy I saw hanging around in the alley."

Embarrassment filled his eyes before his jaw hardened, and he nodded. "Yeah, that was me."

"And the other day, you were looking in the window. What were you doing? Why didn't you just come inside?" Mary asked, though deep down, she thought she already knew.

Matt sighed and pulled his fingers through his sandy-brown hair. "I kept meaning to, I just..." He puffed out his cheeks and took another look at Paige, then back at Mary. "My wife died a couple of years ago. I haven't dated, or wanted to date, anyone since. And then Paige moved to town and I, well, for the first time I thought maybe, except I wasn't sure she was ready since, well, I overheard her and her daughter talking once so I knew she was divorced and—"

Mary laid her hand on his arm to halt the sudden rush of words. He stumbled to a stop and threw an agonized glance at Paige, who was studiously checking items off the list attached to the clipboard.

"Maybe you should talk to her," Mary suggested quietly.

Matt rubbed his hands down his pant legs. "You think?"

Mary shrugged. "To be honest, I have no idea if she's ready to date yet or not, but I know she could use a friend to talk to."

Matt's Adam's apple bobbed as he nodded. "Yeah. Okay."

"Uh, Paige? I'm gonna—" She gestured toward the front. "I'll be over there."

Paige blinked, looked at Matt, then blinked again as Mary moved away. So much for dangerous delivery drivers. Matt was as gentle as they came. Sweet too. And considerate.

Mary stifled a growl. And he was absolutely, positively, beyond a doubt...

Not the person they were looking for.

CHAPTER TWENTY-SEVEN

Mary ran a brush through her hair, each rhythmic stroke slow and measured, and almost without thought. Sighing, she put the brush down. Wade would be arriving soon to take her to the Valentine's Dance. After debating who to ask, she'd settled on Wade, because despite Martha's urging to sort out her feelings, things were still muddy where Bill was concerned. As Paige had predicted, Wade seemed happy she'd called, happy to escort her. She only hoped he wasn't building up any false hopes, because if nothing else, one thing was certain.

Wade wasn't the man for her.

She'd known it the moment he picked up the phone, and a flicker of disappointment had sputtered inside her chest. So then, could it be she was destined to live out the rest of her days alone? Would that really be so bad?

Her phone buzzed on her nightstand, and she rose to check the caller ID. Seeing her daughter's name, she swiped to answer.

"Jennifer, hi."

"Hi, Mom. I hope I didn't catch you at a bad time."

Mary ran her hand over the red off-the-shoulder dress she'd chosen for the dance. The lines were clean, simple, with only a subtle ruffle at the elbow to give it flare. Still, she liked it, and hoped Bill—

Her thoughts ground to a halt. Wade. She hoped Wade would like it.

"Mom?"

"Oh, I'm sorry, honey. No, this isn't a bad time." Mary sank down to sit on the edge of her bed. "How are you doing?"

"I'm good, I guess. I handed in my big research paper."

Mary sucked in a breath. "And?"

"I got an A."

"That's great news."

"Thanks, Mom."

"What about you and Michael?"

Jennifer let out a low groan.

"Oh, honey. Are the two of you still not talking?"

"Let's just say we've still got some stuff to work out."

"But you are trying?"

"Yeah, I'm trying. Not sure I can say the same for Michael."

"Now, Jen."

"I know what you're going to say."

"Oh? And what is that?" Mary bit her lip and waited.

"He's adjusting to his new role. I've got to give him and Heidi time. Things will get back to normal."

"Wrong. I was only going to say half of that."

Jennifer's laughter was music to Mary's ears. She pressed the phone closer. "Sweetheart, why don't you come to the farm for a visit? I'd love to see you, and you know we have plenty of room."

"I would if I could, Mom, but with classes and work, it's just too hard."

"Well then, maybe I could come there."

"And sleep in my dorm room?" Jennifer snorted into the phone. "I can just see you climbing into a bunk."

"Why not?"

Tink sat up in her bed, and a low growl rumbled in her throat. A split second later, she took off out the door, barking all the way down the stairs.

"Someone there? I thought I heard Tink," Jennifer said.

"Actually, that would be my date to the Valentine's Dance."

"Your *what*?" Jennifer's voice rose on a squeal. "Who is he? Why didn't you tell me? Is it that contractor guy?"

"That contractor guy's name is Bill, and no, it's not him. Tonight I have a date with Wade Jameson, the baseball coach at the high school. And before you ask, we're just friends."

"Hmm. Friends who go out on a Valentine's Dance date."

"Just friends, Jennifer," Mary said.

Jennifer chuckled. "Okay. I'll let you go. Oh, Mom, wait! Send me a picture of this Wade guy."

"I will not."

"I'll just ask Aunt Elizabeth to do it."

Mary sighed. "Oh, you know what? Fine. They're taking pictures at the dance. I'll send you that."

"Don't forget."

"I won't."

"Love you, Mom. Have fun."

"I love you too."

Jennifer disconnected before Mary could tell her goodbye. Kids. Always in a hurry.

Mary grabbed a silver clutch from her closet and slid her phone inside, along with her wallet and a small pack of tissues.

By the time she got downstairs, Wade was in the hall, hunkered down to pet Tink, who had forgotten that she was annoyed, and now lay on her back with her tongue hanging out.

"Hi, Wade."

He rose and hitched his thumb over his shoulder. "Martha let me in."

She glanced around. Martha was nowhere to be seen.

Wade's gaze drifted over her. "You look great. Forget the blue. Blond is definitely your color."

Mary reached up to touch her hair. "Thanks." She dropped her hand and motioned to his suit coat and dark slacks. "You look good too."

"Yeah?" He grabbed the lapels of his coat and struck a pose. "What do you think?"

Mary laughed and reached into the closet for her coat. "I think we'll be late if we don't get moving."

Wade helped her with her coat and then moved toward the door. Mary held up her finger. "Can you hold on for one second? I just want to let my sisters know I'm leaving."

He nodded, and Mary slipped off to the kitchen. Martha stood near the sink, Butterscotch in her arms.

"We're heading out," Mary said. "Is Elizabeth outside?"

Martha nodded. "She and Pal went to feed the animals."

"Okay. Well, will you let her know not to wait up?"

Martha stepped toward her. "You look beautiful, Mary."

Surprised, Mary let her mouth drop open. She lowered her gaze to the red dress peeking out from her coat. Martha shook her head.

"It's not the dress. Or your hair. It's you. And the fact that you're going to all this trouble to help your friend. That's what makes you beautiful."

Mary rarely felt speechless, but at this moment, with tears glimmering in Martha's eyes as she stared at her, she couldn't think of a single thing to say.

Martha set Butterscotch on the floor then crossed to Mary and patted her cheek. "Good luck tonight. Let us know if you learn anything that will help."

"I will."

Humming softly, Martha followed Butterscotch out through the kitchen door.

Wade looked up as Mary appeared and once again reached for the doorknob. "All set?"

Mary laid her hand on his arm. "Just one more thing."

He looked down at her hand, and his lips turned up in a tentative smile. "Everything okay?"

She could say yes, after which they would go to dinner. Or she could say nothing, and they would still have dinner. Neither option was the honest one. She removed her hand and squared her shoulders. "Wade, you're a lot of fun, and I like you, but I haven't been quite fair with you. For that, I need to apologize."

As she talked, the confusion gradually cleared from Wade's face, replaced by chagrin and a hint of a blush. "Uh-oh. Is this what I think it is?"

She bit her lip. "That depends. What do you think it is?"

"The 'can we just be friends' speech. Not that I've heard it all that often." He cleared his throat and tugged on his shirt collar. "Usually, it's the other way around, and I'm the one play-ing the bad guy."

Mary held her breath as she studied him. Was he teasing? How could she be sure? Finally, a smile broke out on his face, and she puffed out a sigh.

"I'm sorry, Wade. You really are a great guy." And then, because she felt a little guilty, she added, "It's late notice, I know, but I would totally understand if you decided not go to the Valentine's Dance with me."

"And miss out on a steak dinner?"

She stared. "Are you being serious?"

He chuckled and offered his arm. Before she took it, he held up his palm. "I only have one condition."

Mary narrowed her eyes at him. "Oh? What's that?"

"You're buying."

She laughed and looped her arm through his. "Deal."

Now that the initial awkwardness was behind them, Mary found she could actually enjoy Wade's company. He was funny and kind when he wasn't playing a role, and thanks to the ball-room dancing lessons he'd taken as a kid, he was quite a good dancer. They had just finished a spirited quickstep when Mary motioned to their table.

"All right, time for a break."

"Aww, but I was just getting warmed up," Wade said, flexing his muscles and reaching over his head to stretch out his arms.

"Not me. I'm already warm." Mary fanned her face and tipped her head toward the punch bowl. "I'm going to grab something to drink and then go check on my friend."

"Friend?"

"Dottie." She motioned toward the sign-in table at the door.

"Let me get the drinks." Wade put his hand to her back. "I'll meet you back at our table."

"Thank you," Mary said, relieved for a moment just to cool down. There was a long line at the punch bowl, so she knew it would be a bit before Wade returned. She headed over to Dottie.

"Hey. Anything yet?"

Dottie set her pen down and shook her head. "Nothing, and by now, most everyone should be here."

Mary glanced at her watch. The dance was nearly half over. "Any chance we'll see some stragglers?"

"Not likely. I'm sorry, Mary. I was sure this would work."

"Me too," Mary said, hiding a disappointed frown. "I sure appreciate you keeping an eye out, though."

"Of course." She put her hand on Mary's arm. "One more thing. I did see your friend Paige come in."

Mary raised her brows, and Dottie pointed. "Over there."

She angled her head toward a table near the stage. Paige was there with Matt Zoch seated next to her.

"Hmm. Thanks, Dottie."

"I'll let you know if I see anything strange."

Mary nodded her thanks once again and eased over to greet Matt and Paige. Catching sight of her, Paige's eyes brightened, and she waved Mary closer.

"Hey, you two." Mary caught Paige's gaze and lifted one eyebrow questioningly.

"Hi, Mary." Paige smiled and shook her head. "It's not what you're thinking. Matt has a son the same age as Kailey. We ran into each other dropping the kids off at the Valentine's dance at the high school. Matt asked what I was doing tonight, and since neither of us had plans..." She lifted her hands and shrugged.

Matt smiled. "Just friends. And I promise, no more loitering around the salon."

Mary laughed. "Well, I'm glad it worked out."

The music struck up, and Paige had to cup her hand to her mouth to be heard. "I spoke to Dottie." She signaled with one finger. "Nothing yet?"

Mary shook her head and leaned down to Paige's ear. "Unfortunately, no. She said she'd let me know if she saw anything."

Paige's shoulders slumped, and Mary gave her arm a pat. "Don't worry," she said. She gave a subtle tip of her head. "Try to enjoy yourself."

"I will," Paige said, but the frustration in her eyes said that might be difficult.

Mary wove back to her seat. While she waited for Wade to return, she checked out the couples swaying on the dance floor. She was surprised to realize the crowd had grown while she and Wade had been dancing. Men in suits and women in fancy dresses maneuvered gracefully across the floor in time with a gentle waltz, played by a talented orchestra seated on the stage.

Mary smiled. She had to admit, she was glad she'd come, even if it was more work than play. The decorations were tasteful and elegant—flowers and white lights draped the ceiling to form a romantic canopy, columns stood wrapped in ivy garland,

and there were hearts. Everywhere, hearts. In such a lovely setting, it would be easy to forget that she was here looking for a
culprit with a conspicuous bandage on one hand.

"Here you go." Wade set down a crystal teacup brimming
with frothy punch.

Mary took it gratefully and brought it to her lips for a sip.
"Thank you."

He swallowed from his own cup and then sat back to tug at
his collar. "Is it warm in here?"

Grabbing a napkin to fan him, Mary laughed. "I told you."

"Right." He plucked the napkin from her fingers and
pressed it to his brow.

The music swelled, so they cut off talking until the number
ended. In the meantime, their dessert arrived, and Mary
groaned looking at the mountain of chocolate cake dripping
with hot fudge and strawberries. On either side of it, their
waitress placed a long-handled silver spoon.

Wade's eyes widened. "How did I not hear about this event
sooner?"

From the stage, the microphone popped, and Mary looked
over in time to see Catherine Randall stepping up to speak.
Dressed in a stunning silver floor-length gown, her hair swept
up to expose her gleaming neck, and with white silk opera
gloves reaching over her elbows, Catherine looked like a movie
star, and Mary was just the tiniest smidge envious as she
fidgeted with her hem.

"Wow. Who is that?"

"The theater director," Mary said, her voice dropping to a
whisper as Catherine raised her hands.

"Good evening, everyone, and welcome to the sixth Annual Valentine's Dance, hosted by your very own Bird-in-Hand Stage and Community Players."

Polite applause followed the announcement, and then the house lights dimmed, and a spotlight bathed Catherine in an ethereal glow.

"As you know, the Valentine's Dance is the theater's primary fund-raiser, and is it any wonder why? Take a look around you."

She waited while the crowd expressed its appreciation and then went on. "Over the years, donations from this event have gone to purchase curtains for the stage, dressing tables for the actors, even a new spotlight."

She smiled and swept her hand upward, indicating some person hidden by shadows, high in the rafters. Once again, applause erupted, and Catherine added her own, the clapping muffled by the gloves she wore. After a moment, she bent again toward the microphone.

"This year, however…"

She paused to let the crowd settle. Watching her, Mary was impressed by the expert way she handled herself and the crowd.

"This year," Catherine resumed, "we have an even more daunting task before us. Not only are we hoping to refinish the stage floor, we would also like to update our sound system and increase the theater seating by over fifty places."

A murmur swept through the audience, and Catherine nodded, as though she too was stunned by the concept.

"It is an ambitious project to be sure, but with performances like *A Bird-in-Hand Christmas to Remember...*"

Applause.

"...*Imagine...*"

More applause.

"...and *A Magical Merry Christmas* selling out in record time, we are in definite need of the added room."

Her smile widened as cheers mingled with the applause swelling from the room. At last, she held up one hand, quieting the crowd.

"Thank you. You are all so kind. Many of you have told me tonight that I have played a part in the theater's success."

Though she shook her head, she let the whistles and applause from the audience go on for some time before quieting them again with an uplifted hand.

"The reality is, it is thanks to you, our patrons, that we have enjoyed seeing the theater grow. We are able to bring you fun, wholesome productions because of your generosity and support. And so, tonight, let this evening be all about you... celebrating you, showing our gratitude to you, and yes, telling you all how much we love you. Thank you all so much for coming tonight. Please, enjoy the rest of your evening, and as the sign says"—she pointed to a banner that draped the stage above her head—"let's all 'Dance the Night Away'!"

As if on cue, the orchestra struck up a merry tune. At the same moment, a gentleman in a tuxedo appeared at Catherine's elbow to sweep her onto the dance floor. It was a choreographed moment, certainly, but the timing of it was so beautiful and effortless that Mary couldn't help but be impressed.

She glanced back at the table as Wade scraped up a bite of chocolate cake with his spoon.

He offered it to her with a wry grin. "Bite?"

Sneaking one more glance at Catherine's perfect waistline, Mary shook her head. "No thanks."

Tonight, she planned on working off a few more calories on the dance floor. And tomorrow, she was starting a diet.

CHAPTER TWENTY-EIGHT

Not a single one. Not even so much as a scratch.

Mary placed the last fork on the table and stood back with a sigh. Not a single person at the dance last night had come in with a wound on their hand. By the end of the night, she'd given up looking, and so had Dottie. So, where did that leave them?

"Here's the iced tea." Elizabeth set a pitcher on the table and pulled out a chair. Soon Martha joined them, the scent of a sizzling pot roast wafting from the Dutch oven in her hands.

Elizabeth took a long sniff. "Oh, Martha, that smells delicious."

"I hope so. I added a packet of onion soup, just how you like it."

Elizabeth narrowed her eyes and reached for her napkin. "Hmm. Lasagna last week, pot roast today." She looked from Martha to Mary. "You two are going to have to stop spoiling me."

"Don't look at me." Mary smoothed her napkin over her lap then reached for the iced tea pitcher. "It's all Martha."

Martha chuckled and slipped into her seat. "Shall we ask the blessing?"

Martha's sweet voice filled the dining room while she prayed. Afterward, she took the lid off the pot roast, releasing a cloud of savory steam, and spooned out a large portion for Elizabeth, then Mary, and lastly, one for herself.

"So, tell us about the dance," Martha said, picking up her fork and spearing a tender baby carrot. "We didn't get to talk much about it before church this morning. I heard there was a good turnout."

"Oh, it was well attended," Mary agreed, ladling a bit of gravy over her roast and potatoes. "I was actually pretty surprised at how many people were there."

She named a few of the people she knew, then tapped her fingernail against the side of her glass. "It's a great idea for a fund-raiser, and Catherine did a wonderful job as hostess. All in all, it was a very pleasant night."

Elizabeth swallowed a bite of food. "Except that we're no closer to finding our culprit."

"Except for that." Mary sighed and took a bite. While she chewed, she pondered their options. "I guess I'll go see Paige this afternoon. I hate the idea of admitting to her that we're no closer to solving this mystery than before, but I don't think we have a choice."

She looked hopefully at Martha and Elizabeth, but to her disappointment, they nodded.

"Would you like me to go with you?" Elizabeth asked.

Mary pushed a piece of potato around on her plate while she considered the offer, then shook her head. "No, that's okay. I'll talk to her."

"At least you'll go knowing nothing else has happened," Martha said. "Could it be that all of this was just some sort of nasty prank?"

"Maybe." Mary nibbled a bite of potato and washed it down with a drink of iced tea. Martha and Elizabeth continued talking, mostly about things going on at church, but Mary was too consumed with thoughts of Paige to participate. Once lunch was over, she helped clear the dishes before heading to Paige's apartment.

When she got there, Kailey answered the door, and Mary was pleased to see a smile on her face. Mary asked for Kailey's mother, and Kailey called over her shoulder for her while she slid into her coat.

"See you later, Ms. Baxter." She wiggled her fingers and grabbed her backpack before slipping out the door.

A moment later, Paige appeared. She too had a relaxed look about her that eased some of the tension in Mary's chest. She jabbed her thumb toward the door. "You just missed Kailey."

Paige nodded. "A couple of girls from school are getting together for a study group. They invited Kailey to join."

"Hey, that's good news, right?"

Paige held out her hands while Mary took off her coat. "It sure is. And after she got home from the dance last night, she actually wanted to sit up and talk."

She yawned and rubbed her eyes, and Mary laughed. "Sounds like you need coffee."

Paige grinned and motioned for Mary to follow her to the kitchen. "I was just about to brew a pot."

Paige's kitchen was small, but nicely appointed, with stainless steel appliances and marble countertops. The backsplash was composed of crisp white subway tile, a classy contrast to the periwinkle paint and gleaming crown molding. Mary looked around approvingly.

"What a cute kitchen."

Paige looked up from spooning coffee grounds into a filter. "Do you like it? Kailey helped me paint. Actually, I should rephrase that. Kailey painted. I helped."

She smiled and snapped the lid on the plastic tub of coffee and put it back in the cupboard. "I'm telling you, Mary, the last couple of days have been such a relief. For a while there, I really was questioning my decision to move back, especially after all that stuff at the salon."

"Um, speaking of the salon…"

Paige poured water into the coffee maker and set it to brew, then sat with Mary at a small dinette table tucked into the corner. "What? Did you find out something?"

"Just the opposite, I'm afraid." Mary frowned and rested her arms on the tabletop. "I was so sure we'd get a lead at the dance last night."

"But no luck, huh? I have to admit, I was sort of hoping that would lead to something too." Paige's phone pinged, and she sighed as she took it from her pocket. "Oh, that's my reminder. I'm meeting a lady at the salon early tomorrow morning for a wash and set."

She typed something on her phone and set it aside.

"So, you're getting used to your new phone?"

Paige nodded. "Slowly but surely. I've even gotten most of my client's phone numbers entered. There's a few I'm still missing, of course, but eventually I'll have them all."

The coffee maker beeped, and Paige rose to pour their cups. While she worked, Mary reached for Paige's phone. "Hey, Paige, can I look at this?"

"Sure, go ahead." She took the lid off a sugar bowl, looked inside, then retrieved a bag out of the cupboard to refill it.

Mary swiped across the darkened screen. Instantly, it sprang to life. "What's the name of that app you're using for your appointments?"

Paige told her and carried the cream and sugar bowls to the table. "Are you looking for something to use?"

"Maybe." Mary frowned, a half-formed idea niggling at her brain. With just a few clicks, she maneuvered through the app. "You were right, Paige. This is really easy to use."

"I know. That's why I like it so much." She set the coffee down in front of Mary and laid a spoon next to her cup. "There you go."

"Paige, did you show anyone else this app? Clients, I mean, or maybe Matt?" She cringed saying his name. He and Paige had looked so comfortable last night.

"I don't think so," Paige said, stirring a spoonful of sugar into her coffee. "But anyone could have seen me using it, I guess. Why do you ask?" She tapped the spoon against the side of her cup then laid it on a napkin.

Mary tilted her head as the idea that had been brewing took shape. Filled with excitement, she reached out to pat a drumbeat on Paige's arm. "I knew I was missing something. The connection between the things stolen from your desk? I think I know what it is."

A puzzled frown tugged on Paige's lips. "My phone and my appointment book?"

Mary nodded. "It's the app. Whoever took your phone must have known you kept your appointments on it. They took the book for the same reason." Mary's eyes widened in disbelief. "Paige, what if...?"

"What?" When Mary didn't answer, Paige grabbed her fingers. "Mary, what is it? What are you thinking?"

"I can't believe it, Paige." Mary smacked the heel of her hand against her forehead. "All this time." Smiling, she pushed Paige's coffee cup aside and took hold of her hands. "All this time, we've had it all wrong!"

CHAPTER TWENTY-NINE

Mary let go of Paige's hands and pushed away from the table to pace the small kitchen. "Where did I put that list? I need the names of everyone who came into the salon after my hair was dyed blue."

Paige also stood, wringing her hands as she watched Mary pace. "I emailed it to you."

"Right!" Mary grabbed her phone and scrolled until she found what she was looking for. "Here it is." She looked up at Paige. "You're sure this is everyone?"

"Mary, I already told you, I don't remember everyone who came in. Those are just the ones I could recall."

Mary stopped and shook her head. "You know what? It doesn't matter. I don't need everyone, Paige, just the ones who came in after I—"

Catherine. Catherine Randall had come in immediately following her. And Mary wasn't even supposed to come in that day. Paige had shuffled her appointments to fit her in.

She lifted her head. "Paige, whose appointment did you change in order to see me that day?"

"I...I..." Her mouth worked, but no words came out. Mary crossed to grip her shoulders.

"This is important, Paige. Who was supposed to be in the slot I took?"

Paige's breathing quickened, and she lowered her gaze to the floor. "It was...I think it was..." Her gaze snapped to Mary's. "Eloise Parkhurst. I remember now. Eloise was supposed to come in, but she was on a really tight schedule, so I moved her to the next week to give her more time."

Mary's thoughts spiraled like a tornado. Had the appointments not changed, Catherine would have come in right after Eloise. Eloise denied Catherine's application to the chamber. Catherine questioned Eloise at the chamber meeting. And last night, Catherine wore opera gloves. They couldn't see her hands!

"Mary, what is it? What are you thinking? And what did you mean when you said we had it all wrong?"

Mary forced her breathing to slow. This was a lead, certainly, but much of it was circumstantial. She pulled Paige to the table to sit. "Okay, this is just an idea, but what if you weren't the target of these incidents at all? What if it was someone else?"

Confusion clouded her gaze. "Like who?"

"Eloise Parkhurst," Mary said. "Think about it. Eloise and Catherine have a history."

"Because Catherine wouldn't give Eloise a part in her play," Paige said, recounting what they'd learned from Vanessa at the chamber meeting.

Mary nodded. "And then Eloise denied Catherine's membership application to the chamber."

Paige's eyes widened. "So, my missing phone and appointment book?"

"Catherine took them so she could figure out when Eloise was coming in."

Paige put up her hand. "Wait, why not Eloise? Couldn't she have been just as guilty as Catherine?"

"Possibly, but we saw her hands, remember? At the chamber meeting." Mary wiggled her hands. "No scratches."

"But we didn't see Catherine's." Paige gasped. "She was wearing gloves last night. And she had at least two opportunities."

Mary froze.

Paige nodded. "The first time was a while ago. She wanted a haircut. But the day you came in, she called to ask if she could come in for a color. I told her she didn't really need one yet, and that coloring too often was bad for her hair, but she said she wanted it to look fresh for the Valentine's Dance and, of course, the theater opening next week."

Mary processed this information. "I didn't get a look at her at the chamber meeting. Did you?"

Paige shook her head. "No, sorry. I was focused on Vanessa."

"Me too." Mary frowned.

"So, where does that leave us?" Paige asked.

"I think our only choice is to go and see Catherine at her coffee shop." Mary groaned.

"What?"

"It's Sunday. Is her shop even open?"

"One way to find out." Paige grabbed her phone and tapped the screen. "Here it is." She sighed. "They don't open until tomorrow morning."

"No, no, that's okay," Mary said quickly. "That will give us plenty of time to figure out what we should say."

Paige frowned. "Well, I'm not exactly inclined to be tactful. I say we just march in and ask her."

"Uh, yeah. About that."

Paige's expression darkened. "You're not going to suggest that I stay here."

It wasn't a question, and she didn't phrase it as one. Mary sucked in a breath. "Think about it, Paige. If she sees you coming, she may just clam up and say nothing. Better if I go alone, or with one of my sisters."

"But it's my salon and—"

"Are we even certain she's guilty?"

As she'd intended, the question caught Paige off guard. She crossed her arms. "Fine. I probably couldn't go with you anyway. Chelsea, the new nail tech, is supposed to start tomorrow, and I need to be at the salon to show her around and help her get set up. But I want to hear the moment you've had a chance to talk to Catherine."

"Of course." Mary picked up her coffee cup and took a sip. Going to the coffee shop to see Catherine was easy. Figuring out what she would say was another thing altogether.

CHAPTER THIRTY

The coffee shop Catherine owned was a quaint little place tucked into a historic stone house on the edge of town. Staring up at the list of coffees available on the board above the counter, Mary realized the name suddenly made sense.

She quirked an eyebrow. "Un-Common Grounds."

Elizabeth looked over at her. "What?"

She pointed to the board. "The name of the store. It's Un-Common Grounds. And all the coffees they serve are exotic or unusual. Get it?"

Elizabeth pulled a twenty-dollar bill from her wallet. "Have you decided what you want?"

"I think so. I'll try the maple and bacon blend." She looked around and pushed closer to Elizabeth's side. "I don't see Catherine anywhere."

"Me neither." Elizabeth's gaze darted to the baristas scurrying about behind the counter. "Should we ask them?"

"I guess we'll have to." Mary squared her shoulders. "Ready?"

Elizabeth nodded, and together they stepped toward the counter.

Martha had volunteered to stay behind to tend the store while Mary and Elizabeth went to see Catherine. Mary was glad. Elizabeth was a steadying influence, and when Mary had relayed the conclusion she and Paige had reached, it was Elizabeth who suggested they go in early for coffee and have a look around before confronting Catherine.

A young woman in a starched collared shirt and black apron smiled at them as they approached. "Good morning. Welcome to Un-Common Grounds. What can I get for you ladies today?"

Mary gave her order and then strained for a glimpse of Catherine in the back of the shop. Next to her, Elizabeth pointed to the board.

"I'd like to try something different today. The Chilled Campfire Coffee sounds good."

The barista typed the orders into the computer and looked at Mary. "Will that be for here or to go?"

"To go, please."

"All righty. Can I get you anything else?"

Mary eased over to the glass case where a variety of muffins, pastries, and other delicacies were artfully displayed. She pointed to a tray of frosted scones. "Are those cranberry?"

The young woman nodded.

"I'll take one." She arched a brow at Elizabeth, who drew closer to pay the bill. "Make that two."

The barista grabbed a brown paper bag and a pair of tongs to reach into the display case.

Mary cleared her throat. "So, uh, the lady who owns this place, it's Catherine Randall, right?"

"That's right." She placed both scones in the bag then folded the flap over and handed the bag to Mary. "Your coffee will be right up."

"Thank you." Mary licked her lips. "If you don't mind my asking, how long has Ms. Randall owned the shop?"

The woman took Elizabeth's money. "It's been a while. I've worked here a little over a year." She looked over her shoulder at one of the other baristas. "Hey, Roger, how long has Catherine owned this place?"

Mary cringed as her voice rose. If Catherine was near, she was certain to hear.

Roger stared up at the ceiling. "I don't know, three or four years, I guess?"

Mary tapped her finger on the counter. "Thank you. Is, um, is Ms. Randall here, by any chance?"

The woman shook her head and rested her arms on the top of the display case. "No, sorry. She won't be in at all today. She's over at the theater getting ready for opening night. She's the director, you know. *Stolen* opens Thursday, and they're doing light checks and final dress rehearsals."

"Oh, I wanted to see that play," Elizabeth said.

"Me too." Mary nodded to the barista. "Thanks again." She tugged Elizabeth toward the end of the counter. "Great. She's not even here. We've wasted a trip."

"Not necessarily." Elizabeth pointed toward a narrow hall at the back of the coffee shop. "When we came in, I spotted a door back there marked OFFICE."

Mary's gaze followed the direction she indicated. "You think we should try to get a look inside?"

"Wouldn't hurt. We are still hoping to find Paige's old phone and her appointment book."

Mary stared at her. "You think she kept them?"

"What else would she have done with them?"

Mary thought a moment then touched Elizabeth's arm and nodded toward a vintage-looking sign painted with crisp, white letters. "Looks like the bathrooms are back that way too."

Behind the counter, the barista was just getting started on the second cup. Mary hitched her purse over her shoulder.

"Grab the coffees, will you? I'm gonna head to the restroom but as I go by, I'll see if I can get a peek inside Catherine's office."

"All right, but be careful. And don't get caught snooping."

Seeing the twinkle in Elizabeth's eyes, Mary smiled.

The coffee shop was quite busy this time of the morning, and Mary actually had to stand in line for the restroom, a fact that suited her fine since it put her almost exactly opposite Catherine's office. Thankfully, the door had been left open. A modern metal desk dominated most of the space, but there was also a small bookcase, a couple of chairs, and on the wall behind the desk, a framed one-dollar bill.

"Excuse me." The woman in line behind Mary pointed toward the bathroom door. "Are you in line?"

Mary laughed nervously. "I'm so sorry. I wasn't paying attention. Please, go ahead."

She moved across the hall to let the woman pass. One more step, and she'd be inside Catherine's office. Mary waited until the bathroom door closed behind the woman before muttering, "It's now or never."

Sucking in a breath, she hurried to the desk. She only had a couple of minutes at most, and then the woman would walk out and wonder why she was sneaking around where she didn't belong.

The top of the desk looked like an advertisement for office furniture, everything in place and neatly organized. The bookshelves, too, were perfectly ordered with books alphabetized by author.

What? Mary shook her head. *Who has time for that?*

One of the drawers was slightly open. She stuck her finger inside and nudged it out a bit farther. Paperclips, pens, highlighters, a little box of rubber bands, even a set of chattering teeth.

The last item made Mary smile. And frown. Now that she suspected Paige wasn't the target, nosing through Catherine's things didn't feel right.

She slid the drawer back in place, but despite her best efforts, it screeched its protest loudly. Freezing in place, Mary held her breath and stared at the door. To her relief, no one came to see who was in Catherine's office. She straightened and half turned to go. Arrested by a small triangle of white under the desk, she bent low to investigate. Was it a linen napkin or something else?

After hooking the item with the tip of her finger, Mary pulled out an apron, white, except for a blue stain over the hip pocket. A broken pen, perhaps? Mary bit her lip. Unless she was mistaken, the color was very close to the dye that had been used on her hair.

Her breathing quickened as she took out her phone, snapped a picture, then pushed the apron back and made for the door.

Elizabeth waited for her, a cup of coffee in each hand. "Well?"

"Nothing in the desk, but I didn't poke around too much." She took one of the cups and urged Elizabeth toward the exit. "I did find something under the desk that I want to show you. Come on."

"Where are we going?"

"My car." She threw a harried look around the coffee shop. "Too many people in here. Let's go."

They hadn't been in the coffee shop long, but the chill morning air had already frosted the car windows. Mary started the engine and turned up the heat before pulling up the picture to show Elizabeth. "What do you think?"

Wrinkles formed on Elizabeth's brow as she bent close to examine the stain. "It could be ink, I suppose."

"I thought so too."

"But it could also be dye."

"Uh-huh. Worth investigating?"

"Absolutely." Elizabeth's jaw firmed. "Now what?"

Mary dropped the car into REVERSE. "Now we head to the theater to see Catherine. Busy or not, rehearsals or not, I'm determined to put this mystery behind us once and for all!"

CHAPTER THIRTY-ONE

No trace of the Valentine's Dance remained as Mary and Elizabeth stepped into Bird-in-Hand Stage. Crew and stagehands rushed everywhere. Some hefted pieces of the set on their shoulders, while others swirled by with costumes draped over their arms. And everywhere there was noise and lively chatter as people either gave instructions or took them.

Elizabeth leaned in and grasped Mary's elbow. "Busy place."

"This week usually is—before opening night of a play, I mean."

Mary had done some acting in her day, so the bustle of the stage was not foreign. In fact, it kind of made her yearn for the excitement that always built up among the cast and crew before the first performance.

She motioned toward the darkened seating area. "Let's check out there. If they're getting ready to run a dress rehearsal, Catherine will be seated in the audience taking notes and watching for any last-minute changes that need to be made."

It took several seconds for their eyes to adjust, but it soon became clear that Catherine was not among those waiting for the dress rehearsal to begin.

"Where could she be?" Elizabeth whispered.

Mary swiveled for a better look of the stage. At the front, members of the lighting crew perched on ladders adjusting the overheads. Below them, a man with a clipboard called instructions and checked items off his list.

"She's got to be back there somewhere," Mary said, craning to see around the heavy velvet curtains. "Let's go look."

Though they spent several minutes searching, they found no sign of Catherine.

"Do you think she could have gone somewhere?" Elizabeth asked.

Mary zeroed in on one of the actors pacing the back of the stage as she ran through lines. "One way to find out."

The woman was short and slender and dressed in plain clothes. Were it not for the script in her hand, Mary might easily have mistaken her for Amish.

"Excuse me," she said, and then when the woman didn't look up, she cleared her throat and repeated the words louder. "Could you help us? We're looking for Catherine Randall."

The woman blinked her annoyance at being interrupted. Jabbing her finger toward one of the stage doors, she said, "Back there. The seamstress had a problem with a couple of the costumes, so she's working on some changes to wardrobe."

"Okay. Thank you," Mary said, but the woman had already gone back to her study. "Come on," Mary said, motioning to Elizabeth.

They had to weave their way around sets and miscellaneous props, but the moment Mary opened the stage door,

Catherine's voice pulled them toward the costume room. Bright light spilled onto the walls and floor, which had all been painted flat black to cut down on anything that might be seen whenever there was a performance.

Mary eased forward, and though the door was ajar, she knocked. "Excuse me, Ms. Randall?"

Catherine and a short, stout woman wearing a tape measure looped around her neck and with several pins clamped between her lips looked over at Mary with surprise.

Catherine lowered the man's coat she was holding. "Yes? Can I help you?"

Mary stepped fully through the door. "My name is Mary Baxter. This is my sister, Elizabeth Classen. Could we have a moment of your time?"

Hearing her name, Catherine's face paled. "M-Mary..."

She caught herself and squared to face them. It was then that Mary caught sight of the bandage wrapping her left hand. Seeing her stare, Catherine's lips thinned, and she draped the coat over her arm and hand.

"I'm sorry, Ms. Baxter, I'm afraid we're very busy at the moment. Opening night is in a couple of days. I'm sure you understand."

Mary cast a pointed glance at the seamstress. "This is important. It will only take a moment."

Plucking the pins from her mouth, the seamstress bustled to push them into a pincushion shaped like a tomato. "I'll go and get those measurements we talked about." She eyed Mary and Elizabeth curiously as she passed but said nothing more and hurried out the door.

Catherine breathed an exaggerated sigh and crossed her arms. "All right. What can I do for you, Ms. Baxter? And please, make it quick. I only have a few minutes."

Mary rested her hand on the purse at her hip. "Ms. Randall, are you aware of the accidents that have taken place at Paige Schiller's salon?"

Catherine's gaze flitted to Mary's hair and settled back on her face. "I, um…" She smoothed her hair and then braced her fist on her hip. "I take it you're referring to your unfortunate choice of hair color?"

"That, and a couple of other things, like clippers that were adjusted to cut too short, and chemicals that resulted in a bad perm."

Elizabeth piped up from over Mary's shoulder. "And the hair color wasn't her choice. Someone switched the labels on the bottles."

"That's correct," Mary said.

Catherine's nose rose. "I'm not sure what you think any of that has to do with me."

"Actually, I only just realized it myself," Mary said. "For the longest time, I thought Paige was the target."

"When things started going wrong at the salon, we assumed someone was trying to force her out of business," Elizabeth added.

"But then we heard about how you had applied for membership at the Chamber of Commerce but got turned down because Eloise Parkhurst was still carrying a grudge over not being given a part in the spring play."

Catherine's face had turned to stone. She glared at Mary, and then at Elizabeth, before licking her lips and opening her mouth slowly to speak.

"That is ridiculous. I mean, yes, Eloise did deny my application, and I admit, I was a bit disappointed, but she's not going to be chair of the chamber forever." She shrugged one slim shoulder, and a laugh that was too high-pitched to be natural escaped her lips. "I just figured I would wait until she was gone and then reapply."

"Except you didn't wait, did you?" Mary pulled her phone from her purse and held up the picture of the apron for Catherine to see.

Her eyes narrowed. "How did you get a picture of that?"

"It was in your coffee shop. We stopped by there earlier today." She made the picture larger. "See?" She pointed to the name embroidered across the apron. "Un-Common Grounds. It says so, right there."

Catherine scoffed. "So? I keep several aprons there in my office, just in case one of them gets soiled. It's important to keep a certain image, and I insist that all of my staff wear clean aprons."

Mary looked at her over the phone. "How did you know I took this picture in your office?"

"Well...I...just assumed you did." Catherine crossed her arms. "It's white, which means it's mine. All of the staff wear black."

"I see." Mary pointed to the stain over the pocket. "And what about that?"

Catherine's chest rose and fell faster as she lowered her gaze to look at the stain. "I left a pen in the pocket and didn't realize it until the thing broke." Her gaze drifted to Elizabeth. "You know how hard ink is to get out of fabric? Especially something white. I figured it wasn't worth the effort." She pressed her lips together tightly. "What were you two doing in my office, anyway?"

"We stopped by to talk to you," Mary said. "Your door was open, so I went inside." She motioned toward Catherine's hands. "So, if it was a pen, did you get any of the ink on your hands?"

"No." She shot out both hands. "See? No ink."

"But you do have an injury." Elizabeth directed a pointed glance at the bandage on Catherine's hand.

She pulled her hands back quickly, her gaze bouncing from Mary to Elizabeth.

"How did you cut your hand?" Elizabeth asked her.

"It h-happened at the coffee shop last week," Catherine stammered. "I got careless and sliced it on a can."

"But you didn't have the bandage the day you came into the salon after my hair was dyed blue," Mary insisted. "Or to be more accurate, the *second* time. Are you sure you didn't cut yourself a little more recently on, say, a pair of antique scissors?"

"Before you answer, you should know we found a couple of drops of blood on Paige's desk blotter. It will be easy enough to prove it was you who stole her phone and appointment book if Paige decides to press charges." Elizabeth lowered her voice soothingly. "Which she will be a lot less likely to do if you confess what really happened."

Catherine's chin trembled. "She's thinking of pressing charges?"

"Where are her phone and appointment book, Catherine?" Mary asked quietly.

Her shoulders drooping, Catherine crossed to a closet, opened the door, and took out her purse. She reached into a side pocket, pulled out a phone, and handed it to Mary.

"I've been carrying that thing around ever since I took it from the salon. I'll be glad to be rid of it."

A look of pleading crept into her gaze. "I wasn't going to throw it away. I actually intended to get it back to Paige somehow after things settled down. The appointment book is back at the coffee shop." She replaced the purse in the closet and closed the door with a soft click. For a long moment, she stood with her back to them, her hand on the door. Finally, she turned around.

"I'm sorry Paige thought someone was trying to force her out of business." She looked at Mary. "And you. I'm really sorry about your hair." She lifted her hand weakly. "All of this was supposed to be prank—a way of getting back at Eloise for denying my application to the chamber. I had no idea you would take her time slot."

"I figured that was a mistake," Mary said. "But when you did find out what happened, you weren't ready to give up, were you?"

Catherine shook her head. "I knew Eloise had rescheduled, but I didn't know for what day. I saw Paige inputting appointments on her phone, so I went back to the salon later and snuck into her office to look. Only I heard her drive up before I could find the information so I took the phone and her appointment book to check later. Once I knew what day Eloise was coming into the salon, I went back and switched the perm solution."

"But how did you know what products to tamper with?" Mary asked.

"It was easy. Paige always adds a note next to the appointment about what the client wants done so she knows how much time to block off and which products she's using."

Mary reached up to touch her head. "Eloise and I have the same hair color. That's why Paige used the bottle you tampered with on me."

Elizabeth nodded. "And the clippers? Why did you change the settings?"

"Clippers?" Catherine blinked and looked from Mary to Elizabeth. "I have no idea what you're talking about. I never touched any clippers."

"So they really did just get jostled during the move," Mary said, giving a wry shake of her head. "That threw us off for a while, and it was one of the reasons we were so sure Paige was the target of these attacks. It seemed too calculated to be coincidental."

"But you *do* believe me?" Catherine asked, worry adding hesitancy to her voice.

Mary looked at Elizabeth, who nodded.

Catherine let out a breath in a whoosh. "So, what happens now? Should I go to Paige and try to explain what happened?"

"I think that would be a good idea," Elizabeth said. "And it would probably go a long way toward convincing her to let the matter drop."

Catherine's hands shook as she rubbed them down her sides. "All right. Just let me grab my things."

Mary gestured toward the stage. "But the dress rehearsal?"

Catherine thought a second then shook her head. "This has bothered me long enough. Better to get it settled now. I'll just let the cast and my assistant know to go on without me, and then I'll meet you both at the salon. That is, if you wouldn't mind going with me just so…in case Paige doesn't…"

She looked so forlorn as she trailed off that Mary couldn't help but feel sorry for her. She patted her arm. "We'll be there. And for what it's worth, I think you're doing the right thing by going to her yourself."

Catherine nodded, but Mary had to admit, she had reason to be worried. They had no way of predicting how Paige would react when she heard Catherine's explanation, nor could they say that she'd be willing to let bygones be bygones. In fact, only one thing was certain—all this pride and pettiness had led to a terrible tangle of misunderstanding and hurt feelings.

And it was up to them to at least try to sort it out.

CHAPTER THIRTY-TWO

A sweet sense of peace flowed through Mary as she sipped a cup of peach tea, her feet propped on an ottoman, the only sound in the room the gentle hiss of the fire in the fireplace and Tink's wheezy snore on the couch next to her.

"You two look comfortable."

Tink opened her eyes when Martha entered, but promptly shut them and puffed out a lazy sigh when she realized there was no danger of feline intrusion.

"Mind if I join you?" Martha continued, gesturing to a spot next to Mary on the couch.

Mary tipped her head, and Martha sank down with a weary "Oof."

"Here." Mary pushed the ottoman toward her with her foot. "You sound like you need this more than I do."

"I'll take it," Martha said, putting her feet up with a grateful smile. "I admit, there are times when being on my feet all day makes me rethink my career choices."

Mary laughed. "You know you love it too much to change a thing."

Martha laughed. "So?" She rested her elbow on the arm of the couch and reached out with her other hand to rub Tink's ears. "Any more from Paige?"

Mary curled her fingers around the bottom of the teacup, absorbing its warmth. "No. Mostly, I think she's just so relieved to know she wasn't the target of Catherine's pranks that she's willing to set everything aside and forget it ever happened."

"That's good, I suppose. Not so sure Eloise will agree." Martha's hand stilled over Tink's fur. "I wonder what she'll do when she finds out her bad perm was Catherine's doing."

"Actually, I don't think she'll do anything."

Martha peered at her questioningly. Mary went on. "Catherine claims she was trying to get back at Eloise for denying her membership application, which she claims Eloise did because she didn't get a part in the spring play. I really don't think either of them will be too keen for that story to get around."

Martha snorted and turned her gaze to the crackling fire. "You're probably right. They're both too proud to risk letting their reputations get sullied with talk of tit for tat."

"Mmm." Mary took a sip of her tea and then stared into her cup at the dark swirling liquid lapping at the edges. "'My cup runneth over.'"

Martha's brow arched. "What's that?"

Mary shook free of her thoughts and looked up. "It just occurred to me how much we've been blessed with—family, friends, good health, just to name a few. It would be easy to take all of that for granted and dwell only on the things we think are missing."

A gleam lit Martha's eyes. "Such as?"

Mary fell silent while the seconds ticked by on the clock above the mantel. "I've learned something about myself. You already know what it is."

She paused and looked over at her sister.

"Months ago, I told Bill I wasn't ready for a relationship. I insisted we remain friends. But then, when I saw him with Nettie, something clicked. You knew it was jealousy and warned me to sort out my feelings before things went too far with Wade."

"Yes, I did."

"But even when I thought I understood what you were trying to say, and I still had it wrong, you didn't push."

"Would it have done any good?" Martha asked, a twinkle in her eye.

"Probably not."

"Well then, I'm glad I didn't push."

Mary chuckled. "Me too."

After a moment, Martha asked, "So? What about Wade? Are you going to keep seeing him?"

Mary curled her fingers into the fur on Tink's neck. "Nah. He's not the one for me."

"Hmm."

"What?"

Martha shrugged. "Nothing. Just wondering if maybe someone else *is* the one."

"Someone?"

Martha remained impassive, and Mary stifled a snort. "If you mean Bill, we really are just friends."

Which was true. Somewhat. *For now.*

Martha didn't press, and Mary snuggled into the couch cushions, content to let the smoky scent of the fire and the warmth from its blaze lull her into serene stillness. Martha too fell quiet, until the *swish-swish* of Elizabeth's rubber-soled shoes indicated she'd come to join them.

"There you are," Martha said, sliding over to make room on the couch.

With the three of them, there was no room for Tink. She dropped to the floor and curled up next to Pal on the warm hearth.

"Where were you?" Martha asked.

Elizabeth pushed her hair behind her ear and sat, her gaze fixed appreciatively on the fire. "I was on the phone."

"Anyone we know?" Mary asked. She grabbed a tin of short-bread cookies from the end table and passed them down to Elizabeth.

"Actually, yes." Elizabeth snapped open the lid and removed one of the cookies, then offered the tin to Martha, who shook her head.

"None for me. My jeans are getting way too snug."

Elizabeth shrugged and replaced the lid before setting the tin on the coffee table. "It was Jennifer. She wanted to talk to about Heidi and Michael."

Mary pushed to the edge of the couch. "Oh, then I should go call her."

Elizabeth shook her head, color flaring in her cheeks, and Mary paused, one hand on the arm of the couch.

"No, that's okay," Elizabeth said. She rubbed her palms nervously on her slacks. "Actually, um, she asked to talk to me."

"She did?" Mary and Martha asked together. Mary looked at Martha and then back at Elizabeth. "What did she say? I mean, what did you say? What did she want to know?"

"Ahem." Martha shot her a pointed glare.

Elizabeth chuckled. "It's all right. I was surprised too."

"Oh." Martha nudged her with her knee. "Well then? Are you going to leave us in suspense?"

Mary poked her in the ribs. Obviously, Martha was just as curious as she was. They both looked at Elizabeth.

"Well, at first I just listened," Elizabeth began slowly. "Because the first time Jennifer and I talked, she didn't really want to hear what I had to say. I was afraid that if I offered my opinion too soon, she'd just ignore me again." Her gaze jumped to Mary. "Jennifer told me she'd talked to you, and that you told her things would settle down in time."

"That's right, I did. So? Was she feeling any better about Michael and Heidi not having time for her?"

"Not really," Elizabeth said. "At least, not at first. But after we talked, I think she felt a little better."

Mary frowned. "I don't get it. What did you tell her that I didn't?"

Elizabeth dropped her gaze and folded her hands in her lap. "I...uh...well..." She threw a quick glance at Mary and then Martha. "I told her to stop being so selfish."

"You did what?" Martha's eyes rounded.

She nodded. "I told her she needed to stop thinking about herself and put them first. If she wanted to spend time with Michael and Heidi and the baby, I told her to pack up a suitcase and trot over to their house instead of always expecting them to make time to go see her."

"And what did she say to that?" Mary asked.

Tears sparkled in Elizabeth's eyes. "She didn't take it well at first, to be sure, but then she agreed I was right. She said when we hung up she was going to call Michael and Heidi and let them know she was heading over to see them—not to be entertained, but to help out in any way she could." She bit her lip hesitantly. "What do you think? Was that okay?"

Pride glowed on Martha's face as she looked over at Mary.

"It was more than okay," Mary said, her throat tight. "It was absolutely perfect. Thank you so much."

Elizabeth nodded and glanced over at Martha. "I've been thinking about Jared and Trish too, and praying about their situation."

Martha patted her hand. "I appreciate that, Elizabeth. Thank you."

"Martha." Mary stared at her with a lifted eyebrow. Martha stared back blankly. Finally, Mary sighed and peeked around her at Elizabeth. "What did you come up with?"

Elizabeth cleared her throat. "It seems to me, the problem is one of two things—either Jared needs a new job closer to home, or the family needs a new home closer to Jared's job. Since Trish works from home, I think the obvious answer would be for them to at least consider moving a little closer to work so Jared could spend more time with the family. Of course, he would have to try to cut back on the number of hours he spends there too."

Martha shook her head. "I believe they've already talked about that, but Trish is worried about uprooting the kids."

"That's the hard thing about compromise," Elizabeth said, a gentleness to her tone that removed any possible sting. "It usually costs both sides something. In the end, wouldn't the kids rather they had their dad? They're both young, after all. And really, if they were going to make a move, what better time?"

Martha pondered Elizabeth's words quietly for some time before agreeing with a slow nod. "You're right, Lizzie. Moving to a new town will be hard, but it would definitely be worthwhile if it means the family could spend more time together. I'll talk to Trish and Jared about it tomorrow."

The three of them fell silent while the fire chattered on, popping and hissing and occasionally puffing up a cloud of smoky accord.

"You know, you're pretty wise when it comes to dealing with kids." Martha spoke without looking at either of them.

Mary blinked into the fire. "She's right. And it has nothing to do with being a mom. It's about being the kind of person who has a heart for God, someone willing to love and listen and say the hard stuff other people tend to avoid."

"Is that a nice way of saying I'm nosy?" Elizabeth teased, her voice choked.

Mary didn't have to see it to feel her smile, or Martha's. She shook her head. "Call it what you like. I'm thankful for you exactly the way you are, and I wouldn't have you any other way."

"Me neither," Martha said, then took hold of Mary's hand with one hand and Elizabeth's with the other.

Mary stared at their clasped hands, overcome with the raw truth of something she'd always known but was only recently beginning to understand.

Eyes burning, she gulped down a sudden knot. "Stronger with three?"

When she looked up, she saw the same heartfelt emotion reflected in each of her sisters' eyes.

"Stronger with three," Martha agreed.

Elizabeth nodded. "Most definitely. Stronger with three."

A NOTE FROM THE AUTHOR

For most of my life, I have battled feelings of being less than... less than perfect, less than popular, less than successful. Typically, these feelings come from comparing myself to someone else—either what they are doing or how they look. Instead of seeing myself as rare and beautiful, someone to be sought after and treasured, my heart has whispered lies that led to discouragement and doubt. Certainly, this is not how God would have me measure my self-worth. In His eyes, I am precious and ultimately worth dying for. But even knowing that, I have often indulged in self-pity, wishing I looked a certain way, or acted a certain way, or thought if I could just reach a certain goal, I would finally be rid of my feelings of inferiority. The truth is, the only way to truly be free of this burden is to recognize it for the lie that it is and give it over to the Lord.

Creating this story for Mary was a way for me to examine myself and acknowledge that struggle. Through her, I wanted to show the great value God has placed in each one of us. And just like Mary, I wanted to show how great His love and patience and mercy is for each one of us. I pray we all grasp this truth.

Elizabeth Ludwig

ABOUT THE AUTHOR

Elizabeth Ludwig is an accomplished speaker and teacher, often attending conferences where she lectures on editing for fiction writers, crafting effective novel proposals, and conducting successful editor/agent interviews. Book three in her popular Edge of Freedom series, *Tide and Tempest*, was named a finalist for the Gayle Wilson Award of Excellence. Elizabeth was also named a finalist in the 2015 Selah Awards for her novella *One Holy Night*, part of the bestselling anthology collection *Christmas Comes to Bethlehem, Maine*. Most recently, she was honored to be awarded a HOLT Medallion for her book *A Tempting Taste of Mystery*, part of the Sugarcreek Amish Mysteries series from Guideposts. Her latest releases include *The Coffee Club Mysteries* and *Sheeps Passing in the Night*, part of the Mysteries of Martha's Vineyard series, also from Guideposts. To learn more, visit ElizabethLudwig.com.

BARN FINDS

I have taken an interest in a new-to-me television game show. It involves two teams of contestants scouring flea markets, looking for items that can either be refurbished or turned into something entirely new. Usually, there is a theme that the contestants must follow, but always, it involves looking for the best values and flipping the purchases to make a profit. Many times, I am less than impressed by what the competitors create. But other times, I am completely blown away by their ingenuity and skill. One example is an old clock that contestants turned into an end table. Another was a doggie kennel fashioned from an entertainment center. So clever! Though I don't have the imagination some of these people have, I certainly have learned to look at objects in a new light. Things I used to throw away now get curious perusal as I wonder how they can be repurposed. While this has been a fun experience for me, I must admit, it has not been entirely popular with my husband, who has learned to dread the words, "What can we make out of this?"

Still, flea markets and resale shops are the best places to find hidden treasures. I hope you enjoy browsing through them as much as I do.

FRESH FROM MARTHA'S KITCHEN

Jennie's Chicken Potpie

Ingredients:

⅓ cup butter

⅓ cup chopped yellow onion

1 pound boneless, skinless
  chicken breast, cut into
  small pieces

1 cup chopped carrots

1 cup green peas

½ cup sliced celery

1 small potato, peeled and
  cubed (in bite-sized
  pieces)

⅓ cup all-purpose flour

½ teaspoon salt

¼ teaspoon black pepper

¼ teaspoon celery seed

⅔ cup milk

1¾ cups chicken broth

2 9-inch unbaked
  piecrusts

Directions:

Preheat oven to 425 degrees.

In a saucepan, melt butter over medium heat. Add onions and cook until soft and translucent. Add chicken, carrots, peas, celery, and potato, and cook for 10 to 15 minutes until chicken is cooked through, stirring often.

Add flour, salt, pepper, and celery seed. Stir mixture until there is no visible flour left. Slowly stir in milk, then chicken broth. Simmer over medium-low heat until thick. Remove from heat and set aside.

Place one of the piecrusts into a 9-inch pie pan. Spoon chicken mixture into piecrust. Cover with second crust, seal edges, and cut away excess dough. Make several small slits evenly around top crust to allow steam to escape.

Bake in preheated oven for 30 to 35 minutes, or until pastry is golden brown and filling is bubbly. Cool for 10 minutes before serving.

Read on for a sneak peek of another exciting book
in the Mysteries of Lancaster County series!

By Any Other Name
by Beth Adams

The phone on the counter rang as Martha carried her plate
to the sink.

"Just let it go to voice mail." Elizabeth balanced the bowl of
leftover asparagus and the plate of ham with her own plate as
she walked toward the sink. "It's always robocalls at this hour."

Martha was tempted, but she set her plate down and leaned
over so she could see the name that popped up on the screen.
If it was an unidentified caller, she would let it go. But the
name that showed up on the screen was *Silas Fischer*. She set her
plate in the soapy water and then picked up the phone.

"Hello?"

"This is Ephraim. Is this Mrs. Watts?"

It was their Amish neighbors' sixteen-year-old son. He
sounded out of breath. He must have run to the phone shanty
that stood at the end of the family's driveway. Martha knew
right away that there was something wrong. It was the only way
Ephraim would have forgotten to start with a greeting of some
sort. Those Fischer children were the most polite children
Martha had ever met.

"Yes, this is Martha. What's wrong?"

"There are police here. They say Adam is lying about who he is. *Maam* asked if you or your sisters could come over and explain that he was on your land all day."

What in the world? Adam was Rachel and Silas Fischer's twenty-two-year-old son, who was married and had a baby on the way. He farmed the Classen sisters' land. None of what Ephraim had said made sense. But Martha knew there was only one answer.

"Of course. We'll be right over." They would figure out what was going on when they got there.

"*Danki.*"

She set the phone down and found both Elizabeth and Mary looking at her.

"That was Ephraim. He said the police are there, saying that Adam is not who he says he is, or something. We need to vouch that he was here this afternoon."

Mary's eyes narrowed, and Elizabeth just looked confused.

"I don't know. It wasn't exactly clear what's going on. But Rachel is asking us if we can come."

"Of course." Mary set down the water glasses she was carrying.

"Let's go." Elizabeth was already heading toward the door.

Martha glanced at all the dishes waiting to be dealt with, but then she nodded. The dishes would wait. Their friend needed them.

The sisters pulled on coats and piled into Elizabeth's car. The drive to the neighboring farm took only minutes. Daylight Savings Time had recently begun, and the sky was still light when they pulled into the driveway. They saw that the horses were in the paddock and several buggies lined up against the fence. Through the open barn door, Martha could see Ephraim, as well as twins Matthew and Thomas, tending to the animals. A police car was parked in front of the house. It looked incongruous in this peaceful setting.

"Let's go see what this is all about," Mary said, pushing her door open. The three sisters all walked across the yard to the side door. Before they even got there, the door opened and Phoebe, Rachel's twenty-one-year-old daughter, was ushering them inside.

"Thank you for coming," Phoebe said. "Maam does not know how what they are saying could be true." She closed the door after they all stepped inside and led them through the kitchen, with its wooden cabinets and propane-powered appliances.

"How *what* could be true?" Mary asked. "What happened exactly?"

"Maam and the police will tell you," Phoebe said and showed them to the living room, where Rachel and her husband Silas sat on wooden chairs. Martha was glad to see that one of the police officers was John Marks. John was a close friend of Elizabeth's, and he was a fair and good man. He sat on a couch against one wall and smiled when Elizabeth walked in the room. There was also another police officer, one she hadn't met before, and Adam Fischer sat on a wooden bench across from him. Even under the full Amish beard, Adam looked so young and scared. Adam's wife, Leah, sat in a rocking chair, cradling her growing belly. It wouldn't be long now—probably only a month or so left.

"*Hallo*," Rachel said as she and Silas rose as the sisters entered the room. "Please, sit." She gestured for Adam to move from the bench, and he stood so the three sisters could sit down. Both police officers watched them settle into the seats, and they looked uncertain.

"What brings the three of you here?" John asked, though he was smiling, as if he already knew. Rachel explained that Ephraim had called them. John introduced the other officer as Officer Hooper, and he nodded, though he seemed confused by their appearance.

"Thank you so much for coming," Rachel said, and then she turned to the officers. "Adam was working on the Classen land this afternoon," Rachel said. "They can tell you. He could not have done this thing."

"He was," Mary said. "Adam leases our land, and he was out there plowing today." Martha and Elizabeth nodded along with her, but Martha was bewildered. What was all this about?

"What is going on?" Elizabeth asked.

Officer Hooper spoke first. "There was a hit-and-run accident this afternoon over on Cherry Hill Road, out by Oak Hill Road. A car was driving far too fast and hit a buggy as it came over the rise."

"Oh dear," Mary said.

Elizabeth felt her stomach drop. Accidents like these were becoming far too common. Cars drove too quickly over these rural roads and often didn't see the slow-moving buggies until it was too late. The Amish buggies didn't stand a chance against thousands of pounds of metal, and there had been several fatal crashes in recent years.

"It was the Mast family," Rachel said. "Abner and Miriam and their three-year-old son, Abel. Coming back from a visit to see her sister's new baby."

Martha didn't even need to ask how Rachel knew this. She had never understood how news spread so quickly in the Amish community, but it always did.

"Are they okay?" Elizabeth asked, echoing the question that was in Martha's own mind.

"They were transferred to Lancaster General Hospital," Officer Hooper said. "We do not know their condition at this time."

"The car sustained substantial damage and was abandoned at the scene," John said. "It was registered to Adam Fischer at this address."

Elizabeth and Mary looked as confused as she felt. "But Adam doesn't have a car," she said.

"He's Amish," Mary added, as if the officers hadn't figured that out already.

"Nevertheless, the car was registered in his name," Officer Hooper said. "And this was listed as the address."

"But Adam does not even live here," Silas said quietly. "He has not for several years."

"He lives on another piece of the property, on Herr Road," Elizabeth explained to the officers. "Since he got married. With a totally different address."

"That may well be." Officer Hooper had that thin, wiry look of a long-distance runner and thinning gray hair. He had a small notebook open in his lap, and he made a note before looking up. "But when we ran the name through the system, we came up with a laundry list of other offenses committed by Adam, including public intoxication and a DUI."

"As well as a restraining order taken out against him," John added.

"This came up as his most recent address," Officer Hooper said.

Martha wanted to laugh. It was ludicrous to imagine Adam, with his horse and buggy and his suspenders, drinking and driving a car. But the officers weren't laughing, so Martha held it in.

"It wasn't him," Martha said. "That's obvious, right?" Neither of the officers gave anything away. "If what you're saying is true—"

"It is," Officer Hooper said, with no trace of humor.

"Then it was someone else pretending to be Adam," Martha finished. "There's no way it could have been him. He doesn't drink. He doesn't drive. And he certainly doesn't need a restraining order."

"Plus, like we said, he was working in the fields this afternoon," Elizabeth said. "I can vouch for the fact that he was out there all afternoon."

"I saw him there too," Martha added.

"Have you ever been to State College?" Officer Hooper asked Adam.

Adam shook his head. "No, sir. That is quite far from here."

It was only a two-hour drive, but it would take all day or longer in a buggy.

"What's in State College?" Elizabeth asked.

Neither officer answered the question. Officer Hooper wrote something down in his notebook.

Martha knew State College was the home of Penn State, a huge university with a football team and a party culture. The officers had to see how funny it was to imagine Adam there. The Amish were only educated through eighth grade, so he hadn't exactly gone on a college tour.

"This is crazy," Mary said. "There's no way Adam could have caused that crash."

Martha glanced at Rachel and saw that her lips were pressed together, and her face was pale. Silas's shoulders were hitched and his knuckles were white where they gripped the arm of the couch.

The two police officers glanced at one another, and Officer Hooper nodded at Adam, then said, "And you don't own a car that you loaned to someone else to use?"

"No, sir," Adam replied, shaking his head.

"Well then, as it turns out, it appears as though you aren't the one responsible for this crime," John said slowly.

Martha heard Elizabeth let out a breath she must have been holding. Rachel's face relaxed, but only a little.

"If this is Adam Fischer—" Officer Hooper started.

"This *is* Adam Fischer," Rachel said.

"Then it seems pretty unlikely to us that he was behind the crash, or the other offenses," John continued.

"Which begs the question, who *was* behind them?" Martha wondered.

"And why was he using Adam's name and address?" Mary asked.

"And how?" Elizabeth added.

"That just about sums it up." Officer Hooper was nodding. "I guess that's what we'll be looking into."

"Do you have any idea at all how someone could have stolen your identity?" Officer Hooper asked.

"No," Adam said. "I did not even know this was possible."

"Someone must have gotten a driver's license in your name," John said.

"And you need a Social Security number to get a driver's license," Officer Hooper said. "But you don't have one of those either, correct?"

"Actually, I have both a Social Security number and a driver's license," Adam said.

Officer Hooper's face registered surprise, but John seemed to understand.

"I thought you were against those kinds of things," Officer Hooper said. "Government registration, taxes, and all that."

"We are not against cooperating with our government," Silas said. "We pay taxes just like everybody else. What we do not approve of is insurance, like this Social Security."

John nodded, but the older officer looked confused, so Martha jumped in.

"The Amish don't use insurance. They believe it is up to their community to provide for one another in times of need. And Social Security is a form of insurance, right?"

"I guess so," Officer Hooper said.

"So in their community, they opt out of Social Security," Martha said.

"I didn't know you could do that," Officer Hooper said.

"Most people can't," Elizabeth said. "The Amish have a special exemption through the courts."

"But you must register for a Social Security number to be able to say you do not want to take part in it," Silas said. "So most of us have these numbers."

Officer Hooper was nodding, but he still looked confused. "Did you say you have a driver's license?"

"That is right." Adam nodded. "I did, in any case. I do not drive anymore. Not since I joined the church."

"When was that?" John asked.

"More than two years ago." Adam shifted on his feet.

"You got it while you were on *rumspringa*?" John asked.

"That's right."

Even Officer Hooper was nodding now. Everyone around these parts knew about rumspringa, or the teenage years, when Amish youth were allowed to experience the Englisch world before deciding whether they wanted to join the Amish church and commit to the lifestyle for good. Many television shows and documentaries had portrayed this as the time many Amish youth went wild, but the truth was that most did nothing of the sort. They might get a cell phone and try to dress Englisch sometimes, but most were able to enjoy their taste of freedom without going too far off the deep end.

"That's quite unusual, isn't it?" John asked. "To get a driver's license?"

"I suppose it is," Adam said.

"He works very hard. He is very responsible," Rachel added.

"How does an Amish person even get a driver's license?" Officer Hooper asked. "How is that possible?"

"Before they join the church, the Amish are allowed to learn to drive," Mary explained.

"But it is unusual because of the work and cost involved in learning to drive a car," Martha said. "Adam is a very determined young man."

"What made you want to drive?" Officer Hooper asked Adam. Martha thought it was a silly question. What teenage boy didn't want to get behind the wheel of a car? But Adam's answer surprised her.

"Back then, I was thinking I might become a veterinarian," Adam said.

"Wait. Really?" Mary looked as surprised as Martha felt. Becoming a vet would mean years of schooling beyond the eighth-grade education most Amish received. Martha wasn't even sure you could be Amish and have an advanced degree like that.

"I was not sure if I was going to join the church and farm or become a veterinarian and help animals," Adam said. "I thought I might be able to do more good helping many people's animals than I could by staying here and raising my own."

"That's admirable," Mary said.

"So I got a job helping out at a clinic in Lancaster to see what it was like. And I wanted a car for an easy way to get there regularly, rather than use the family's horse and buggy all the time."

Martha looked at Rachel, who was nodding.

It showed a tremendous amount of initiative on Adam's part, Martha thought. Not many young men in his position would even know where to start, even if they had the desire to get themselves a job and a car to get there.

"But you decided to join the church instead," Officer Hooper said incredulously.

"Yes. In the end I could not leave my family and my church," Adam said. Martha wasn't sure, but she thought she detected a bit of uncertainty in his voice. She wondered if there was ever a small part of him that regretted his choice, but knew that she could never ask. "And I wanted to marry Leah." He glanced at his wife, who let a slow smile spread across her face.

Ah. There it was. He'd made his decision for love, as so many young people did. Well, you couldn't fault him for that. Martha had also chosen to marry Chuck and have children over the promise of a career in nursing.

"And what happened to your driver's license when you joined the church?" Officer Hooper asked.

"I do not know," Adam said. "I had lost the card a few weeks earlier, but I figured it did not matter, since I would not be driving anyway."

Martha couldn't imagine losing such an important piece of documentation and not doing anything about it. Once, many years ago, she'd lost her wallet, and within hours she'd cancelled every credit card and reported her license lost and had a replacement on the way. How could you not take something like that seriously? But then, maybe Adam hadn't realized what could happen if your identification got into the wrong hands.

"You lost it?" John's eyes met Officer Hooper's. "Where?"

"I do not know," Adam said. "If I knew, it would not be lost."

Martha couldn't help laughing at that, though Officer Hooper seemed stunned. Many people underestimated the Amish sense of humor, she knew, and this seemed to be the case for this police officer. John was fighting back a smile.

"How could someone else be using his license?" Leah asked from the corner. Her dark hair was combed back under her *kapp*, and her brown eyes were sleepy. "I thought the whole point was that it tells who you are."

"That's true," John said. "But in this case, I'm guessing there was no photo?" He looked at Adam, who nodded.

Martha knew that the Amish church did not allow its members to be photographed, and that the Commonwealth of Pennsylvania had granted a special exemption to members of the Amish community who got licenses and state-issued identification cards. The corner where the photo usually went was just a white square.

"In that case, it wouldn't have been hard for whoever took the ID to have put his own photo on your card and have started using it as his own," John said.

"So it could be anyone," Mary said, shaking her head.

"Just about," Officer Hooper said. "Anyone who could pass for a man around Adam's age, that is."

That was a whole lot of people, Martha thought.

"Do you have any ideas where you might have lost the physical license?" Officer Hooper asked. "Given what we know so far, I'm guessing that whoever is calling himself Adam Fischer is using your lost license. If we can find out where you might have lost it, we might be able to figure out who has it."

"I do not know," Adam said.

It had been over two years ago, Martha thought. How could he possibly know at this point?

But Adam continued. "Though I do not think there could have been too many places. I did not go very many places when I was driving."

"Let's start by thinking about places you went regularly," Officer Hooper said. "Where did you go?"

"There was the veterinary clinic," Adam said.

"And the racetrack," Silas said.

"The...what?" Officer Hooper's eyes were wide.

"Lancaster Speedway," Adam said reluctantly. "I liked to watch the car races."

Martha wasn't sure she'd heard correctly. She'd never heard of an Amish person who went to watch car races. "Seriously?"

"Seriously." Adam nodded. "I was on rumspringa, and I got to experience the Englisch world. And I had always been fascinated by fast cars."

Maybe she shouldn't have been surprised. Her own sons Craig and Kyle had both been into cars. Maybe it was a genetic thing, something about that Y chromosome? But she had never thought about Amish men having the same fascination.

"That's unusual, isn't it?" Officer Hooper asked.

"I suppose," Adam said. "Then again, if you had spent as much time in a slow-moving buggy as I had, being passed by cars right and left, you might find yourself dreaming of racing cars someday too."

John laughed, though Officer Hooper still just seemed incredulous.

"It does not mean that he was driving that car quickly today," Rachel added. "He does not drive anymore."

"I understand," John said with a smile. "Is there anywhere else you went regularly?"

Adam looked around the room, his eyes darting from the officers to his wife and then back at the officers. Leah cleared her throat, and Rachel shifted in her seat and looked down. There was a pause, just a fraction of a second too long, and then he continued. "That's it, really. The vet clinic and the racetrack."

Something had passed between the Amish people in the room, something that they all understood and didn't want to say. Martha wanted to ask what it was but decided she would follow up with Rachel about it later. Right now, John was asking Adam about where the vet's office was, and what his address was and how long he'd lived there, and then, after a few more questions, he and his partner promised to look into the matter.

"You will find the man who is pretending to be Adam?" Silas asked.

"We will do our absolute best," Officer Hooper said. He tucked his notebook into his pocket and stood. "We'll find him and bring him to justice."

Rachel and Adam nodded but didn't say anything. Silas stood and walked the police officers to the door. John cast a glance back at Elizabeth and then stepped out. Adam and Leah also stood. Leah looked exhausted, as most women did at this point in their pregnancies.

Rachel hugged them both, and after they'd left, she turned to the sisters. "Thank you for coming. I appreciate your help."

"Of course," Elizabeth said, pushing herself up. "I'm just sorry about this awful situation."

"It's ridiculous," Mary agreed, also standing up to go.

"I'm sure they'll figure out who is pretending to be Adam very quickly," Martha said.

"I hope they will," Rachel said with a sigh. She looked like she wanted to say more, but she didn't.

"If there is anything else we can do to help, please do let us know," Martha said.

"I will," Rachel said. Again, there was a look on her face, like she wanted to say something more, but she simply ushered the sisters to the door.

Neither of Martha's sisters said a word as they crossed the yard. Night had fallen while they were inside, and she could see eighteen-year-old Luke in the barn, silhouetted against the light from a lantern. He'd led the horses into their stalls and was tossing hay in for them. Martha pulled her coat closed around her. The days may have been getting longer, but winter had not let go of its grasp completely yet.

"So," Mary said, as soon as they were all buckled in to Elizabeth's car, heat pouring out of the vents. "Are we going to figure out who stole Adam's identity?"

"I was just about to ask the same thing," Elizabeth said as she put the car in REVERSE.

"The police are looking into it," Martha said. She was crammed into the backseat, and she tried to shift to find more space for her legs. "I'm sure they'll find him."

"But what if they don't?" Mary asked. "What if he gets away with it, whoever he is?"

"I think we should do our own investigation," Elizabeth said. "We won't interfere with the police. Just do some digging on the side."

Martha knew her sisters loved mysteries, and she had also enjoyed solving several puzzling situations since she'd moved home last year. But this seemed like a clear case when their help wasn't needed.

"Look, girls. I'm sure there is an established protocol for looking into identity theft," Martha said. "And I'm pretty sure it doesn't involve the victims figuring it out on their own."

"I think this is probably a pretty unique case," Elizabeth said. "I can't imagine there are many times when the identity theft victim is Amish."

"Officer Hooper didn't seem to know a whole lot about the Amish," Mary said. "He might not see some things that would be clear to someone who grew up around here."

"But John knows this world well," Martha said. "He'll make sure to clarify anything Officer Hooper doesn't understand."

"It's not like this is some victimless crime," Elizabeth said. "Whoever the man using Adam's identity is, he landed a family in the hospital. He crashed into a buggy, and then he left. He needs to be found and brought to justice."

"I agree with you, of course," Martha said. "I'm just not sure we need to get involved in this." But even as the words came out of her mouth, she knew they were futile. Her sisters had already made up their minds that they were going to "help" in this case, she could already see that. Well, for her part, Martha was going to do her best to stay out of it and let the police do their job. Maybe there was something she could do to help the Mast family. Martha didn't know how badly they were injured, but they would no doubt have significant hospital bills no matter what, and she knew they didn't have insurance. Martha would talk to Rachel about how she could help with that.

Still, as they pulled into the driveway at their own home just a moment later, she couldn't help but wonder who was behind the crash and the stolen identity. She prayed that whoever it was would be found and stopped right away.